CHEATING THE HANGMAN

The Reverend Tobias Campion returns from morning service on Easter Day and makes a grisly discovery: a corpse nailed to a tree. Together with his old friend, Dr Hansard, he pledges to expose the truth — though it means uncovering secrets the hostile villagers would prefer to keep hidden. Questioning the offended and resentful gentry as well, the pair hears whispers of Satanism, unsavoury pasts, and sinister obsessions. Before long, an attempt is made to silence their enquiries; Tobias, injured but no less determined, realises he must be close to the truth if someone wants him dead. With friends and colleagues either unable or unwilling to help, Tobias is forced to confront his own demons, and ask for help from the last person on earth he wants to meet again . . .

CHEATING THE HANGMAN

JUDITH CUTLER

LARGE
PRINT

First published in Great Britain 2015
by
Allison & Busby

First Isis Edition
published 2016
by arrangement with
Allison & Busby Limited

A catalogue record for this book is available
from the British Library.

ISBN 978–1–78541–196–0 (hb)
ISBN 978–1–78541–202–8 (pb)

Published by
F. A. Thorpe (Publishing)
Anstey, Leicestershire

Set by Words & Graphics Ltd.
Anstey, Leicestershire
Printed and bound in Great Britain by
T. J. International Ltd., Padstow, Cornwall

This book is printed on acid-free paper

*To my dear friend Marion Roberts,
to thank her for her years of private kindness
and public service*

THE KEEPER OF SECRETS

Judith Cutler

England, 1810. Young Parson Tobias Campion is excited to be starting at the small parish of Moreton Priory. But his first night in the village brings excitement of the wrong kind when he has to intervene in the attempted rape of housemaid Lizzie Woodman.

Even in the normal course of events, village life is far from quiet, and soon Tobias has to deal with suspicious deaths. Matters come to a head when Lizzie disappears from her employers' home. What has become of the girl and who is responsible? As Tobias searches for answers, he finds himself delving into the dark secrets that haunt Lizzie's past.

COLD PURSUIT

Judith Cutler

When a colleague becomes seriously ill, Chief Superintendent Frances Harman delays her retirement to oversee an investigation into a recent spate of "happy slappings". Initially, she takes a back seat, but it is not long before she is close to the action again.

The wave of assaults has ignited a media furore. Fran soon finds herself having to spend as much time trying to control the media as trying to catch the criminals.

As the crimes gradually escalate, and the line between "happy slapping" and serious sexual assault becomes blurred, all mention of retirement is postponed until Fran can resolve the nightmare that has enveloped around her.

Prologue

They stop before the oak tree. There is no argument. They must carry out their task, no matter how heavy their hearts, no matter how even the most hardened man is sickened by the grievous sound of the nails being knocked through still warm flesh. Those holding the limbs in place wince with each blow: nails pierce the hands, then the feet.

The birds have gone silent; the trees are still; no animals scurry. It is as if nature itself abhors the deed.

At last they stand back, wiping their hands on the bright grass. They might be admiring their handiwork; in truth they are merely making sure that the nails will hold the corpse above the reach of scavenging creatures — though it cannot be long before the birds peck out the eyes.

Still no one speaks. No one seeks another's glance. To a man they shift their feet, as if waiting for some sign that they may quit the troubled place and creep home. Everyone will know where they have been, but no one will speak of it. The enormity of the act, conceived in righteous fury, is beginning to press upon them, one by one: at all costs it must be kept secret in the depths of the dense, neglected woodland.

As country men, in their hearts they know that that is impossible. If they can track game, how much easier it will be to follow their heavy paces, which crushed alike bright celandines and delicate tendrils of wood anemone. Yet by the time the stench drifts on the wind to some hamlet they hardly know of and have certainly never travelled to, maybe bluebells, and certainly more grass, will have shot up to hide the maimed undergrowth.

The noon sky darkens, heavy clouds gathering so fiercely that in summer they would know it heralded thunder. To their terror, even in the chill March, it does indeed. The sky is cleft by a fork of lightning; the clap of thunder makes them reel. One man turns towards the distant church spire, afraid it may have been sundered. What is to be done with the pile of clothes? In these hardest of times, it seems sinful to destroy such fine linen. Many are tempted. Someone mentions dicing for it. But Adam Blacksmith has promised to feed everything into the fire in his forge, and few would argue with a man with forearms like the hams they can barely imagine after the long winter's hunger.

It is not until they are trudging wearily home, to face the swift, underbrowed glance of the silent waiting women, that the strongest amongst them asks the question that they might have posed earlier: "Why didn't we just bury the bastard?"

CHAPTER
ONE

Wherever I was going, it always gave me enormous pleasure, tempered with guilt, to ride Titus. He had always been far too grand for a parish priest, but I found he was one indulgence I could not deny myself. Nor, since today I was riding to meet my mother at Radway Park in Worcestershire, could I restrain myself from wearing my most fashionable buckskins. My hat was well brushed, and my boots polished to perfection — without, I must say, the use of champagne — by the stable lad, Robert, until recently a workhouse orphan.

Tomorrow I would have the pleasure of escorting Mama to my cousin's home near Banbury, part of her journey to London. But I would be going no further. To think that once my heart would have beaten harder at the thought of all the excitements of the capital: the theatre, the concerts, even riding in the park. Now I —

"Stand! Stand and deliver!"

How could I be so stupid as to fall into a reverie on this deserted stretch of road and expose myself to the attentions of a highwayman? Not that this man was the handsome be-masked gentleman that my sisters would have naively expected. He was a poor, starved wretch, hardly able to hold still the pistol he was trying to aim at my head.

Holding Titus with my knees, I raised both hands. There was no point in doing anything else: my pistol holsters were empty. "You shall have all I carry, my friend," I said, "and my blessing with it."

"And be hanged for dressing like a lord?"

He had a point.

"I might dress like a lord," I said, "but I am a man of God, serving the parish of Moreton St Jude's. If you want money, let me reach for it — I promise you I am unarmed." Do not think that because I spoke calmly my pulses were not racing. What had a man in his position to lose by killing me? He would be hanged for taking my few gold coins; he might as well be hanged for taking my life, since alive I constituted a threat.

"You don't look much like a parson," he objected reasonably. But he lowered his pistol. I tried to place his accent — it was not from around here.

"I don't, do I? But you have my word that I am. Should your travels take you into Warwickshire, I can promise you shelter and food. Work, if you have the right skills. The village of Moreton St Jude's, remember. I am the parson there. Meanwhile, my friend, let me give you —"

My words were interrupted by shouts and halloos. It seemed that help was at hand, but at what cost? The man's life, assuredly. I leant down. "Give me your pistol and I will save your neck. Quickly. Butt first, of course." Quickly I slipped the offending weapon into my holster. "Thank you, kind sir," I said, in the carrying voice I use

4

to make sure that even those lurking in the side aisles of St Jude's can hear my words. "I will be sure of my way from now on. No! Pray wait." I pressed a few pence into his palm, which barely closed on them he was so surprised. "Moreton St Jude's," I repeated softly.

By now my rescuers were upon us. His arrest was imminent unless he played his part as well as I was playing mine. One man, carrying a cudgel, was probably, from his assured air, the parish constable. "We saw you from yon hill, sir, and have sped to your rescue," he panted, tugging his forelock.

At his behest the motley group behind him surrounded my attacker, grappling him to the ground. My few pence were torn from his grasp, and the constable seized on them as evidence of robbery.

"My dear sir," I said, affecting my father's drawl, "you are too generous in your rescue. But you are sadly mistaken — had I been robbed, do you not think he would have a great deal more in those ragged pockets?" If only I carried, like so many of my contemporaries in the *ton*, a quizzing glass to depress pretension. "I merely stopped to ask the way. The hayseed took forever to fathom the answer, but at last he gave me the information I needed and I rewarded him with those few pence." Only now did I see that I had perhaps been overgenerous, even in the circumstance I had invented. But my father was renowned for his largesse. Perhaps I had inherited this tendency; my dear friend Dr Hansard would no doubt venture some worthwhile opinion. I felt in my purse again. "Gentlemen, since you have been put to such needless trouble, perhaps I

5

might reimburse you. But return those paltry coins to the man and send him on his way first. I fear he has already been delayed too long."

How much of my tale they believed, I do not know. I doubt it was much. But their credulity was oiled by the sight of two bright half-sovereigns. My would-be assailant loped off into woodland the far side of the road from which they had appeared. Soon my rescuers dawdled away, no doubt reflecting on the eccentricity of the Quality.

But it was not only aristocrats who were eccentric. The highwayman had tried to ply his trade without loading his gun.

The rest of my journey was uneventful enough, possibly because I now kept my eyes and ears open. If I had hoped for a glimpse of the man, to reassure him that I would keep my promises, I was disappointed.

Naturally I would say nothing of this to my mother. She always found plenty to worry about without my giving her genuine cause.

"I do not like to see you looking so thin, Tobias," Mama told me, as she drew me down on to the sofa beside her. She paused as Lady Radway graciously passed us our tea. We were both guests at Radway Park in Worcestershire, whence I would accompany her to the Mintons' seat. Thence she would progress to the family's London house, for the best part of the Season, and I would return to the rectory I was honoured to call home.

As our hostess moved away, Mama added, "I fear you may be ill. You ate so very sparingly — and rarely have I seen so many tempting dishes at an informal dinner party."

"You know, Mama, that Lady Radway can never let slip the opportunity to feed her guests so that they resemble nothing so much as oven-ready capons."

"She is the most generous of hostesses. But you did not share in the general indulgence, Tobias." She looked at me searchingly. "Is it your stomach that ails you? Or is it your heart?" She touched the back of my hand with her fan.

"I assure you, my dearest Mama, that my heart is intact." My response was too abrupt. I added thoughtfully and by no means untruthfully, "In fact, I might commission you to find me a suitable wife amongst your acquaintance."

My mother had the most expressive smiles of any lady I knew; you might say indeed that she had a range of smiles at her disposal. This one indicated a most unladylike cynicism. "And I suppose I have an absolutely free range?" She counted off attributes on her fingers. "An heiress? Yes — provided that she would not mind giving up her life in the *ton* and her ten thousand a year so that her new husband might feed the poor? Yes, certainly an heiress." Her smile changed subtly: "A light and elegant dancer? I know you would have no other, but I must find one familiar with the works of all the philosophers? A great reader? She would love your library, but rarely sit in it, since she must constantly devote herself to good works amongst your flock. Have I missed anything? Ah, yes! You require a notable musician — but one whose nimble fingers would surrender their rightful place on an elegant harp in a warm parlour to wrestle with the mysteries of ecclesiastical music, as manifest by some wheezing organ in an ice-cold church."

"Indeed, Mama," I said, rising to her bait just as she knew I would, "the one that graces our otherwise humble St Jude's is accounted by the cognoscenti to be amongst the finest provincial instruments in the country." I sighed. Was it a sin to have such an extravagance that was hardly ever played, let alone listened to with any understanding, in such a poor parish? I once suggested it should be sold, the proceeds being given to those who were literally starving, but the churchwardens had greeted my proposal with a most decided negative. Taking the long view, I knew that they were right.

"If your heart is whole," Mama persisted, returning to her original theory, "it must be the case that you are ill. The truth, if you please."

"How could that be the case, with my dear friends Dr and Mrs Hansard to care for me?" I parried. Were I to tell her of my self-imposed rules for Lent, she would be even more alarmed. There was nothing in the Church's teaching that required me to give up so many of the delights of the table. But how could I indulge myself with a clear conscience when my Master gave up everything in the wilderness? "I promise you, Mama, that their dining room is more familiar to me than my own, much to poor Mrs Trent's despair. In many respects, she is a most admirable housekeeper: her care of linen is unsurpassed, I believe; the rooms are spotless; she rules my little maidservant with a rod of iron."

"You have omitted one essential in a woman not merely the housekeeper but also, in an establishment your size, the cook," Mama pointed out dryly. "The ability to produce a palatable meal. I infer, Tobias, that the reason you dine so often with your friends is that you are barely able to eat your own cook's offerings. But that should not have prevented you from indulging yourself tonight." She looked at me shrewdly.

"I will confess that I have strangely lost the ability to feast without stinting." It was true: the less I ate the less I wanted to eat. But I might go on the offensive: "I will not sully the evening's entertainment by disclosing to you how much port we gentlemen consumed tonight before we joined you ladies here in the drawing room. Whereas Lord Merrivale and his brothers are still steady enough on their feet to play billiards, I truly believe that I would be under their table, snoring loudly, had I taken a quarter of what they had imbibed."

"Your father fears you are turning Methodist," she observed, so quietly that I had to lean towards her.

"Then you may tell him how much I enjoyed the Chablis with the fish, and the port with the excellent Stilton," I said coldly. I feared that if I did not check her enquiries she would discover that I took no tithes from the parishioners; even if I had been so desirous, it did not take a mathematician's brain to tell me that a tenth of nothing was — nothing.

Never had I been so pleased to see our hostess sailing towards us again, her turban more like the crest on a knight's helmet than a piece of innocent silk. Her figure, according to the Gainsborough portrait of her that graced the morning room, had once been sylph-like, and she had been, by Mama's account, a most wonderful dancer, always the first to have her hand claimed at a ball or assembly, though that might have owed a little to the circumstance of her having been the most notable heiress of the season; all too clearly, over the last quarter of a century she had enjoyed the dishes that made her table groan.

"My dear Lord . . . Oh, I still find it hard to call you Dr Campion," she said, with the vestiges of a winsome smile showing regrettable teeth. "My dear sir, it deeply grieves me to see a handsome gentleman such as yourself sitting apart from my other guests, even if — perhaps especially if — the lady to whom he is dedicating himself is his mother. Now," she continued, looking about her with satisfaction. "There are enough young people here to set up a country dance or two, and the governess has fingers that will make your feet fly. And I know that dear Lady Hartland is the most proficient of whist players: my husband craves the indulgence of partnering you in a rubber or two."

"You mistake, ma'am," I said with a smile. "My mother is not merely proficient: she enjoys most extraordinary good fortune. It is to be trusted that her opponents play for no more than pence." Truth to tell,

10

were my father ever to lose all his money on 'Change, Mama would have been more than capable of running a profitable gaming house, with no weighted dice and not a single bent card in the establishment.

"And if Lady Hartland is to be otherwise occupied, might I present you to a partner?"

I hesitated.

My mother spoke swiftly. "Tobias, you might wish to mortify your flesh by declining to join the set, but I tell you straight that you should not mortify the flesh of a poor young lady by making her a wallflower. Of course my son needs a partner, Lady Radway." Turning so that only I could see, she mouthed the words, "And a saintly wife!"

Much as I might wish my heart to be saintly, the moment I took my place with a pretty blonde Miss Chisholm for the first country dance, my feet took over. I had always enjoyed dancing, probably even more for the movement than for the chance to become acquainted with a charming young lady. Miss Chisholm gave way in time to a fubsy-faced Miss Fairclough, and she to a red-haired Miss Anne — I never learnt her surname. Alas for my mother's hopes, they were interchangeable in their determined smiles and insipid conversation, and none had dainty feet.

But Lady Julia Pendragon was altogether different. She emerged from a bruising encounter with Lady Radway's nephew, a lad about to go up to Oxford, still managing a smile, though I would conjecture that it concealed gritted teeth. Tall, dark and lithe, Lady Julia was the younger sister of a college friend of mine; my recollections of her included her climbing an illicit but tempting tree to rescue the housekeeper's cat and a failed attempt to teach me to skate. Now, however, she appeared perilously like any other demure young lady, determined to talk vapid nothings.

It was clearly time to remind her of the time when her scapegrace elder brother put a lowly domestic article on the head of a particularly ugly Roman statue on the terrace of one of their country seats — was it in Radnorshire or perhaps in Herefordshire?

She flushed becomingly, shaking her head and failing to suppress a laugh. "Indeed, Tobias — Oh, I beg your pardon . . ."

"Tobias is my name, Lady Julia, and I am more than happy for you to use it. However, I prefer to be known to strangers simply as Dr Campion — as Henry may have told you."

I fancied the pressure on my hand might have increased as she said, "Indeed, Tobias. I honour you for it. But I must tell you that there are incidents which it is entirely inappropriate for a man of the cloth to allude to." This time her chuckle was open. "And I have to confess that I am no longer so adept with a cricket ball." It was she, after all, who had thrown the missile that had mercifully despatched the piece of china.

The dance separated us, but each time we returned to each other we found another happy memory to amuse us. Then, I know not how, the conversation moved forward of its own accord as we found our way to the green saloon where our kind hostess had ordered further refreshments to be laid out: over a glass of champagne we found that we were charmed by the same music, the same books. Naturally we also spoke of her brother's new life, and of mine. "Do you recollect, Julia, an earnest young groom who did his best to make sure I never broke more than my collarbone? Jem?"

"The one who insisted I train my puppy properly? Jem by name and gem by nature, my old nurse used to say."

"The very one. He moved with me to Moreton St Jude's."

"I would have expected nothing less — although I collect yours is a very small establishment and he might reasonably have expected a better post on a great estate . . . I'm sorry. You and your father —"

I declared swiftly, "A better post Jem has. He is no longer a man subject to the whims of a selfish employer. He has quit caring for horses and puppies. He has become our village schoolmaster, with his own cottage. My dear Julia, I wish you could see how he is transforming the young and ignorant minds of his charges."

Her bright dimpled smile rewarded me — but her face clouded. "But Tobias, it must be a very lonely existence for him. Consider, before he always had his fellow servants for company, even if his prime duty was to you. How does he pass his leisure time?"

"He has the best-kept cottage garden in the village," I said. This was true, but not the whole truth. Was Lady Julia ready to hear that whenever I dined with Dr and Mrs Hansard, Jem would be there too, as an honoured guest and our social and intellectual equal? On the whole, I thought not. In any case I had to relinquish her to the hands of another dancer.

"I hope to hear more of Jem tomorrow," she declared over her shoulder as the pimply youth made his bow and took her hand. "Like Scheherazade in reverse."

"Alas, Julia, I shall have quit Radway Park before your maid even pulls back your curtains. My mother is an early riser, and expects others to follow her lead." Perhaps I nursed a fledgling hope that she rose early too. But she said nothing, and I smiled her on her way.

My next three partners were enough to drive anyone into the dismals.

My mother shook her head as I lit her candle at the foot of the stairs. "You do not look around hopefully at any of these young ladies, Tobias: you do not need to tell me that your heart is still whole. But one day," she added, with the roguish dimple that must have bewitched my father in his youth, "I wager you my winnings tonight —" she shook her reticule — "that ere the year is out, I will have made a match for you."

"With your talent for gambling, Mama, I would not dare bet against you." I might not have made the wager, but I suspected that after all I should have won it, until, that is, the following morning as I handed Mama into her carriage I chanced to look back at the house and saw an open window and Julia Pendragon waving from it.

Since Passion Week, the most solemn period of the Christian calendar, was now almost upon us, I could do little more than consign my mother to my cousin's care and return to my parish. To please Mama I stayed one night. Cousin Bromwich was a harmless enough man, so long as a good dinner burdened his table. His wife indulged him in this — overindulged, one might say — and he suffered terribly from gout. No matter where he had taken the waters, there was no sign of a cure. As I set out the following morning, Mama, holding Titus's bridle herself, hissed that she was sure that a regime like mine would be perfectly efficacious.

"I must remember to invite him to stay with me," I said, my eyes gleaming, "next Lent."

"And would you invite me and your Papa? Tobias, your face looks like thunder at the very mention of him. This is no way to behave — and you a man of the cloth, charged with reminding people to forgive fellow sinners that they might be forgiven!"

"My dearest Mama, I remember him every time I kneel in prayer. God knows that I forgive him. But he has not forgiven me, as you are all too well aware."

She dropped her eyes: she found it hard to lie.

I laughed gently. "Never once, when you have signed your letters to me, have you written that Papa joined you in your good wishes. My dearest Mama, it was he who broke his foot as he tried to kick me down the stairs."

"Only because you had broken his heart, going against his express desire that you took a commission, and insisting on being ordained."

Titus, aware of conflicting pressures, from the one at his head and the other on his back, shuffled uneasily.

"When my earthly father desires one thing and my heavenly Father another, whom should I obey?"

Her hand flew in an impatient gesture. "I fear you are not aware how priggish you can sound."

I tried not to flinch, but now to my ears my voice sounded greasy with self-justification. "Mama, you know full well that I could never, ever have fulfilled my Lord Hartland's ambitions for me —"

"Lord Hartland?" she repeated sharply, unsettling Titus still further. "Indeed, Tobias —"

"He disowned me — said I was no longer his son. How else should I refer to him? He dismissed me from his sight forever, and indeed, Mama, much as I would like to return to the fold, I fear another attack of the fury with which he despatched me from his presence would bring about another seizure. His heart —"

"Is already in pieces. Well, Tobias, I can see that in common parlance I should save my breath to cool my porridge." Her voice cracked.

"I promise you, Mama, that the moment my father is ready to treat me as his son, I will be before him on my knees entreating his blessing."

She nodded, as if but partially satisfied. She added pettishly, as Titus made it clear he wanted to be on his way, "I do not like you to jaunter around the country on your own like —"

"Like the country parson I am," I finished for her, to her obvious chagrin, but also dry amusement.

"At least you do not look like one today. In those buckskins and boots you look quite the gentleman again. And such a smart hat!"

16

By now, feeling a traitor to my calling, I was as anxious as Titus to depart.

"Find me a wife, Mama. The paragon you spoke of the other evening. She does not even need to be an heiress."

CHAPTER
TWO

As if even at that distance he knew which route would take him most quickly to his stable, Titus set off at a brisk but sustainable pace, with the minimum of guidance from me. He had always been in the care of Jem, of whom I had spoken to Lady Julia. Even now my heart glowed at the delights of our conversation and our time dancing together. Could she possibly even consider . . . But the last time I had allowed myself a reverie, I had been accosted. I had been lucky the other day but might not be again. So I dragged my thoughts from her, and tried to be alert to any possible dangers.

Had he been a human friend, Titus would have given a knowing laugh. As it was, he made it subtly clear that he was glad I was in control again, and I found myself talking to him as if he could reply.

We agreed that he might have missed the attentions of Jem, of whom I had spoken to Julia, when Jem took his new position. Now he was technically in the hands of Robert, a silent mouse of a workhouse orphan, though Jem, as much out of affection for Titus as any sense of duty, paid almost daily visits to ensure his standards were being maintained.

Had they not been, I'm sure Titus would have made his feelings clear. However, Jem declared that until he had taught Robert to speak, something he steadfastly refused to do in my presence, there was little point in even attempting to teach him his letters. Accordingly, though he should have been well above mucking out a stable, Jem talked as he shovelled and helped the lad brush Titus till he was glossier than ever. Their labour done, Robert was submitted to a cleansing under the pump, which Mrs Trent thought entirely appropriate in one so young. At this point Jem would often but not always join me in my parlour for a glass of Mrs Trent's home-brewed ale. He insisted that he did not wish to be seen in the village as in some way *presuming*, a term which denoted complete disapproval of any notion of social equality.

Titus pricked his ears. What had he heard or seen? But it was only the familiar profile of the church in which I was privileged to lead the worship. Had I not been very much aware of my old friend's desire to reach his stable, I would have stopped there for a few minutes, even in my travel-stained state, to thank God for the delights of my daily life. However, I could do that as well in the privacy of my own chamber, which called me as loudly as the loose box called Titus.

Between them, Mrs Trent and Susan, the maid of all work, had spring-cleaned the rectory yet again; they rarely confined their activities to the spring, although I had to admit that this time their choice of season was apposite. At least they had remembered to replace each item in my study in its rightful place, rather than tidying it away out of sight, so I could find the drafts of the sermons I was to deliver on Palm Sunday and on Good Friday and Easter Day. However, I would postpone revising them until I had shed my fine travelling attire and donned something more appropriate to my calling. As usual, with no more qualms than if I had been Robert, I sluiced myself down under the pump in the yard, inevitably shocking poor Mrs Trent. I could hear Robert talking to Titus as he rubbed him down. Perhaps one day, when Mrs Trent's very homely cooking had done its work and he was filling out the clothes she had so kindly made him, he might talk to me. As yet, however, he confined himself to tugging his forelock, his eyes firmly locked on the ground, though his smile whenever Titus appeared was a pleasure to see.

My skin a-quiver with gooseflesh, I considered I had mortified it enough, and was grateful that Mrs Trent had serenely disregarded my taste and lit a bright fire in my bedchamber, and one in every other room I might use. At least she had my direct order that if my quarters were warm, hers and Susan's must be too. As for Robert, for some reason he eschewed the bedchamber we had allocated him over the kitchen, a room small but always snug. Instead he silently insisted in sleeping either on a heap of straw in the loose box next to Titus's, a practice I discouraged, though I could understand how reassuring he must find the smell and sound of what he clearly considered his best friend, or curled up on the rag rug in front of the new kitchen range.

I had installed this on Maria Hansard's advice. It might be — was! — an extravagance for someone in my position and had at first challenged Mrs Trent to the point of her despair — and mine. But dear Mrs Hansard had feigned equal ignorance and the two had learnt how to use it together. Dr Hansard was outraged, hating his wife to do anything that reminded him, and no doubt others, that once she had been no more than a housekeeper.

She, however, had insisted, pointing out that mastering such a contraption, a smaller version of one she demanded for Langley Park's kitchen, meant that she would brook no excuses from any new cook who came their way in the future.

I was still before the bedroom fire securing my bands when the sound of horses drew me to the window. A very fine curricle and pair, the horses beautifully matched: who could be driving such a natty equipage? Could it be — could it truly be — that my father had against all the odds decided to visit me? But he would have stood on greater ceremony, dumbfounding my poor neighbours with all his formal and lordly splendour in his favourite coach, attended by outriders and liveried footmen.

Deducing that it must be one of my old school or university friends who had strayed so far from the main road to come to see me, I finished my toilette hastily, still watching with eagerness, though endeavouring not to be seen. The tiger jumped down to take the leader's head. His coat was sufficiently well cut to suggest that his master must have money to burn. Was it Edmund Walton, always a bit of a dandy? Or Tom Alleyne?

Thanking goodness for Mrs Trent's cleaning frenzy, I ran downstairs to my study, anxious in a childish way to demonstrate a serious endeavour suitable to my calling. I quickly laid on my beautifully polished desk my pile of draft sermons; a couple of volumes suitable for such a spiritual endeavour; my Bible; clean paper; and a trimmed pen.

In the event, I was relieved that I had thus prepared. The visitor whom Mrs Trent ushered punctiliously into my presence was no college friend but a man ten or fifteen years my senior, Archdeacon Giles Cornforth. He too had eschewed clerical garb for travelling. My clothes had been ideal for riding; his were far smarter. In his exquisitely tailored coat he could have been on his way to some select London club.

My face must have shown considerable surprise, which, since I had taken care that no one could see my spying, he interpreted as an appropriate confusion from one so lowly in the ecclesiastical hierarchy in the presence of a veritable prince of the Church. He looked for some few moments at the ink on my fingers. Nonetheless he deigned to shake my hand, for all he thought it the paw of some grubby schoolboy.

Over a glass of Madeira, and some of Mrs Trent's biscuits, baked to surprising perfection, thanks, perhaps, to that new stove, we exchanged suitably meaningless pleasantries. At last, however, Archdeacon Cornforth withdrew his pocket watch, as if not trusting the handsome timepiece on the mantelpiece, and declared that he really ought to be on his way to Lichfield. He was to dine with the bishop.

"Now, Tobias, my dear fellow, I have a request to make. You will be conducting all the appropriate services this Eastertide, I make no doubt? And I perceive that you are already preparing your sermons." He raised a fashionable quizzing glass and peered at what now seemed all too rough and ready a pile of paper. He picked up one of the volumes of others' sermons: it was a collection by a cousin of Lady Julia's, as it happened, Lucius Allardyce, chaplain at an Oxford college.

I tried not to sound defensive, and may have overreacted. "Indeed, Archdeacon, and with the greatest of joy."

He nodded as if I was some puppy whose overeager prancing both amused and irritated him. "In that case, I feel it not inappropriate to ask you to take extra services. Not here, man, but over in Clavercote. In — what's the name of the church?"

"All Souls'. The rector is the Reverend Adolphus Coates, as I recall." Clavercote was about ten miles distant, and to my chagrin I found I did not feel the enthusiasm I ought for journeying back and forth to a distant parish with which I had no connection.

"The very man. To cut to the chase, Tobias, he has written to the bishop: briefly and at the shortest of notice he informed him that he was about to travel on the Continent for the sake of his health."

"The Continent?" I echoed in disbelief.

"Quite," the Archdeacon said with asperity. "Why, with Europe in its present chaotic state, Mr Coates does not choose to repair to Bath or to Cheltenham, I for one do not know. Nor do I know how long he proposes to recover from whatever ailment he fancies afflicts him. Apparently the rectory is locked up and the servants dispersed. Now, you have a reputation, Tobias, for — shall we say — going the extra mile? So it is to you that the bishop has turned. Palm Sunday; Good Friday; Easter Day. We will endeavour to prise a curate or two away from other parishes after that." He shot a surprisingly shrewd look under his well-shaped eyebrows. "I did not think, Tobias, that you would want our Easter celebrations to be conducted by anyone second-rate."

"It is not for me to judge —" I protested.

"No. But it is for the bishop and my humble self to do so. I will tell him that you have agreed, then." He looked me in the eye. "If you will forgive the observation, my young friend, there are times when your righteousness teeters towards self-righteousness. Just a friendly word of warning, nothing more." He nodded home the point with as much authority as if he was wearing alb and cassock. "And here is a note for the Clavercote churchwardens," he added with a slightly curious inflection, "to say that everything is in hand."

Taking this as an exit line, I rang for Mrs Trent to request my visitor's hat and gloves. Then I escorted him myself to his equipage, which had gathered a small crowd of scrawny village lads, alternately jeering at the young tiger, who was far too high in the instep even to acknowledge their presence, and offering knowledge-able appraisals of the horseflesh.

For a moment, the archdeacon's face clouded. "Pray God this year will see better crops," he said. "And lower corn prices, of course." Reaching into the leather squabs of the curricle, he pulled forth an almost feminine knitted purse. From it he drew a fistful of coins, which he threw towards the lads. To my shame, Robert was amongst the first to dive for them. He, who at least had a roof over his head, and three good meals a day, in addition to all the apples and cakes Mrs Trent thrust into his grubby hands! To do this while some of the other lads were from some of the poorest homes in the village. I must rebuke him.

Then I perceived that other equally fortunate boys were also scrabbling in the dirt: two of the churchwardens' sons were there, elbowing others in the ribs with a will.

I hung my head. I had forgotten any boy's absolute need to compete for anything, especially if it involved falling over and writhing in mud to obtain it. My mother's word rang in my ears: what a prig I was becoming indeed.

Waving the archdeacon on his regal way I reflected that if nothing else I had a theme for a forthcoming sermon. *Judge not that ye be not judged.*

CHAPTER
THREE

Despite the bitter cold, the next day was so fine I decided to make the journey myself. Successive landlords in my parish had invested enough in their land to ensure it was well drained and in good heart. Soon, however, I rode through lanes in such a state of disrepair I was worried that even the sure-footed Titus might miss his step, and was far more alert in the saddle than yesterday.

The outskirts of Clavercote were deserted, with no sign of anyone within the sad, mean dwellings or working outside. And yet I had the curious sensation of being watched, which continued the deeper into the village I penetrated. There was not so much as the shout of a child or the bark of a dog.

Since I did not know the names, let alone the whereabouts of the churchwardens, I had perforce to rap on a door. There was no reply. At last I located the church noticeboard torn from its rotting supports and lying half hidden in a ditch. Although I did not trust the bank of the ditch to support me if I tried to rescue the board, I could at least read most of it, and was directed to the key keeper, Mr Powell. His door was opened a mere crack by a slatternly creature who, holding her apron to her face and backing from me as if I carried the plague, tried to slam the door in my face. At last, assisted by a few coins, she directed me to the cottage of the nearest churchwarden, a man rejoicing in the name of Mr Boddice, if my ears were to be believed. However, the poor creature had so few teeth and such bad cold-sores that I had every cause to doubt them.

The cottage stood at a little distance from the others. It looked more prosperous, in that there was an obviously productive kitchen garden, presently scratched over by glossy-plumaged hens. There was also the decided smell of at least one pig. Tying Titus firmly to the gatepost, I stepped up to the front door, though I suspected that most visitors presented themselves at the kitchen door round the back. However, a little ceremony never came amiss.

It seemed that Mr Boddice was not at home, at least according to an adenoidal maid — or daughter, it was hard to tell. Regarding me with what seemed almost like distaste, she directed me to Mr Lawton's place, just up the lane yonder.

If the so-called lane was naught more than a shallow stream, who was I to argue? Titus picked his way delicately if disdainfully through the foul water, but then shied unexpectedly as a stone flew past. It was followed by another. Neither was large enough to do harm, I told Titus, but the image of the tiny stone from David's sling hitting Goliath's temple filled my mind. Without much prompting from me, Titus decided a moving target would be harder to hit than a stationary one, and our progress to the warden's house was brisk.

I arrived breathless and more than a little splashed. The house was about the same size as St Jude's rectory — four-square, solidly built, sitting confidently on a slight rise. Another horse was already tied up outside. The chill wind and absence of stable boy to escort Titus to temporary quarters made me resolve to keep my visit as short as was polite. Being out in all weathers, and never knowing if there would be any shelter for Titus, I had got into the habit of carrying a thick rug to throw over him. Usually there was an urchin at hand to guard both rug and horse. Here there was no one in sight. On the other hand, Titus, well trained by Jem, had ways of dealing with strangers, so I covered him and, leaving him to make the acquaintance of his fellow creature, I strode to the front door.

This time I was greeted with a curtsy by a young woman whose cap and apron were pleasingly clean. Telling me she would fetch the master, she relieved me of my hat, gloves and whip, and showed me swiftly into a sunny parlour, in which the lingering smell of coffee with an undertone of beef suggested it doubled as a breakfast room. So far, so good. But I kicked my heels there for nearly twenty minutes before the master in question deigned to appear, closely followed by another middle-aged man. Both were rotund, their noses and cheeks swollen and in hue the bluish-red that implies the consumption of a great deal of port and roast beef. For a moment I wished I was dressed as I had been yesterday, as a gentleman, and that I might slap my whip impatiently against my buckskins. But I was here as a parson, was I not, so I fixed on a benevolent smile and awaited their apologies for the unconscionable delay. None came. To my astonishment — my clerical attire usually elicited politeness, if not respect — they stared at me as if the pig had wandered in from his sty.

Despite myself I pulled rank. "The Reverend Dr Tobias Campion at your service, gentlemen. And whom do I have the honour of addressing?" My father could not have looked down his nose with more *hauteur*.

The older, more prosperous man declared himself to be Squire Lawton. His companion was indeed Mr Boddice.

"You are the churchwardens of All Souls', I believe, gentlemen? The archdeacon has sent me to you."

The news obviously gave them little pleasure. "Has he indeed?" ventured Mr Boddice.

"He has asked me to lead your Holy Week worship," I pursued, "in the unavoidable absence of your own rector. I was sorry to hear of Mr Coates' indisposition — I hope and pray that his travels will restore his health," I added as a matter of form.

What had I said to give offence? I verily believe that had he been outside, Mr Boddice would have spat on the ground.

"Yes," he grunted. "All the windows barred and locked and the servants sent away."

Just as the archdeacon had said.

Squire Lawton's face remained stony. At last he asked, "And how many services were you planning to lead, Rector?"

At last I felt on firmer ground. With a smile, I said, "All those that Mr Coates proposed, of course. Though

I fear that in view of my own parish duties we may have to negotiate the times of the services themselves. I have noted on this sheet of paper the hours I am engaged in Moreton St Jude's."

They exchanged the tiniest of glances, as if the name of the parish meant more than my own. So be it: my role was more important than any name. But Boddice had taken the paper, holding it by the extreme edges as if it might contaminate him. He jabbed a thick finger. Lawton nodded ponderously, his jowls undulating with the movement.

"These are the same times as we'd expect to hold our own services, so I'm afraid you won't do, Parson Campion. So we'll say thank'ee and wish you good day."

Although shamefully relieved to have been excused from the duty, I said, passing over the archdeacon's note, "Perhaps you should communicate your decision to the archdeacon. He asked me to deliver this."

At no point had I been asked to sit, but at this point chose to find a chair myself, adopting my father's pose, which always conveyed a nice blend of patience and irritation via the angle of his folded arms and the slight movement of the leg crossing the other.

Lawton's face empurpled further. "This is a damned instruction!"

"Saving your presence, Parson," Boddice added ingratiatingly.

Lawton shoved the sheet under my nose. It did indeed read like an edict.

"All I can say is that I am as bound by his request as you are," I said. I got to my feet. "So it seems we must negotiate our service times after all, gentlemen . . ."

As far as I knew, young Robert had seen no sign of my disapproval when the previous day he had scrabbled for the archdeacon's largesse. Ought I, however, to make some sort of apology to him for my small-minded criticism? Or was I making a mental mountain out of a non-existent molehill?

Between periods of pondering my encounter with the bitter souls of Clavercote, I wondered how I could make life better for the unhappy lad under my own roof. How might I make him feel valued? How could I make him feel he deserved the warmth and comfort I was trying to offer him? My usual exchanges with him were — as had been this morning's — simple commands, expressed courteously, and always followed by warm and genuine thanks. But talking to a stone wall might have been as profitable. And more enjoyable for the wall: poor Robert evinced a visible distaste for human interlocution.

At last, returning Titus to his silent care, I turned to the One to whom I took all my cares. Stepping into the calm of St Jude's, I said matins and spent a long period in silent prayer, offering to God my earthly problems. I had long learnt not to expect an instant response, knowing that any divine revelation would come in the Lord's good time. At last I rose, and walked slowly back to the rectory, relishing the calling of the birds and the sight of bobbing daffodils. What a blessed time Easter was. No wonder the ancients had chosen it for one of their festivals long before our Lord walked on the earth.

I made my way not into the house but to the stables, where Titus was having the rubbing down of his life. Jem had clearly taught Robert most if not all of his skills. Soon — if ever the lad discovered his tongue — he could learn his letters, and I was sure he would make a good pupil.

As usual, Robert had carefully moved to the far side of Titus.

"You'll take any amount of brushing like that, won't you, old boy?" I asked, rubbing his nose, which was as usual searching for an apple or a carrot. "But I wonder if all is well with that right foreleg of yours. I fancied it felt a little tight. Do you think it needs a poultice?" I spoke to Titus, but as I had hoped, Robert responded.

He paused in his activities and ran his small, thin hands expertly over the leg I really thought was perfectly sound. So, it seemed, did he. Staring at the ground, he shook his head.

"It seemed a mite . . . when I was riding," I lied. "Why not mount him yourself and see?"

Eyes round, he stared.

"Do you need a saddle? When I was your age, Jem made sure that I could ride my pony bareback, and I wager he has also taught you."

"Not Titus," he breathed to the nearest bale of straw.

No, not Titus. "Well, today is the day you shall ride Titus and surprise Jem," I declared, shrugging off my coat and rolling up my sleeves.

32

I do not know how many times we had been round the paddock when I espied Mrs Hansard's handsome new gig outside the rectory. "Robert, we have work to do," I declared, lengthening my stride. Titus did likewise, and I feared for Robert's safety. But he might have been glued to the horse's willing back, and soon I had to run to keep up. Within moments Titus and Mrs Hansard's pony were secure in their loose boxes. Robert would be agreeably busy for the next few minutes.

"My dear Tobias," Maria greeted me with an affectionate squeeze of the hands, as I led her into the house, "it is to be hoped that Mrs Trent has a large quantity of hot water to hand. Look at the mud! Whatever possessed you?" It was hard to tell whether she mocked or was genuinely shocked. "Now, upstairs with you, and I will send Susan up with as much water as she can carry. And you will be well served if it is cold and if your bedchamber fire is out."

"Maria, if you will engage to remain in the kitchen with Mrs Trent, both averting your gaze from the yard, there is a much quicker way of dealing with my dirt."

Fortified by a glass of Madeira and some of those excellent biscuits, Mrs Hansard told me that she had been distributing food to the poorest of the villagers. She had also no doubt been offering work to able-bodied men. Regardless of the expense, Edmund and she had paid teams of villagers to repair their walls and fences, and other workers had pressed stones into muddy tracks to make decent paths. They were paid largely in kind, Maria being especially anxious that every member of each family would benefit. Any housewife feeding her rations to her husband, or denying her daughters to the benefit of sons would be sternly but kindly rebuked. After all, she would point out prosaically, the womenfolk needed energy to sew the veritable acres of flannel she had persuaded one of Edmund's grateful patients to pay for, and to knit worsted stockings. To be sure it was spring, and the maidens should have been looking forward to making pretty summer dresses, but as long as they were hungry, they were cold.

"Edmund labours night and day," she continued. "I fear it is only the needs of Moreton St Jude's that keep him here, not dashing off like some raw recruit to tend our soldiers in Spain. I collect that the casualties have been severe indeed at Badajoz. They say that Wellesley wept at the sight of the men whose lives were so terribly lost, heaped in the trenches and the breaches. And those poor men who survived, but who have lost limbs and will be unable to fight again — they will be returning home hoping to be treated as heroes and given work, or even pensions . . ."

"And will in all likelihood merely swell the numbers begging or simply starving," I concluded for her. Perhaps the man who had accosted me had been a soldier. Pray God he was not a deserter: the army was not kind to those who had strayed from their ranks.

"These are hard times, Maria. I should pray for victory, I know, but all I want is a prosperous peace."

"Amen to that," she said reverently. Then she smiled. "But now I must take my leave of you and make sure that Cook is aware that you will be joining us at Langley Park for supper — which of course you will, will you not?"

"What Mrs Trent called a good healthy spit-roasting bird, Tobias, I would consider to be no more than a scrawny fowl fit only for the pot," Mrs Hansard declared, raising her glass of sherry in emphasis. She settled more comfortably in her favourite chair, a little distance from the bright fire that illumined her elegant drawing room. "So by dining with us you do her a favour: she will not have to apologise to you once again for the inadequacy of your dinner and she, Susan and Robert will at least get the less stringy breast meat to chew on. As for the legs — I declare the poor bird must have walked to market . . ."

"And a parson really needs to keep his finger on the pulse of his parish," Edmund declared. "What better source of information than the doctor? So eat and drink your fill with us. Heavens, man," he added with asperity as I gestured away the decanter that their butler, Burns, was proffering, "I shall be glad when Easter is come and gone and you can start eating again like an Englishman. Not that you will," he continued, looking at me sternly under his brows. "Not until the spring brings a more abundant supply of food for your parishioners, eh? Why do folk not realise what a hard time it is, when all the winter supplies have long since been eaten and that which is in the ground has yet to grow?"

"We cannot change Nature," Mrs Hansard reflected. "But it would be good to find a better way to distribute her bounty, so that all might share and there were less hardship."

"Pray, my love, take care where you utter sentiments like that, or they will take you as a veritable revolutionary, keen to raise a guillotine or two over here."

"When one hears of goings on like those at Orebury House," she retorted, "one is surprised that our poor did not take arms as the French did."

"My dear Maria," Hansard said, raising a hand, "pray do not take rumours as facts. Or servants' gossip as gospel."

I stared at him, amazed that he should rebuke her so publicly. A glance at Burns's normally inscrutable countenance suggested that he was shocked, but I knew that he would have bitten off his tongue rather than reveal any domestic secret. Though younger than I, and the most vicious bowler and attacking batsman in the village team, here he was the embodiment of sober respectability and discretion.

Within a heartbeat, however, Hansard was apologising. "I beg your pardon, my dear. I should not have uttered those words, especially in such a tone. In truth, I lost yet another babe this morning — delivered well before term, and with no hope of survival even had it ever drawn breath." He raised his eyes in challenge. "I trust you will make no objection to burying it in hallowed ground, Tobias?"

36

"*Suffer the little children to come unto me.*" I drained my sherry as if defying those who would argue, and did not protest when the silent Burns refilled it.

Once Burns, whose skills as he served at the table improved by the day, was no longer present, we lingered over our port, Maria sipping what always seemed to me her only real indulgence, a glass of champagne. Only then did I venture to refer to the issue that had caused controversy before dinner. "You spoke, my dear friends, of gossip about Orebury House. Even if it is no more than servants' tittle-tattle, I should be glad to hear it. Forewarned is forearmed." Perhaps I spoke disingenuously. Lord Hasbury, who withdrew to his country seat, Orebury, when his creditors pressed too hard in London, was an old friend of my father's — and not, according to Mama, a good influence. What if my father were present?

"Oh, as to that, it is little more than the most idle of talk. The *on dit* is that there is a large house party gathered there: tons of food and gallons of champagne have naturally arrived by the cartload. Furthermore, coaches full of light-skirts have hurtled through the night, depriving honest folk of their sleep. In short, Tobias, an orgy is planned if not already in progress." His raised eyebrow indicated how much he believed the rumour. "Orebury's doings are not illegal, and possibly not even immoral — but given the hunger hereabouts, they are tactless. But when did the Upper Ten Thousand ever consider much apart from their pleasure? Nor," he said, with a wink, "do I want them

37

to. Where would I be without their gout and their vapours?"

There was a scratch at the door. Burns padded to Edmund's side. We held our breath: most likely this was another summons to a sickbed. But he announced another visitor.

"Oh, bid him come in, Burns — I do not know why he or you should stand on such ceremony! Jem, dear friend, welcome! I dare say Cook can find you a crumb of cheese. A crust of bread. The lees of our wine."

Mrs Hansard embraced him as if he were her son; Edmund and I shook him warmly by the hand.

"Now our circle is complete," Maria declared.

"I am sorry to come so between-times," Jem said. "Too late for dinner and too early for supper. In truth, I had rather lost count of time, as you do when you are thinking about something else."

"Something is troubling you, Jem," Mrs Hansard said: it was a statement, not a question. As Burns withdrew, she stretched out her hand, and seated him beside her. "Tell us how we may help."

CHAPTER
FOUR

"So it is too late for me to offer my services gratis?" Edmund said sadly. "Both the young mother and her baby? Dead and buried?"

Jem bowed his head. "Both. Both done to death by the mother's own hand. A maiden from near Clavercote. Molly Fowler, and the child unnamed. Despair drove her to it, they said: she was dead within a week of being brought to bed. The mill race." Edmund mouthed something to his wife, who nodded in sad agreement. "The villagers probably thought that the girl had brought disgrace on her family. So I know not that your help would have been accepted even had you been in time to offer it."

"Damned for having a child in her belly before she had a ring on her finger? Pshaw! I would wager that at most ten per cent of country girls are virgins when they are married: am I right, Tobias?"

It was Edmund's way to fend off emotion with intellectual truculence, so I indulged him. "In my limited experience you are. But there is a consensus that, by wedding her, the young man is making an honest woman of his bride, is there not? And in country eyes, I fear it makes sense to prove that both man and

39

woman are fertile before they are irrevocably bound together."

Jem stared. "Do I hear aright? You are usually the most morally upright of men, Tobias!" He sounded as much outraged as surprised.

I raised a mollifying hand. This was not the place to burden him and the Hansards with the pungent opinions of both my mother and the archdeacon and my reflections upon my treatment of Robert. Who was I to cast the first stone? "As Mrs Trent says when Susan drops yet another plate, 'What can't be cured must be endured.' I suspect that however much I disapprove of the practice, I can never change it. And at least the potential parents turn to the church to regularise the situation. I must thank God for that." I could not resist the urge to add with a smile of hopeful joy, "And every couple I bind at the altar brings to the font the infant that appears six months later." I added ruefully, before Edmund could voice the same thought, "Though that might owe less to a reverent desire to ask for the blessing of baptism than to Mrs Trent's good offices with the layette box." My housekeeper's skill with the needle was far superior to her uneven accomplishments in the kitchen. Each new mother received a sturdy box full of vital items of tiny clothing. As the child grew, the mother would launder the clothes one last time and return them to Mrs Trent, who would supply the next size. As for the box itself, it was big enough for the infant to sleep in for a few weeks. Mrs Trent liked to think that the idea was her own; Maria and I had long ago tacitly agreed not to remind her of its true origin.

Jem's jaw tightened stubbornly.

Hansard laid a hand on his arm. "For my part, I cannot fault the injunction I am surprised that Tobias has not already repeated: 'Judge not that ye be not judged.' But we digress. The poor young woman, I collect, was not betrothed to some village lad desirous of wedding her?"

If anything, Jem's face became even grimmer. "'Tis said that the maid was the paramour of a gentleman — one of Lord Wychbold's cronies, maybe. Him of Lambert Place."

It was indeed not unlikely that a man of the *ton* had taken advantage of an innocent maid, as I was about to observe when Hansard thundered, "Accursed rumour once again! And is there any evidence?" Nonetheless he placed a glass of port beside our friend.

It took Jem a few moments to reply. When he did so it was with the uncomfortable shift in his chair that he must have seen many of his young charges make when posed an awkward question. "There are always tales flying round about the noble lord," he said, his voice weighing down the last two words with irony, "and his devil worship."

"There have been ever since I moved to Moreton," Mrs Hansard corroborated. "And indeed his choice of society is to say the least unconventional, though not to my knowledge actually depraved. You cannot accuse him of belonging to the Hellfire set, surely? Look at that poet, for instance: he's a mere boy. Mr Julius Longstaff. The worst that is said of him is that he spends more time peering at his flowing locks in a looking-glass than worrying about his metre and his rhyme."

"The vanity if not the talent of Lord Byron," Edmund agreed. "Apart, however, from rumours that he has a regrettable penchant for recondite words and laboured rhymes, I too have heard nothing truly ill of him. Or, before you ask, of his two neighbours. Provided one does not pay any attention to their clothing."

"It is hard to do anything else. At least to Lady Blaenavon's, I understand, if not to Miss Witheridge's. By all accounts she at least is as conventional in dress as you or I," Maria said. "Lady Blaenavon, however . . ." She shrugged. "The *on dit* is that she is a great ugly woman given to wearing a strange mishmash of clothes. There is, of course, something eminently practical about jacket, cravat and heavy skirt divided into two like very wide sailors' trousers if one is striding about one's land. Especially were one to tuck them into one's boots . . . Consider," she continued, apparently blissfully unaware of the impropriety of her opinions, "how the toil of the poor laundrymaid would be eased, did she not have to wash the muddied flounces of her ladyship and the young ladies of the house when they returned from walks down dirty lanes. And in truth I will say that other housemaids would be able to accomplish other tasks with more decorum if they could wear them." She cast an impish glance at us all. "Before you upbraid me, dear Tobias, consider the inconvenience if you have to wear your surplice at all times. On horseback — what would Titus make of a

42

side-saddle? Your ablutions under the pump? And to my mind, breeches might be no less indecent than the dampened muslin gowns of certain fast young ladies who wish to leave nothing of their figure to the imagination." Her smile gathered us up. "Now I have shocked you all to the core, let us adjourn to the drawing room." She did not add, though it was true, that there our tea drinking would be watched over by ladies from the distant past, whose painted selves suggested no major preoccupation with modest attire.

Poor Molly Fowler — at fourteen no more than a child herself — had been one of Mr Coates's parishioners. Since it was clear that he was in no position to pay a visit of condolence to her family, I went myself, taking a discreet package containing flour, cheese, part of one of Mrs Trent's home-cured hams, and a little money. I did not wish them to feel patronised by any excess, but I had no doubt that like all the villagers they would welcome honest sustenance.

There was a straggle of ragged children eager to guard Titus, unaware, of course, that Titus had his own way of dealing with would-be riders yet to make his acquaintance. I warned them to keep clear of his hooves. Hallooing but getting no response from within the dwelling that the urchins assured me was occupied by the Fowlers, I stooped almost double to enter, via a doorway secured by nothing more solid than a sheep hurdle, what was little more than a gloomy hovel. A hole in the bedraggled thatch passed, no doubt, for a chimney when there was a fire on the cold hearth but currently admitting occasional flurries of the unseasonably cold rain that had squalled across my path this morning. Only a couple of crude shelves occupied by some primitive earthenware showed that this was a habitation meant for man, not beasts.

It was indeed unoccupied. Or did something stir in that bundle of rags in the deepest corner? Something? Or someone!

As my eyes grew accustomed to the gloom I understood the origin of those groans, those ill-suppressed screams. And knew that the woman — for that was what this creature was — needed more help than I could provide.

Shouting to the boys to fetch a woman to the hovel, I summoned Titus to me, and threw myself on to his back. This was a case for my dear friend Edmund and his medical instruments, and possibly for the precious case I kept ready by my own door: I knew not whether I would have to offer Holy Communion to a dying woman or to baptise a child emerging dying or even dead from the womb.

Whenever there was a situation like this, Edmund and I would make our independent ways, speed being more important than companionship. Both of us would ride what my young sister romantically described as *ventre à terre*: not for her the concept of two ordinary men doing their best to ride swiftly on not always easy terrain. Assuredly as he got older, and was now blessed with a wife, Edmund was more circumspect than he was wont to be; I fully expected him to be there perhaps fifteen minutes later than I. What I could not therefore comprehend was a horse and rider heading away from the hovel. From this distance — I was still over half a mile from the hamlet — I could recognise neither the rider nor his mount, a handsome grey. Who but a rich gentleman could afford an animal flying with such ease and grace over hedges and ditches? And why should a rich man appear as eager to get away from the hamlet as I was to reach it? And what might such a man be doing in such a sad forgotten corner of God's good earth in the first place?

The track was now so deeply rutted that it was time to offer guidance to Titus, who took my advice as if he really needed it. We picked a delicate route through mud and worse, arriving once again outside the hovel. As before, we attracted urchins, probably of both sexes. Mrs Trent — or Robert — had filled any space in my saddlebags with last autumn's apples, many too wizened to be eaten by anything except a hopeful horse or starving children. I tossed a few around as I threw balls at cricket practice, soft, easy catches, but, picking out the most likely child, passed not one apple but two. One was for Titus, the other for himself. As I mentally girded myself to enter the place of suffering, a figure emerged, carrying a bundle, from which a thin mewling struggled to emerge.

"'Tis Eliza Fowler's babe, Your Reverence," she declared, bobbing a hurried curtsy. "There's a woman down yonder as has just lost her own. Sarey Tump. I thought — but I'd best be quick."

"I'll be with you on the instant. First I must look to the poor mother." Fortunately I was not called on to do this alone. The sound of hooves heralded Edmund's arrival.

The woman looked at him bleakly, sniffed, and scurried off with her tiny burden.

Having said prayers I could not be sure the dying woman could hear or comprehend, I baptised her puny infant with the swiftly chosen name of Joseph, Sarey, the newly bereaved mother, standing as godmother. Her bemused daughter, a child of perhaps seven, set off to find her father in the coppice, wherever that might be. Feeling that for the moment I could do no more, I returned to see if I could assist Edmund, but he had already pulled what passed for a sheet over the dead mother's face and was forcing a little brandy down the throat of a man so begrimed and wizened it was impossible to attribute an age to him. Assuring him that I would conduct the funeral free of charge and that Edmund would pay for the grave, and leaving to hand the food I'd brought, we waited as he slid into a brandy-induced slumber.

Edmund had other calls to make in the area so when we reached our horses, still guarded by a platoon of half-starved children to whom we distributed a shower of pennies, we parted company. Titus picked his way disdainfully to the home of Mr Boddice, the churchwarden, with whom I had a short and forceful conversation concerning Mrs Fowler's burial service and interment.

Once again I mounted Titus, startling him by not turning for home. To be sure, it was late for a morning call, and I had not done him the courtesy of leaving my card beforehand. But I had a few observations to make to the landlord of this pitiable apology for a village and they would not wait for a more eligible occasion.

CHAPTER
FIVE

Lord Wychbold, a man in his later forties whose pallor suggested an aversion to outdoor activity, permitted himself a sneer of surprise at my precipitate arrival at Lambert Place, a huge establishment dating back to Elizabeth's time, but now in sad want of repair. Ensconced in his library, an untidy room one end of which he clearly used as his study, he raised his eyeglass at my travel-stained garments as he bade me, with clear reluctance, to take a seat. A pile of folios tottered on the floor beside him; with an irritated sigh he closed the one on his lap and placed it on the others. On the vast and elegant range of shelves, the books in regular use could be distinguished from the others by the presence of fingermarks on the spines; the rest were covered in a rich patina of dust. Mrs Trent would have spring-cleaned this every day until well into the autumn before she could declare herself satisfied. Meanwhile my coat would act as duster for the leather armchair to which he gestured me.

Since he had a glass of Madeira on the reading stand beside his chair, I felt it would be churlish to decline when he raised the decanter in my direction. The aged butler who had grudgingly admitted me reappeared with a glass — I cannot say a *clean* glass — on a salver that only its tarnish told me was silver.

"Without roundaboutation, Wychbold," I said, suspecting that to implore him as a humble clergyman would be less effective than to exhort him as an equal, "I am come to tell you that more must be done for your meanest tenants. I do not suggest you are obliged to build a model village for them, but the very least they need is a supply of fresh water and adequate drains. You treat them less well than the beasts of your fields, sir!" Truth to be told, they too were unhealthy enough, with very poor pasturage to sustain them.

He peered at me, though with little evidence of real interest. He might have been a tortoise, sniffing the air before sallying forth. But his eyes were sharper than they appeared. "Ah, Hartland's errant son. I heard you were wont to tell your betters how to conduct themselves. Well, sir, I tell you that what happens on my land is none of your business. It was good enough for Adolphus Coates. It should be good enough for a mere curate."

I stifled an absurd desire to point out that I was no curate but a fully-fledged rector. "It is the duty of any Christian man to love his neighbour as himself. These people are more than neighbours: they are your tenants, whom it is your privilege to aid and protect. For heaven's sake, My Lord, do you really want their death by starvation on your conscience?" I knew his sort all too well. By giving his labourers a huge Harvest Home feast and their children a few sugar plums at Christmas, he prided himself on his generosity sufficiently to be able to ignore them for the rest of the year.

He muttered something, and rang the bell. For a moment I feared I was to be unceremoniously ejected; instead, he pushed my card in the direction of the butler. "See that Eacott waits upon Dr — what do you call yourself? — Dr Campion. And now, sir, good day to you." Donning a pair of spectacles, their tiny lenses like full stops between me and his hooded eyes, he turned his attention once again to the tome he had been perusing when I arrived.

I would in courtesy have asked any other man the object of his scholarship, but it was clear that to give an explanation would have given him no pleasure at all.

Whatever his instructions, no one from Lord Wychbold's estate ventured to see me during Holy Week; the most charitable interpretation, if not one I clung to, was that Eacott had no wish to disturb me during such a sombre and prayerful period. A more prosaic explanation might lie in the weather, blowing up unseasonable thunderstorms despite the cold, particularly on the day I buried Eliza. There were no mourners except Edmund and her poor widower, who clutched a miserable bundle containing all his worldly wealth and muttered that since he had nothing in the area he might as well go and die a soldier.

Both Good Friday services being concluded in Lenten bare, stripped-down churches, my own dear St Jude's and All Souls', Clavercote, I looked forward with solemn joy to the greatest day of the Christian calendar, Easter Day, when the very fabric of the buildings would be celebrating Christ's resurrection. My engagement at All Souls' meant I would miss the innocent pleasure of the egg-rolling competition on the village green, in anticipation of which Mrs Trent and Susan had been hard at work boiling and dyeing a vast quantity of eggs, our chickens not having heard that they were not supposed to lay during Lent. Mrs Trent, unsure what celebration might take place in Clavercote, pressed me to fill my saddlebags with enough for the youngsters there to eat, if not race. She also produced an attenuated version of her famous box for the new baby, which still, according to Edmund, clung desperately to life; not expecting any of the garments to be returned, she picked out the least good, though she made sure that each was laundered to within an inch of its life.

Sunday had dawned with the total perfection of a spring day. The sun was warm, trees were throwing out their blossom, birds sang as sweetly as any choir and all my congregation seemed to share my joy. All Souls' was but half full, and the singing was sadly perfunctory. The few farmers' daughters flaunted their spring finery; of the poor cottagers there was unsurprisingly no sign. Accepting, with a reluctance I hoped I concealed, an invitation to return to Squire Lawton's home for a festive sherry, I asked as I sipped if Lord Wychbold had shown any sign of improving the dwellings on his land.

"Wychbold? Up at Lambert Place? A curst rum touch if ever there was one. All that book learning has

51

fair addled his brain, if you ask me, with all those break-teeth words. There are those," he added judiciously, sucking his teeth and looking around to see that no one in the empty room might overhear — the rest of the household were preparing a tempting-smelling repast to which I was not invited — "who say it's more to do with what he got up to when he was young." He gave the most enormous wink, touching the side of his nose with a dirt-engrained index finger. "Goings on, they say. Devil worship," he clarified ghoulishly.

"The rumours have not escaped me. This is surely not a suitable topic for such a day as this, Mr Lawton."

Not quelled at all by my repressive tone and words, he added, "And now there's all that to-do at Orebury House. Rakes and barques of frailty turning the fine old place into a brothel. And every man jack with a fine title to his name, as well as a fine —" He made an indecent joke.

For nothing would I have pointed out that by insulting Lord Hasbury and his friends he was insulting friends of my father — and, heaven forbid, my father himself. As it was, I verily believe that he could not fathom the reason for my real displeasure at his unsavoury humour. Thanking him tepidly for his hospitality, I made my excuses and left.

Wishful to cleanse my head of his sullying conversation, I resolved to ride home not via the lanes but through the healing verdure of fields and woodlands. While not entirely embracing Mr Wordsworth's fervour, I truly felt the cares of the last few days lifted from my shoulders as I felt the sun on my face. Titus, in tune with my mood, had relaxed to the slowest of walks.

However, as we approached the path through the woods, which was our nearest way home, it became clear that his reluctance to move forward was nothing to do with his attunement to my current humour, but to something that offended him. His ears and nostrils flared. He knapped. However much I might urge him forward with kind words, he resisted.

At last I dismounted, going to his head and talking softly but firmly to him. Still he resisted my blandishments, though he reluctantly consented to let me lead him on a tight rein into the wood. Fifty yards we walked — and no further. Him having veritably dragged me back whence we had come, I tied him to a sapling, fearing that for once his obvious anxieties would inspire him to return to his stable without me on his back.

I had penetrated perhaps a hundred yards beyond the point at which Titus had dug in his heels when I first noticed the smell. At first it was simply a sweet tinge to the verdant air. Then the sweetness became unmistakeably sickly. I was in the presence of a dead creature, one beginning to putrefy. Covering my nose and mouth with my handkerchief, I moved gingerly forward.

I cannot tell how long it took me to come to my senses so that I could run from the sight, and I believe that were it not for Titus's anxiously nuzzling my face I

53

might have swooned again, as the vile smell seemed to have followed me. And I had to return: somehow I must protect what remained of the dead man. All I had with me was my surplice. That would cover at least his face, though I had to disperse a million flies to do it. God would give me the strength to do it.

I clung to Titus on my return as a drowning man to a log. Now at last I could heave myself on to his saddle and quit this awful place. It would of course be but a temporary reprieve: I would have to guide Edmund and a party of servants to carry the body to a place of decent privacy. At least I had the sense to tie my handkerchief to a sapling to remind myself precisely where I entered the woods.

I was on Lord Wychbold's land: perhaps the information I had to impart would shake him out of his book-fuelled complacency. But as far as I knew he was not a magistrate — for that I must seek out Lord Hasbury, over at Orebury House, since the nearest, Lord Chase, had been living in retirement in Wales for some time. Would I see scenes to shock me? Would any of his guests be sober and decent? Just now I cared not: all I wanted was to remove myself from this accursed place.

Tumbling from Titus, I cared not for my appearance as I ran up the elegant semicircular flight of steps to the front door of Hasbury's superb Palladian house. But the butler who responded to my vicious tug on the bell obviously did. The epitome of disdain, he gestured to the side of the house. I was being sent to the servants' entrance.

"My man," I said, in my best imitation of my father's tones, "I am here to see Lord Hasbury in his capacity of magistrate in order to report a murder. You will kindly inform His Lordship of my presence — and there is to be no leaving me to cool my heels because you are too lily-livered to disturb him," I added as he showed me with the greatest reluctance into the library — a room as tidy and pristine as Wychbold's was chaotic and filthy. There was, in fact, no evidence that it might ever have been used for its intended purpose. Meanwhile, it appeared that no orgies were currently in train.

"Good God, man, you look as queer as Dick's hatband," Lord Hasbury announced as he swept into the room. He stopped abruptly. "And a parson, too. I thought Coates had flit the coop."

"I have the honour of being his temporary replacement. Tobias Campion of Moreton St Jude's at your service, My Lord."

A slight frown edged between his eyebrows, but he did not indicate what it might signify. In any case it disappeared as swiftly as it had come. All courtesy, he stepped forward to offer me his hand. He might be in his fifties, but he had the complexion of a much younger man, and though he was plump he did not need the Cumberland corsets so vital to improve the outline of so many of his cronies. His light step suggested he was free from gout, the complaint that so afflicted my father.

"And you want to report a murder? Surely this is the day when you should be celebrating the very opposite of death?"

I chose to take seriously what I feared he had meant as a jest. "Indeed so. And what makes this heinous crime even worse, My Lord, is the way the victim met his end."

Seeing that I could barely frame the words, he poured me a bumper of brandy. "Here. Pull yourself together. Sit down before you fall down."

I complied. Indeed I could do nothing else. At last, fortified by a second burning gulp of brandy, I said, "I would ask you to send a servant to summon Dr Edmund Hansard of Langley Park. It is too late for his services as a doctor, but he has extraordinary skill in deducing the circumstances of a person's death." Not that it would take a genius to work out how the man had died — but Edmund would bring with him his calm common sense. "When he has arrived, and only then, we need a party of men to — to deal with the corpse."

His face might be bland and unlined, but his eyes showed a clear comprehension. "You believe that the circumstances will reveal who perpetrated the act?"

"So I would hope. But I know that like Moreton St Jude's, Clavercote lacks a village constable. Would your steward deputise? However it is done, I must ask that you use your authority to instigate enquiries amongst local menfolk. Every tenant, every labourer, every beggar must be questioned: this is not a murder a man could have committed on his own. I found the victim as

I rode between Clavercote and Moreton St Jude's. I will undertake to have the inhabitants of the latter village interrogated, but as you are aware, over here I am no more than a visiting parson."

"Very well, Dr Campion, I will do as you ask." Perhaps there was an ironic stress on the last word. "All that you ask." Now there was no doubt of the irony. "Meanwhile my advice to you would be that you avail yourself of a modest nuncheon my butler will bring to you here. You will understand that I do not wish this news to reach my guests, to whom it would cause undoubted distress."

His guests. For a moment I had forgotten them. I bowed, acknowledging the wisdom of his advice by pushing away the rest of the spirit. "But it must reach Wychbold's ears, and in a proper manner. Would one of your servants convey a note to him?"

Nodding carelessly, he pointed to a standish and paper, and left the room. Trimming the pen, I gave careful thought to what I might say to Wychbold. At last I wrote something of which I was not ashamed, though the pile of discarded paper testified to the difficulty of the task. For good measure, I wrote notes to my new and sadly inexperienced churchwardens, Mr Mead and Mr Tufnell, asking them to interrupt the good cheer of the egg-rolling and other celebrations by speaking to every male in the village. I should be there myself! But how could I be, when only I knew the location of the body? I was torn indeed, covering my face with my hands in my distress.

To my horror, although I had not actually touched the poor corpse, whiff of mortality seemed to have lingered on my hands. The smell . . . The vile, vile smell . . .

A servant padded in with a tray of wine, cold meats and fruit.

The thought of touching food with my tainted skin made the bile surge into my gorge. Breathing deeply, I managed to control myself. If the servant was alarmed he was too well trained to show it. I think he was glad to bolt from the room to fetch the soap and water I requested.

When at last I could persuade myself to try it, the food was surprisingly welcome, even if I could do no more than pick at a few morsels. Still left to my own devices, I was fortunate to find, tucked away on an obscure shelf, a fine old Bible. So I was able to while away the rest of the time in a mixture of heartfelt prayer and invaluable wisdom. Then, as Hasbury's butler announced that Dr Hansard had arrived and was already addressing the work party the steward had organised, I made my reluctant feet take me to them. The men were on foot, apart from two on a cart, which carried the wooden planks favoured by Edmund to transport a cadaver and a heavy tarpaulin with which to cover it decently. There was no immediate sign of Titus. Then I saw him walking contentedly beside the groom bringing him from the stables, unaware that I was about to direct him towards a place he clearly loathed.

Hansard brought his horse into step alongside us as we led the way back to the woods, asking questions not about the corpse but about my conspicuously absent host who had made no effort to wish me good day. This was not the moment for jocular speculation about barques of frailty but I was sure his interest was piqued by the rumours.

He nodded with apparent approval as I dismounted some two hundred yards from my still fluttering handkerchief, and did likewise. But he directed the men on the cart to approach as close as their horse would let them. We all moved forward, our silence more apprehensive, I suspected, than reverent.

We reached the clearing.

"Dear God, man," Edmund exploded, coming to abrupt halt. "No one told me the man had been crucified."

CHAPTER
SIX

No one argued when my dear friend decreed that he would not ask them to move the poor corpse any further than he had to in order to examine it, lest the rough lanes jolted it so much it disintegrated. The head gamekeeper, a man who seemed to be the unofficial leader of Lord Hasbury's men, suggested a woodman's shelter not far from the ice house, and was sure that Lord Wychbold would have no objection to some ice deemed not good enough for the kitchen being used to keep the cadaver cool as long as possible. I despatched one of his team to speak to Wychbold's steward, faintly surprised that neither he nor his representative had already arrived to see what we were doing on his land.

All these suggestions met with Edmund's undoubted approval. Goodness knew how he could bear the task, but he would examine the corpse, which he assured me had been dead before its final humiliation. Then he would record its injuries in the hope of obtaining some hint as to the means of death and thus perhaps the assailant. "I wish to God I could ask Maria's help in recording all the details of the body, but it would create scandal amongst the villagers and even the gentry, to which I will not expose her," he declared. "Dare not."

I could not argue. Instead, writhing with embarrassment, I said, "I cannot draw, but I could act as your amanuensis."

He responded with kind amusement: "And how many times have you cast up your accounts since discovering the crime? But I know that you want action to rid your mind of what you have seen. I believe Doctor Toone to be staying near Stratford. I would value his opinion greatly, but would prefer not to entrust the task of explaining the situation to a mere servant." He shot a shrewd look at me.

"Nothing would give me greater pleasure than to fetch him — provided his paschal potations have left him fit to sit on a horse," I declared. In fact, the nasty schoolboy lurking within me would have enjoyed holding his head under the pump to sober him up — a belated revenge for all the times Gussie Toone had plunged my head into altogether viler liquids. But now he was Augustus, a most distinguished physician by choice, not financial necessity, and I was Tobias, an ordained clergyman, enjoined to forgive. It was time for us to put away the follies of childhood. He was now only ever known as Toone to his intimates, and as Doctor Toone by those he treated for fashionable ailments.

Hansard glanced at the ice the men had accumulated and at his watch. "If you can persuade him to undertake a moonlit drive, it would be well for our investigation. Burns, who has a countryman's nose for such things, promises a crisp frost, but a bright warm day tomorrow, alas."

61

Toone might already smell strongly of wine but he was sober enough to send immediately to the stables for his curricle. I made his excuses to his hosts while he made swift preparations for the journey. Within minutes he had run downstairs again, and was shrugging on his driving coat, a garment with so many fashionable capes I thought he must be mistaking Warwickshire for Hyde Park.

At times like this, Binns, his deceptively sour-faced groom, acted as his valet. He had already stowed his master's medical and personal bags ready for Toone to take the ribbons. He drove a beautiful matched pair of greys, as elegant as the archdeacon's. Titus and I became his escort, an arrangement that had the advantage of precluding conversation I might prefer Binns not to overhear, however discreet he might be.

Mrs Hansard had left instructions with her housekeeper that we travellers must be provided with a late supper; the guest bedchamber would no doubt be warm — the night had turned as cold as Burns had predicted — and the bed aired. The room I had come to regard as mine would be equally welcoming. But what was clearly not welcome to our visitor was the news that I had suppressed for the duration of the journey — that Mrs Hansard would not be venturing forth to make notes and sketch any salient detail as an aide-memoire.

"You joke me! As an artist of such subjects — I do not presume to judge what I am sure are delightful paintings meant for a drawing room — she is unsurpassed!"

"Indeed. But it would be entirely ineligible for her to be seen anywhere near the corpse. Imagine, Toone, a lady in such circumstances. Sketching a naked man's body!"

"I suppose you have never heard of Madame Kauffman? Or Miss Moser?"

"And I presume that you have conveniently forgotten that when Zoffany painted the members of the Royal Academy surrounding the nude male, the two ladies were present only by means of their portraits on the wall?"

"All arrant poppycock."

"Not to lowly members of country society, I fear, Toone." I sat down again, hoping he would do likewise. Dropping my voice, I added, "And Hansard has a particular care for Maria's reputation, given that however much of a lady she undoubtedly is, she was not nobly born."

"And what care you for noble birth? You, who are a marquis of somewhere or other, call yourself plain Mister! Or less plain Doctor. You at least appear to have learnt something from the events in France in the last century. As for the others — pouf! Damn them!"

"They are the people amongst whom I live, Toone. I may not always share their opinions any more than Edmund and Maria do — but we have to respect them, whilst, one hopes, leading them to hold more enlightened views."

"Hmph. Meanwhile, I lack an artist. Are there any drawing masters in the area, sick of teaching damsels to draw daffodils, who might assist?"

I spread my hands. "Apparently a poet is to hand."

Toone laughed, as I hoped he would. "So he could write a sonnet on blowflies and maggots. I wish him joy of his rhymes. In all seriousness, Tobias, I need someone to record what I find — and I collect that your skill with the pencil is no greater than mine?"

"Not one jot. And my stomach is a great deal more delicate."

It occurred to me as I retired to my chamber that perhaps My Lord Wychbold might, as a scholar, have need of someone who could copy for him items of interest. Even one of Lord Hasbury's guests at Orebury House might be accompanied by a secretary numbering sketching amongst his skills. Accordingly, as soon as I had completed a speedy toilette the following morning — which had dawned with skies as blue and clear as Burns had predicted, the sun already melting the dusting of frost on the south lawn — I put the idea to Edmund, alone in the south-facing breakfast room. Maria entered as I was speaking, and exchanged a wry smile with her husband.

"You may gather that this subject has already been the topic of some animated discussion, my dear friend," she said, giving me her hand to kiss. "And I think your suggestion may come closest to resolve it, assuming it has a happy outcome. Write your notes while I ask Burns for fresh coffee, and he shall see they are despatched instanter."

Edmund spread his hands in mock surrender, as I excused myself to make free of the writing materials in his library. There was still no sign of Toone when I returned, to find Maria already pouring coffee. Now that Lent was over and we had celebrated the joy of the Resurrection, tempered somewhat, of course, by a less blessed corpse, I was happy to carve myself a generous slice of home-cured ham and, when I caught Edmund's laughing eye, a second.

Even allowing for his hasty journey and the lateness of the hour when he had sought his bed, Toone's delayed appearance at the breakfast table was beyond the line of pleasing. His host and hostess were on the verge of quitting it, to embark on their daily duties, as was I. However, he was all handsome apologies, turning the fact that he had overslept to a compliment to his excellent bed and the gentleness of the housemaid's knock when she had first brought his hot water. Apparently he had slept through her first call, and only awoken when she brought a second can half an hour later.

My plan to find him an artist was met with gruff cynicism, as he applied himself to a plate of roast beef liberally spread with mustard. However, he soon had to eat not only his meat but his words, as Burns announced that he had shown a visitor into the library.

"A gentleman concerning Dr Campion's note, sir."

Hansard excused himself from the table immediately, inviting me, as the instigator of the idea, to accompany him.

Our visitor was on his feet, his back to the room, as he surveyed the delightful springtime garden, which the room overlooked. To his left lay the shrubbery that Maria was restoring to its former glory: some of the bushes were laden with pink or white blossom, others bursting with buds of the most vivid green. It must indeed have delighted an artist's eye.

It dawned on me, giving rise to very mixed emotions, that although I had never been introduced to the young man, I might not be unacquainted with him. With his elegant riding apparel, the coat assuredly by Weston, and dishevelled hair à la Brutus, could this be the very person I had seen riding swiftly away from Eliza Fowler's dreadful cottage? At the time I feared he might be the cause of Molly's downfall: could I now be about to address him? And how might I frame any accusation? Perhaps I should wait to see what had brought him here: perhaps my note had quickened a guilty conscience.

But there seemed to be nothing about him except a gentlemanly openness. Turning to face us and making his bow, in his buckskins and mirror-bright boots he confirmed my impression of a fashionable young man, but by no means a fribble, so I was tempted to dismiss the notion that he was Mr Julius Longstaff, the effeminate poet, whose hair was in any case alleged to be flowing. It was hard to estimate his age. His figure was slender enough to suggest padding in the shoulders of that coat, and his voice boyishly light.

"Will Snowdon at your service, Dr Hansard," he declared, offering Edmund his hand. "And at yours, Dr Campion. I hear, gentlemen, that the skills of an artist are required. Might I offer you mine?" he added with a polite smile. "I assure you that I had the very best of drawing masters when I was young, and have seen enough accidents on the hunting field not to swoon at the sight of gore. I am staying with a distant cousin, who lives in general a retired life, so you need not fear any indiscreet gossip emanating from my lips."

As one, Edmund and I bowed.

But Edmund raised a warning finger. "I must warn you, Snowdon, that the corpse we have is not . . . freshly injured. Decomposition has set in. It is currently packed in ice, but even so . . ."

"If I shoot the cat, gentlemen, I will do even that with discretion. But I thank you for your warning. I understand a warm day is likely. Presumably the sooner we embark on this enterprise the better. My horse is waiting."

I marvelled at such assurance in one so young. "Will you be able to make notes as well as draw what Dr Toone requests?"

Hansard laughed. "Worry not, Tobias. I will do that."

Should I speak to Snowdon now, in front of Edmund? But that would be to embarrass him and to divert attention from the urgent matter in hand. I would — must! — question him later, and in private.

Edmund sensed that something was troubling me, and patted my shoulder. "You return to your parish duties, Tobias — which will soon include conducting a burial service, of course."

Indeed, nothing sounded more pleasing than giving young Robert another riding lesson and then visiting my parishioners. Having shaken both warmly by the hand, I returned to the breakfast room to bid a temporary farewell to Toone and Maria, accepting with alacrity her invitation to return to sup with them later.

"While Dr Toone is here, and while you all have so much work to do, we will keep town hours," she said. "So we will look for you at six this evening."

I was about to leave when there came a thunderous knocking at the front door. In silence we listened as Burns admitted someone.

There was an immediate soft scratch on the door. "It's from Orebury House, ma'am," Burns declared. "One of Lord Hasbury's guests has been taken ill and His Lordship desires Dr Hansard's immediate attendance."

Maria raised an expressive eyebrow. "My dear Burns, you must learn to give messages more accurately. I believe I heard not *desires* but *demands*, did I not?" Her smile forgave Burns, but not the man cooling his heels in the hallway. She turned to me. "So, Tobias, it looks as if your secretarial skills may be needed after all."

Despite the beauty of the day, the experience was as vile as I had feared. Toone, who had borrowed one of Hansard's hacks, did his best to ameliorate the stench, soaking thick wads of linen in some sort of herbal decoction, in which lavender predominated. With these he bade us cover our mouths and noses. Neither of us assistants demurred, though Snowdon surprised me by recollecting an Arabian souk where visitors to a leatherworks had been offered sprigs of mint to crush against their noses. Next Toone swathed us in garments not unlike the surplice with which I had forced myself to cover the remains of the man now before us. Then he began to examine, Snowdon to sketch and me to write. His carrying voice meant I was spared close contact, but Snowdon must needs be in immediate attendance; to speak the truth, I doubt if any older man could have dealt with the situation with more efficiency and less emotion.

Toone dictated many and detailed notes. In short, he confirmed Hansard's opinion that the crucifixion had taken place after death — neither the hands nor the feet had bled. Probably the blows to the back of the skull, which I had been fortunate enough not to see, had killed him. The attack on his face had probably been simply to prevent anyone identifying him. But the killers had been unable to obliterate some clues. The man, who Toone put in his forties or fifties, was decidedly well fed, with soft muscles and hands clearly unused to any sort of manual labour.

"A gentleman?" Snowdon ventured. "At very least, not a labourer."

Toone shot an ironic glance at me. "It depends on how one defines a gentleman. Given the fact that he has been emasculated and the relevant organs thrust into his mouth, we might hazard that someone considers him guilty of ungentlemanly behaviour."

"That would be a terrible vengeance!" Snowdon gasped. "So many of our class may treat their social inferiors as mere playthings, but they assume, usually correctly, that a fat purse will buy off a furious swain or father. Punishment like this — it is beyond the bounds of civilisation."

"What if his sin was beyond the bounds of civilisation?" a quiet voice demanded.

As one we wheeled round. "Hansard!" Toone was the first to speak. "Come, Tobias, if Hansard is right, what sort of crime might it be?"

"I think," I said slowly, "that Edmund might be close to the mark. Someone must have done great evil to be dealt with like this."

CHAPTER
SEVEN

Our work done, Hansard invited Snowdon to take pot luck with the rest of us, telling him cheerfully that we would not be changing our dress. He seemed to be on the point of accepting when Toone declared that he for one would rid himself of the odours that had soaked into his very skin by spending ten minutes under the pump, and suggested we might want to do the same.

"We know no relationship between foul miasmas and illness, but I for one deem it as necessary to be rid of them as it is to remove the scent of the stables when one dines." He looked round, as if challenging us to dispute with him.

Snowdon nodded his agreement, but said, "Forgive me, my friends, if I do not join you in your ablutions, but already my kind hostess will be looking for me. I would thank you for a most enjoyable day, but we all know that the epithet is inaccurate. But it has been most stimulating, and a surprising pleasure to recover skills I so rarely use these days."

"Another day, then Snowdon —"

"Alas, provided that my relative's health improves I shall soon be quitting the county. Your servant, Hansard

— gentlemen." He made an elegant bow, retrieved his horse, and left at a canter.

Leaving the county — without my having established if he had actually been the young man galloping from Eliza Fowler's deathbed. I cursed my stupidity. Should I ride after him? Even as I whistled for Titus, I realised that to do so would look very particular. But he had left none of us with means of contacting him again. All I could do was follow the rapidly retreating figure with my eyes, trying to not lose which direction he was following.

I raised my anxiety with some embarrassment as we headed wearily back to Langley Park.

"I am hardly surprised you felt unable to challenge him," Toone said. "A well set-up young man may ride where he pleases, Toby."

"Even if he has seduced and abandoned a maiden who then takes her own life and that of her babe?"

"But you have no evidence of that. Just that a girl has been betrayed by someone. It might be — Dear God, we know what it is like in these remote villages! There is one in Staffordshire where inbreeding is so pronounced that I am surprised that Hansard here has not studied it in connection of those damned pink or blue flowers of his."

Hansard flushed. He had long since abandoned his genetic experiments to spend more time with his beloved wife.

"So you think it would have been ungentlemanly to raise the issue?"

72

"In front of us, tactless in the extreme — which is why I am sure you did not attempt it. Tell me, Hansard, what did you make of . . ."

From then they exchanged medical observations I preferred not to hear. Soon, however, as the three of us operated the Hansards' pump for each other, we were laughing and joking like overgrown schoolboys and good fellowship was restored.

Maria had made sure there were blazing fires in our chambers; another was filling the drawing room with warmth when we gathered. The only chill came from Toone, when Burns announced Jem. Jem and Toone did not find it easy to be in one another's company: for all his protestations of French egalitarianism, Toone was one of the *bon ton* in drawling accent and indeed behaviour. Jem, however, while still very much aware of the dangers of putting himself forward, enjoyed such social freedom at Langley Park that he was ready to prickle at Toone's unconsciously patronising attitude.

Maria treated Jem as she treated me — as the favourite son or nephew she had never had. "The very least I could do," she declared, summoning Jem to sit beside her, "was to invite you to this cadaver party of ours: you will be as interested to hear the results of Toone's post-mortem examination as I."

"Indeed I will. And I come with my own contribution, which is a message for Toby from Mead and Tufnell, the churchwardens: they have spoken to every able-bodied man in the village — indeed, they questioned me, most thoroughly — but to no avail. No one has seen or heard anything of the crime; no one has anything unusual or untoward to report."

"I am heartily glad of it. I would not want any in my flock to have been associated with a crime like this."

As Burns entered to pass round sherry or Madeira, the conversation turned to Hansard's chief business of the day — his visit to Orebury House's guest.

"Alas, I saw no Paphians in states of undress. No young sprigs sliding drunkenly down banister rails. No one rode his horse up the staircase. All I saw was a patient with a case of gout. A gentleman with more hair than wit suffering an attack of gout. The worst gout in the world. And I was to provide an instant cure. A tale I hear so often, Toone — and you? And what, pray, is your most popular cure?"

"Tinted water. At the same price as the best claret. Popular because my patients believe that exorbitant cost means extreme efficaciousness. And if they drink more of it than they do of claret it does indeed seem to be efficacious." Toone eyed the sherry decanter, but declined another glass.

As if by common consent we kept conversation general during the excellent supper, which included, after soup and a plate of salmagundi, a fricasse of chicken, some tiny buttered potatoes and a raised ham and leek pie. Should the occasion merit it, Maria was more than capable of producing a table overburdened with delights; for more intimate dinners such as tonight's, she confined her cook to producing a few dishes of total excellence. The wine as always was the best Hansard could afford, it being his express opinion that poor wine was bad for the health. He never did square this with the amount of vintage wine and port consumed by gout sufferers from the Upper Ten Thousand.

The covers removed, and Burns, having set fruit and nuts on the table, withdrawn, Toone rose, no doubt expecting Maria to adjourn to the drawing room, there to pick at a piece of embroidery until we gentlemen had deemed our conversation at an end. However, this was not the way in the Hansard establishment when there were no female guests. Maria, neither moving from her place nor favouring him with an explanation of her unconventional preference for champagne over port, declared, her voice and mouth prim, but her eyes alive with curiosity, "And now, gentlemen, you may report to those of us not privileged to be with you today what you have found out about the poor man Tobias found in the wood. Jem, confined in his school, has probably heard nothing but the wildest gossip, while I was forced to spend the day examining the contents of my linen press so that I could not walk down to the village and make sly enquiries."

She and Jem listened intently as Toone gave a succinct and intelligible account of our findings and his conclusions. To illustrate his first point he passed round one of Snowdon's sketches.

Jem stared in disbelief. "My dear Mrs Hansard —"

She took it and examined it carefully, as much, I suspect, for the draughtsmanship as for the anatomical detail. "This is very fine work, Toone. You have found an admirable illustrator." She turned to Jem. "I wish I could have done as well."

He blushed deeply. "But if not you —"

"A chance visitor to the area, Jem," Edmund cut in, aware of Toone's irritation at the prolonged interruption.

Swiftly Toone resumed his narrative, tactfully refraining from passing round any further illustrations, and veiling his account of the mutilation in Latin terms. "To sum up," he said at last, "we believe that the man was dead when he was nailed to the tree."

Maria coughed. "He was not a small man. No one man could have inflicted so many injuries, nor, of course, lifted him up and driven in those nails. To drive so many to this collective madness . . . Does not this suggest that he had done enormous harm, perhaps to more than one person?"

Jem appeared understandably reluctant to voice his observation. At last, with a sigh, he said, "Surely this evil crucifixion, at such a sacred time of year, suggests only one thing! Devil worship! I did warn you of rumours about Lord Wychbold and his evil cronies, did I not?"

"Devil worship? What sort of ignorant superstition is that?" Toone demanded.

"Come, man, you have heard of Lord Wharton and of Sir Francis Dashwood! The Hellfire Club?" Whether Edmund wished simply to defend Jem or actually agreed with his theory I could not say.

"But that was disbanded fifty years ago!" Toone exclaimed. "We live in different times now."

"Of course." Hansard bowed. "But in the absence of a village constable to investigate the crime —"

"And what would a mere chawbacon do anyway?"

Hansard ignored the interruption. "It is incumbent on us to explain fully to both Hasbury and Wychbold exactly what we have been doing. You, Campion, alerted Wychbold to the situation immediately, did you not, but he has shown surprisingly little interest in our activities. To be sure, I did not expect him to come himself to ensure our depredations on his ice were kept to a minimum, but I would have expected regular enquiries."

"And indeed," Maria added, "regular offers of refreshment. He was not to know that I sent you off well provided for."

Maria could not know that none of us had been able to eat a crumb. Not even Toone, who had shamefacedly admitted that he felt unable to touch bread with a hand so tainted by his work. Moreover, he had spent as much time as Hansard and me cleansing himself of the nauseating odours. The good food we had handed over, still in its basket, to the workers come to consign the corpse to the rough coffin made by Lord Hasbury's men and carry it to St Jude's for burial. Needless to say, Edmund bade them make vigorous and immediate use of the village pump before they touched any.

"Indeed not," I said tactfully. "So it seems to me that in all courtesy we should pay a morning call to apprise him of the latest developments."

"In other words, to question him. Excellent. Now, I really feel that we gentlemen have earned a glass of my favourite brandy. It was a present from a grateful patient so I cannot tell whether duty was ever paid on it, I fear." He rang for Burns, who returned with the decanter and glasses, and, without being asked, another glass of champagne for Maria.

It was she who, contemplating the pretty play of bubbles, asked, "How came Mr Snowdon to know of your need of assistance? He arrived remarkably swiftly after you wrote to Hasbury and Wychbold. I wonder which of them suggested he came."

Burns, who had been attending the fire, made almost visible attempts not to eavesdrop.

Toone, who had already downed his brandy and was waiting for Burns to offer him more, turned astounded eyes on her. "What the devil has that to do with anything?"

As Burns bowed himself swiftly from the room, she permitted herself the slightest twitch of her right eyebrow, which I had seen reduce pert housemaids to tears and now brought an unlikely blush to Toone's cheeks. Then she replied equably, "I know not. But as a keen student of the relations between different households in a parish, I would like to know. Which of the noble lords whom you asked for assistance is on sufficiently good terms with him or his hostess to know of his genius with a pencil? You tell me that his hostess is supposed to live a quiet life away from society, yet the talents of a guest are known. Furthermore, her acquaintance did not wait till their next meeting to reveal casually that her guest might be interested.

Hasbury or Wychbold must have either told her to her face or sent a messenger with wings on his heels."

Jem looked merely puzzled. Toone's frown deepened. Afraid that the brandy might talk again, I said quietly, "It is a question I might not be able to put directly when I see Wychbold. But as we all know, indirect questions are often more effective than a direct interrogation. Pray, Edmund, will you wish to accompany me tomorrow morning?"

"I fear not. My services are already bespoken by the aristocratic toe at Orebury House. Toone, a second opinion — and some of your coloured water — might suggest how serious the present condition is. Unless, that is, you wish to resume your visit to your Stratford friends?"

"They do not look for me for a day or so — or more. So I would be honoured to accompany you."

"As would I," Maria interjected. "I have some pickled eggs that Mrs Heath may find of use. It is a long time since we spoke."

Hansard and I exchanged a glance: this signified that Maria was going to press for backstairs gossip, something of which he wanted to disapprove, since it allied her with a class she had now left, thanks to their union. I had no such strong feelings, sometimes suspecting that did she not keep herself so busy, she might have experienced pangs of loneliness, so short was she of having a close confidante. No one could doubt the strength of her and Edmund's mutual passion, but I recalled how isolated I had felt without a friend of the same sex until Edmund had absorbed me into his life. On the whole, then, I thought her visits to women continuing in the profession she had left did her good, not harm.

Jem's post as schoolmaster prevented him from joining us in our investigations but for once he did not look wistful. "Two of my brightest pupils are the sons of Lord Wychbold's steward, and both could talk the hind legs off a donkey. Normally, of course, I discourage them. However, I may be altogether more lenient tomorrow." He looked at the pretty clock on the mantelpiece and rose to his feet. To Toone's astonishment, after he had made his farewells to us men, Maria linked arms with him and escorted him to the hallway, from where we heard a low-voiced but clearly affectionate conversation, ending in ripples of laughter.

CHAPTER
EIGHT

Since he had suffered so very much indignity in his death, the least we could do was bury the unknown man with as much reverence as we could before the sun brought us another unseasonably warm day. So Hansard and Toone, stunned by having to quit his bed so early, were the mourners as I read the full service. I made the verger mark the grave carefully: one day we might find family and friends of the man who might wish to visit the spot to pay their respects.

Our breakfast was subdued, as one would expect after such a solemn half-hour, but then we parted, to carry out our appointed tasks.

Receiving me in his library once more, Lord Wychbold regarded me with very little enthusiasm as I gave him at first hand the details of the uninvited guest on his land and how it had behoved us to deal with the corpse more or less *in situ*. I might have been speaking about the death of one of his sheep for all his eagerness to know the identity of the victim.

"Damned trespassers! My keeper should have shot him! It was only some damned sermon of yours that stopped him setting mantraps. I take it the body has been removed?"

I clenched my fists in an effort to speak politely to a man with such contempt for the life of a fellow human being. "It has. At Lord Hasbury's expense. But there will of course be a coroner's inquest."

"Conducted by some clunch who fancies he knows the law."

"Indeed, Mr Vernon, lately of Nuneaton, has proved a very thorough and efficient gentleman. He will be looking for a suitably large room to house the inquest," I said, a sudden and singularly inappropriate imp of mischief thrusting itself into my brain. But it was better to laugh inwardly at him than lose my temper.

Wychbold looked hunted. "I have no such room here," he lied.

Looking about me with appraising eyes, I gave the impression that I was estimating the size of the room in which we were seated. Imagine the villagers, of all ranks and of none, seated amongst these tomes, filling the scholarly air with sweat and bad breath. I fancy the same vision appeared before his own eyes.

"One understands you have a singularly lovely ballroom," I said, in a conciliatory voice. I might have been a ferret confronting a studious rabbit.

"Books. Full of books. Boxes of priceless books." He wet his lips in his anxiety.

"Very well. I will see what Lord Hasbury can suggest. Now," I continued, my voice stern, "a man of your intelligence will understand that the singular manner of the victim's death has given rise to all sorts of tittle-tattle. Your retired, scholarly existence has always bemused your more ignorant neighbours. There

82

are many who believe you once practised devil worship: there are murmurings that this obscene crucifixion has something to do with you."

"I? I have anything to do with such a thing? Are you out of your mind?" His furious spittle bespattered his table.

"Is not Rumour the many-headed monster? I believe you are simply a man obsessed with books and scholarship, to the exclusion of other important matters. Hoi polloi — some of them your own tenants, your own workers — clearly have a different, ignorant view. I have no idea what they may attempt — it may be nothing but a continuation of their sullen resentment, fuelled by hunger, for which few could blame them. But it may take an altogether more shocking form. Who knows? But in all seriousness, I would beg you at very least to make sure that all your doors are locked, all your shutters barred, at night." Nodding home my point, I stood up. "Take care of your books." I touched one with my index finger.

"Take your hand away! How dare you! Never touch my books. No one — no one but me ever handles them. Ever."

The lugubrious butler responded to Wychbold's violent tug of the bell rope. My host glared at me, shaking with anger.

I bowed. "My unreserved apologies. I did not mean so to offend you. Now, before I go, Wychbold, permit me to thank you for your kindness in sending Mr Snowdon to Langley Park in response to my plea for a capable artist. A most talented young man." I bowed, and left him to his studies, whatever they might be.

"Snowdon? Do I know a man called Snowdon?"

Did his eyes truly show the same bemusement as his words? This time I was inclined to believe him. We parted with considerable mutual dissatisfaction.

Once again on Wednesday evening, Dr and Mrs Hansard insisted that we meet, as we had the night before, for dinner; once again the conversation was light and general until Burns had cleared the table and brought in the port and champagne. I suspected that although he must by now be used to the unconventional practice in the Hansards' establishment of Maria remaining with the gentlemen, Toone felt a frisson of unease. So much for his revolutionary tendencies.

I was the first to recount my day's doings; like one of Jem's naughty schoolboys, I set out to make the class laugh at my victim, Lord Wychbold. Better he be a ridiculous figure than one engendering fear. Jem, however, scowled at me as I finished my narrative.

"You think it acceptable merely to mock evil?"

"Personally, I have seen no evidence of devil worship or any other reprehensible practices. I think he is just a misanthropic scholar. However, he was adamant that his ballroom was full of boxes of books, and something told me that in this he lied."

"And you did not challenge him?"

"On what grounds? I was there as a visiting clergyman apologising for activity on his estate he clearly did not welcome. He could have insisted we move the corpse away before Toone was allowed to examine it. Maria would have had another extremely unwelcome visitor to her cellar."

"The corpse would have arrived in pieces — no use to anyone," Toone growled. "We drift from the point, Campion. Hansard, will you talk about our visit to Hasbury or shall I?"

In the matter of providing a room for the inquest, Hansard reported that Hasbury had been more willing but no more able to help, given the size of his house party, members of which must not be incommoded. We rather thought that Mr Vernon, not known for his tactful handling of those who did not deserve it, might have an opinion on the matter, which we would lay before him in due course. He might even require Lord Hasbury's guests to present themselves to say on oath whether they had seen any plump gentlemen wandering round their host's estate. As to Mr Snowdon, Hasbury absolutely denied knowing anyone of that name, let alone sending for him.

"I heard nothing worthwhile this morning," Maria said. "When I tried to question Mrs Heath, all she would say was something about servants not being what they once were. Apparently yesterday there had been some unseemly commotion in the kitchen, though she would not specify the cause. She had to speak firmly with all her staff, and threaten dismissal if anything like it ever happened again. Today everything was very quiet: whatever she said must have struck home. So the sum total of my success was to rid us of a jar of pickled eggs, which might better have gone to the poor, and receive in exchange a trusted recipe for pressed tongue —"

"Which I trust you will not set on any table of mine!" Hansard exclaimed, pulling his mouth down comically at the corners.

"My dear husband, how many families would delight to be given offal?"

"Many. But not yours."

She got to her feet, laughing; we men rose in concert.

For a moment, however, Edmund detained me. His face showed both embarrassment and deep concern, and he gestured me back to a chair, seating himself beside me.

Even then he did not speak immediately. "Tobias," he said quietly at last, "there is something I should perhaps have told you earlier, and indeed would have done had Toone not been constantly with us. He finds the situation richly amusing. I only hope that you may. The patient we are attending at Orebury House is none other than Lord Hartland. Your father," he added, when I said nothing.

"He keeps his room? Will he not be riding abroad for the purposes of sneering at my parish and my vocation? In that case, dear friend, unless he speaks of me, keep your counsel. Unless he speaks of me," I repeated.

"And if he does?"

"In that case . . . in that case . . ." Drawing away from him I took a hasty turn about the room.

"In that case, I shall assure him that he has a son to be proud of, one whom his parishioners love and respect. But what would you have me tell him?"

"That I love and honour him. That I pray for him every day." I paused. "Alas, Edmund, I cannot tell him that I have any regrets, except for the manner of our parting. I cannot leave the life to which I have been called and adopt the one that would please him."

"Would you like me to broach the subject first?"

I had a moment of clarity. "Tell me, Edmund, how does he treat you? As a fellow gentleman or as a lowly sawbones barely worth notice?"

His silence was statement in itself. "But he is in a great deal of pain. Perhaps he will be more courteous after a prolonged sojourn in his room away from the pleasures of Hasbury's table and with a great deal of Toone's coloured water replacing the claret and brandy he enjoys so much. A very great deal of coloured water," he mused.

From the drawing room came the sound of the fortepiano.

"Forgive me, Tobias, but there is clearly going to be music. And I find I cannot bear the thought of Maria singing without my being there to listen."

The following day dawned warm and fine. Edmund had his bread-and-butter patients amongst the local gentry to visit, taking the opportunity as he felt their pulses to ask about a mysterious plump gentleman. Maria would be busy in her herb garden. Toone took it into his head to ask to accompany me on some of my parish work, borrowing once more Edmund's spare hack. Clearly he did not anticipate a day spent prowling round my study while I planned next Sunday's sermon.

As far as I knew, there was nothing urgent to attend to in Moreton St Jude's, and since I had discovered the body as I rode home from Clavercote, it was to that village that we would repair. Mrs Trent, insisting that Sarey Tump would need a more plentiful diet if she and little Joseph Fowler were to prosper, a sentiment with which Toone concurred, pressed on us string bags of supplies: bread, bacon, cheese and a little brandy. Then there were more wrinkled apples. Lastly a small bundle appeared, produced from behind Susan's apron.

"The food's from your own larder, so it's not right you should thank me," Mrs Trent said awkwardly. "But what young Susan here's got is from us. Ourselves. It's not much. The little mite has clothes from the box. But these are a few garments for the poor wench. And young Robert — he's made his own gift. Show Dr Campion, Susan."

I believe all our eyes filled. Robert, who had nothing of his own, had whittled a little teething ring.

Even Toone was moved, coughing quietly behind his hand.

I felt it better to visit Sarey on my own, lest the sight of a well-dressed stranger overcome her. Meanwhile, Toone, armed with the apples, attracted a mob of urchins; I was quite certain that the doctor within him would notice and treat any obvious injuries and ailments, and that the gentleman within would decline any payment.

Sarey was nursing little Joseph when she called to bid me enter the apology for a cottage. An Old Master might have seen her as a latter-day Virgin with her infant Son. I saw her as an exhausted woman, old before her time, her hair lank and grimy, dirt in her very skin. Her dress had obviously been turned at least once, the blue in the seams showing what colour the grey, washed-out garment had once been.

I was reluctant to embarrass her by referring to the contents of the bundle, which I left wordlessly beside her. I hung the bags of supplies alongside the pitiful bundles of herbs that seemed to constitute her larder: rats were always on the lookout for free meals, even in a house as well-regulated as the rectory. Her eyes followed me: clearly she was famished.

Cutting a slice of bread and a hunk of cheese for her — Toone had drummed into me that I must not let her overeat after so much involuntary fasting — I dandled the baby for a few minutes. I did not have it in me to delay her further by demanding we say grace, instead waiting till she had finished every last crumb to thank God for the food. Only then did I ask her if she knew anything of young Snowdon's activities in the village.

"Mr Snowdon?" Sarey looked baffled.

"The day young Joseph was born, I saw a young gentleman riding fast from the village. It might not be Will Snowdon, of course. He might be someone completely different."

This time her reaction was less clear. "Young gentleman? Hereabouts?"

"He rides a grey horse."

"And why might you be wanting to see this man on a grey horse?"

"To ask him a few questions — nothing more."

Her face told me clearly that in her experience a few questions always meant more. "Don't know nothing about any man on a horse."

"Young Molly Fowler's baby — it must have had a father. And in my experience a village lad would do the right thing by his sweetheart. That baby's father didn't."

"You're thinking this young man of yours might be the one as . . .? But why should he come a-visiting when she was lying cold in the earth?"

Pale and sick this young woman might be, but she did not lack native wit. If only she and more like her had had the benefit of a school like Jem's.

"Do you think he might have wanted to make reparation to her family — tell them he was sorry and offer them . . . compensation?"

"Pay them blood money, you mean?" she asked, through narrowed eyes. "No, I've not heard tell of any young man — but I was sickly myself, being confined, as you know." Her eyes filled, but as Joseph whimpered she gathered him up tenderly. "Best you asks others that knows more than me."

Clearly I would get no more information from her. In any case, I needed to speak of her churching, and to ask what else she might need.

"Looks like someone's sent a lot already," she said, as if registering the bundle for the first time. "As well as the food."

"Good people from my village. There's a special present in there for Joseph, made by an orphan lad.

90

You'll know it from the love he has put into it," I added foolishly, but was rewarded by her smile when she dug it out and held it aloft.

By the time I returned to him, Toone had found someone to bring him a stool on which he stood his youngest patients to examine them, and was surrounded by a small but growing crowd of silent adults.

"There is hardly any illness here that good food wouldn't more readily cure than any medicine of mine," he said sadly. "I have done all that I can for the children, at least. I have told *enceinte* women to drink plenty of milk; I have told men to wash dirt out of their cuts when they injure themselves in the field. But they eye me with resentment, as you can see. And I do not feel that they like you any more than they like me. Let us be on our way."

I had been about to ask the gathering for the information I had sought but he was right: the muttering we now heard was ugly. For all that, I led us to the church, which I found locked.

"You would enjoy making the acquaintance of the churchwardens, I fancy," I said, as we returned to our horses. "Squire Lawton and Mr Boddice. The squire keeps a better establishment and serves a decent sherry. We will try him first."

The arrival of two riders created sufficient stir to bring a lad running from the stables, and reasonably swift attendance from our rubicund host, with Boddice in tow. Toone greeted both men as if they were earls, to which they responded with almost maidenly blushes, their behaviour soon clotting into obsequiousness. We were seated, and offered a nuncheon, which we declined. Leaning back, one elegantly booted leg over the other as he sipped Lawton's sherry, Toone played the part of a Pink of the Ton with such relish that I let him take the lead in questioning them about unknown men in the area. Their smiles soon congealed.

"Gentlemen," he said, producing his quizzing glass, "I find it impossible to believe that you should have a stranger in your midst without someone bringing the information to the two most important men in the village. Come, you must have your fingers on the pulse of life here — you know who wants to wed whom, who owes whom what debt."

"We had some paupers," Boddice told him. "Sent them to the right-about, we did. Back to their own parishes to be a burden on them, not us. 'Tisn't as if we haven't our own poor to worry about," he said, with a furtive glance at me. "Well, you must have seen the state of things with your own eyes. And Lord Wychbold too busy with his damned books to see what poor heart his land is in."

I nodded soberly. I had often inveighed against the practice of sending the poorest, weakest men and women on journeys they might never complete, but rarely had I seen so much native-born poverty in such a prosperous county. "I have spoken to His Lordship," I said quietly, "and will speak again. But it will take years to improve his land, not weeks. Meanwhile, turn your minds to this other man."

Toone stepped forward. "Think, a plump middle-aged man, probably well-dressed and most certainly better fed than most of your fellow parishioners, lurking in the area. You must have thought him up to no good."

They remained as stubbornly silent as Robert, without his excuse.

"What about the young gentleman who hangs about the village?" I asked. "I have seen him with my own eyes."

They listened with more interest to my description of Will Snowdon and his distinctive mount.

At last, Boddice spoke. "Quality sniffing round here? There's only one reason, saving your presence, gentlemen, for a man behaving smoky-like. Some hoyden in the case."

The squire sucked his teeth. "Nay. Could be some loose fish thinking some respectable woman is no more than a bit of muslin."

Mr Snowdon did not strike me as a loose fish, but I kept my counsel.

"Squire's right. Mayhap he was young Molly's wicked seducer," Lawton conjectured.

Nodding sagely, Toone set down his empty glass, and got to his feet. "Thank you, gentlemen, for your assistance. Now, I look to you, as senior representatives of the church in your rector's absence, to ensure that the children in the parish are better fed. I have seen too much hunger here, with inevitable consequences to growth and general health. If you want Wychbold to invest in his land, you must invest in the village's future too. Without healthy children, you will not get healthy adults."

The wardens scrabbled to their feet, standing almost to attention. "Yes, My Lord," Lawton said.

Toone nodded as if he were indeed his father's heir, not a younger son. "Excellent. I shall expect to hear better reports from Dr Campion."

They stared. Boddice spoke first. "Be you a medical man and all, Rector?"

I shook my head. "I am called doctor because I passed certain examinations in theology. Dr Toone and Dr Hansard are both doctors of medicine. I am happy for you to address me as Mr Campion if you prefer to avoid confusion."

On that note we were bowed out of the house, waiting barely a moment before our horses appeared. So impressed had the wardens been by Toone's superb manner that Lawton rebuked the stable boy firmly for bringing Titus to me; clearly a man of quality deserved a mount of equal pedigree. What effect would we have made if we had travelled in Toone's curricle? I verily believe they would have cast down their coats for us to walk on.

CHAPTER
NINE

"In the absence of any precise information," Mrs Hansard mused over tea that evening, "do you not think it time to make further enquiries about this Mr Snowdon of yours? A man cannot appear so promptly, so pat, from nowhere and disappear equally quickly. Surely he must have said something to help you place him? Surely he gave some indication of how he knew he was needed?" she added with some asperity — and some courage, given Toone's previous reaction.

"We were too grateful and then too preoccupied," I admitted. "And I was too much of a coward to force the issue. To all intents and purposes he was a gentleman freely giving his services. I could think of no way to ask him."

"There was no occasion for any niceties," Hansard said. "I will confess it now, and hang my head as I do it, Maria, but none of us could face the picnic you sent us. Even tough-stomached Toone here simply wanted to do what he had to and see the poor man laid in his coffin."

"Of course. But if Snowdon received no message from Hasbury or Wychbold, how could he have known?" she repeated, as if daring Toone to be as insolent as he was when she first posed the question.

I suspect it was more her reaction on that occasion than any fear of Hansard that kept him silent.

"Servants," she answered her own question with an irritated snap of the fingers. "Servants' gossip."

"That takes days. Hours at least," I objected, adding with less assurance, "does it not?"

By now, however, she had rung for Burns. With the same cool raised eyebrow that had silenced Toone, she reduced him from a proud, poised young man to a schoolboy accused of cheating in class. "Burns, do you recall anything about Monday morning — the day Mr Snowdon called?"

"Mr Snowdon? I showed him directly into the library, madam. Then I summoned Dr Hansard and Dr Campion. Dr Toone was still at breakfast with you, if you recall."

"Excellent. Now, earlier that morning you had been given two messages. Did you open either before you found servants to despatch them?"

He looked truly appalled. "Madam, had they both been open sheets, not sealed, can you believe that I would have broken the gentlemen's confidence? As it happens," he added slowly, "the seal on one was less secure than on the other. I recall pressing it lightly with my thumb in the hopes of securing it. Then I sent young Henry to Lord Wychbold with one, and William to Lord Hasbury. As far as I am aware, neither can read or write yet, though Mr Jem is teaching them their letters — he spends an hour with them every time he dines with you."

"You will ask them, if you please, to whom they handed their missives, and report back to me. Thank you, Burns. Pray, before you leave the room, may I remind you that you and any other of the cricketers amongst your colleagues have our express permission to play any match, provided you tell us beforehand, and make arrangements, if necessary, for others to do their tasks? You, I fear, will never find a substitute here," she added with the sweetest of smiles, "but that does not mean you should not play. The honour of the team is at stake!"

"And by all means have the east meadow mown early, so that you may practise there whenever you are at liberty," Edmund added with a broad wink. "There are several of last season's games that call for revenge."

Toone waited until Burns had quitted the room. "Fascinating as it may be to discover the whereabouts of our artist friend, albeit one connected with the village of two dead children, I cannot but feel we are searching for a gnat when we should be concentrating on finding a killer. That man was killed horribly, whether or not the contents of his mouth were placed there before or after death. And we should make greater push to discover the identity of both victim and perpetrators. So far we have been genteelly delicate in our enquiries. Now I believe we must make greater exertions, lest, believing themselves safe from the law, the miscreants make an attempt on another victim."

"I have spoken to every patient in my practice," Hansard declared, "both those who have summoned me and those who frankly had no need of a visit. And none of them admits to having any knowledge of a plump middle-aged man, living or dead. Maria, you have that expression on your face that tells me you have an idea of which I may not approve."

She laughed. "Indeed, husband, even I may not approve of this idea. Do you recall how on one occasion, with Dr Toone's advice, I was able to sketch what the victim might have looked like in life?"

"Maria, you realise that this man is already interred? You are not asking at this stage for permission to exhume him?"

She looked appalled. "Indeed no! But after all this talk of Mr Snowdon's identity, we forget that he has left his excellent sketches with us. Might I not work from them?" She looked from one of us to another. "Do I deduce that there are some you consider inappropriate for my eyes?" There was a decided note of challenge in her voice.

Toone spoke first. "It is easy enough to select the most appropriate for your task, Mrs Hansard. But I tell you truly that had I known him in life, I would have found it hard to recognise him after the death he endured. But I would willingly, gladly, spend an hour with you in an attempt, even if it would ultimately prove in vain."

Maria glanced at her husband, who responded with a tiny nod and smile. "I shall be at your disposal immediately after breakfast tomorrow." Perhaps a little embarrassed, she turned to us. "And you, Edmund? And Tobias?"

Hansard spoke first. "I have to attend Lord Hasbury's patient. By now he will surely need a good deal more coloured water. Do we have enough beetroot for me to add my artistic touch? Excellent."

"And tomorrow, well before breakfast, I have to be in St Jude's, for matins. I would be the first to admit that I will probably be the only human in the church, but I will read the service, nonetheless. And I will pray most earnestly for guidance for us all."

St Jude's was indeed deserted when I entered, but it was clear that someone had watered the glorious arrangements of flowers and set up the altar for worship. Our good verger, no doubt. I must make a point of thanking him.

I had just knelt in private prayer before beginning the service itself when a figure slipped into the church, hastening to a back corner behind a pillar, as if anxious to avoid attention. For a moment I hesitated: should I simply ignore him, as seemed to be his desire? And indeed at that moment another had a greater call on my attention. I would speak to the stranger through the words of the liturgy.

Would he seek to slip quietly away at the end? No. As I concluded the service he stepped forward. I almost dropped my prayer book: it was none other than Archdeacon Cornforth.

He responded with alacrity to my suggestion that he adjourn with me to the rectory, where Mrs Trent, forewarned of my return, would be preparing breakfast: she always overwhelmed me with the quantity, if not the quality, of her food, so I had no doubt of the archdeacon being fed to repletion. None could fault her home-brewed ale, though it transpired that we both preferred coffee. There was a profusion of fresh eggs and some excellent ham; the bread was as good as the new stove could bake. I would make sure that the archdeacon thanked her in person.

Encouraging me to address him less formally as Archdeacon Giles, my guest made inroads into all set before him. It was only as he wiped the last crumb from his lips that he broached the problem before him. "These people from Clavercote, Campion: their latest demand is that none but you should minister to them. They spurn the thought of a curate, no matter how usual that situation is. Having seen, if you will forgive the analogy, the Lord Mayor's Procession, they have no desire to watch the man sweeping up after it."

"I am very flattered. But for once I feel unable to oblige them. As you are no doubt aware, there has been a vile murder in their parish." Receiving a shocked negative, I was obliged to recount what had happened and my part in the proceedings.

He looked truly appalled. "But you are no mere parish constable, my dear Campion — you are a man of God!"

"And perhaps, as on previous occasions, an instrument of justice," I retorted.

He bit his lip. "Perhaps this little country backwater is not sufficient for a man of your abilities. Perhaps your abilities would be better suited to something less out of the public eye."

"I am more than happy here. And there is God's work to be done whether one is seen doing it or not."

"Of course, of course. So long as this playing-at-being-constable game of yours is subservient to your other work."

"Archdeacon, all over the country I see men of the cloth delegating all their responsibilities to curates to whom they pay such niggardly stipends that they have to lodge with farmers because they cannot afford their own home. It is with them you should be remonstrating, not I! My apologies," I added hastily. "I spoke too warmly."

"You spoke with a good deal of feeling and a regrettable amount of accuracy. Which is why I am all the more disappointed that you will not take up the care of Clavercote's souls. Sadly disappointed, Campion. A man cannot serve two masters, you know."

As if my father were pressing my shoulder, I remained silent, merely raising one cool eyebrow, much in the manner of dear Maria.

At last he said, "Perhaps a compromise might be reached. Curates may take the services, but you will undertake to continue with your pastoral work there. I hear great things of you from Boddice and Lawton. Dear me, they sound like a particularly unreliable firm of tailors, do they not?"

I laughed, and it seemed that our previous good relations were restored.

Over fresh coffee he questioned me further on the murder, gasping in horror as I relayed the least savoury details, one in particular drawing all the colour from his face. "Can men behave like that?" he breathed. "You are in the right: such a crime must not go unpunished, whoever is responsible." He jumped visibly as the clock struck, and made to depart.

Summoning not Susan but Mrs Trent, I indicated that she was the source of all this morning's good food. Her curtsy was modest, but I wagered she would not be in the kitchen two seconds before she checked the coin that he had passed her. However, she would have to wait a moment longer: the archdeacon should know of her personal kindness in the matter of Joseph, the box, and the clothes for Sarey.

As she bobbed her acknowledgement of his renewed thanks, to my joy she added that Susan and Robert had also played a part. They were included in the sonorous blessing he bestowed upon her. Both might have preferred a less spiritual and more material reward, I fear.

As I accompanied him to his curricle, once again guarded by his little tiger, I admitted my contact with Sarey and Joseph was instrumental in my agreeing to maintain contact with Clavercote, and told him of Joseph's father's despairing departure.

"So the child is to be brought up by strangers?"

"Sarey no longer considers him a stranger: indeed, his arrival in her arms may have saved her reason, since she had but hours before lost her own infant."

He produced his purse once again. "His new family — can they afford an additional mouth? Pray, Tobias, do not give them all this at once, lest others begrudge what they may see as good fortune. You will know when to provide, when to withhold, whether to give in kind, whether to give in cash."

Like Mrs Trent, I refrained from looking at the gold. "I will keep a detailed account for you," I promised.

His horses were more than ready to depart.

"I will see to the curates for all the services; and — Tobias — the bishop will hear of your service to the ailing families. But I will spare him the news of your inexplicable impersonation of a parish constable." He left with his hand raised in blessing.

The sum that Archdeacon Cornforth had entrusted to me would, if husbanded well, keep Sarey and her family in some prosperity. I found a box to keep it in, just big enough to hold a notebook for the accounts I had promised to keep. Both Mrs Hansard and Mrs Trent should advise me, the latter because she had already given as much as she could afford and probably more — the archdeacon's half-guinea apart, of course.

"Clothes for Sarey," she declared as I went to the kitchen to consult her. "And shoes and pattens. Soap for the baby. Bedlinen — though I was about to give her your old sheets now I've turned them." She laughed at my puzzled expression. "Sheets wear out in the middle first — stands to reason — so you cut them in half and sew the two original edges together. Then you hem the new edges."

"But the ridge down the middle . . ." I felt like the princess complaining about the pea.

"Easier to bear than the cost of new sheets, and that I will declare. New sheets slung on the bushes on washday would cause talk in the village, you mark my words. I tell you straight, Dr Campion, Sarey won't want that. She'd see our old ones as a kindness, but new ones as an embarrassment. And if you don't believe me, you ask Mrs Hansard." Was there a tinge of resentment in her voice? How must she feel about my constant attendance at Langley Park? I must give the matter thought and prayer.

"I am happy to take your advice. And what about the matter of clothes? Would it not look particular if I, a bachelor, showed a knowledge of women's wear?"

She laughed. "Truly you need a wife, Rector, to make yourself respectable — and to do all this sort of work for you."

"Until I have one, Mrs Trent, perhaps you would lend me countenance by accompanying me next time I go to Clavercote. In fact, I see that the sun is breaking through at last. I fear my equipage is not as grand as the archdeacon's, and Robert is not so top-lofty as his tiger, but we would make a fine couple, so long as we conceal the bundle of sheets."

To be sure, we were but a pale imitation of either Toone or the archdeacon, but the journey undoubtedly gave Mrs Trent pleasure, as she sat beside me, fine as fivepence in her new spring dress, pelisse and bonnet. Since she was to discuss intimate matters with Sarey, I did no more than make the introductions before returning to Robert, who was plying the horses with apples and affection. I joined him, exchanging an occasional smile. At last the breeze stirred the well-brushed manes and created a little miracle.

"Seems the wind is getting cold, Master. Best if I walk them a while?"

"I'm sure you should." Then from the corner of my eye I saw movement. I laid a hand on his shoulder, and drew him close to my side. His heart was racing. "But perhaps not yet."

Although it was the busiest time of day, when you would expect the hamlet to be deserted and all its able-bodied inhabitants in the field, a crowd of men was gathering, with the same air of menace as before. None spoke to me directly, though one, painfully thin with wild eyes, was clearly the most agitated. Eventually, pushed forward by some of his colleagues, he stepped forward, his arm jerkily emphasising each point.

"Haven't you learnt nothing? We don't want your sort round here. You and your gentleman's ways, thinking that just because you're full of juice you can have anything you fancy. There's Molly dead because of your like, and her mother, of a broken heart. And now it's my Sarey you're a-visiting. Food and fine clothes. We know what you're after. And I'm telling you, you lay so much as a finger on my wife and I'll —"

"You'll what, Jim Tump?" Mrs Trent emerged from the cottage, arms akimbo. "The good rector brought food I cooked and clothes I made. Aye, and a toy that lad whittled too," she said. "How else did you expect them to get here? And don't say you didn't need them, because if ever a wench needs some nourishment and

105

some half-decent clothes 'tis your Sarey. Yes, and you shut your mouth too, John Broadwell. Could your good wife afford to give her sheets? Mended sheets, 'tis true, but sheets and shoes. Kindly step inside, Jim, and tell her how fine she looks with her hair combed and a clean shift. Or are you afraid to look her in the eye, with all your crude suspicionings?" She gestured to the doorway.

Like a naughty child, he did as he was bid. There was absolute silence.

At last he emerged, actually carrying Joseph, wrapped in a shawl that was clean but clearly not new or expensive. "Thank'ee, Mrs Trent. And thank'ee for the other stuff, Master," he muttered to the ground, as if that was what Sarey had ordered him to say. Then he actually looked at her. "And is it really ours to keep?"

Her smile was stern. "As long as you look after that lad the best you can, which I shall check on, you can rest assured. And I'll bring other stuff when I come, because he'll grow, and with a bit of food inside her, Sarey will fill out. There's a nice pork pie in that basket. You might want to try a bit yourself." She let me hand her into the gig and take my place beside her before nodding graciously. "I still have ears in this village, don't you forget. Thank you, Dr Campion."

I think it was meant as a signal to drive off, but poor Jim took it as a cue for him. Tugging his forelock, he said humbly, "Thank you, Dr Campion."

It was not until we were clear of the village that I allowed the horses to slacken their speed.

"Thank you, Mrs Trent, for saving our bacon back there. And thank you for your excellent counsel. Everything we saw there bears witness to its wisdom. It grieves me that neither the mother nor the child will enjoy the luxury of new clothes —"

"As to that," she interrupted me with a quiet laugh, "I think I can recall that Sarey's godmother, who went into service at the same time as I did, had a nice little position in the north. I shall write to her and suggest it is time to be generous, if she can. And who will know if she is rich or as poor as a church mouse? Because it's all England to a China orange that Sarey can't read."

"And you intend to practise a little harmless deception? My dear Mrs Trent, how can I ever thank you enough?"

CHAPTER
TEN

Burns, having served us all to sherry, did not withdraw to the side of the room, but took up an authoritative position by the fireplace. In response to his quiet but meaningful cough, Hansard smiled and gestured: the butler was one of us, temporarily, with information to impart.

"As you know, I sent young Henry to Lord Wychbold with one of your notes, Dr Campion, and William to Lord Hasbury with the other. I understand that both went straight to the servants' halls, but that while Henry delivered his directly to Mr Clopton, the butler, William accepted a mug of ale, meanwhile leaving the message on the table. I understand that horseplay took place."

"Something very deeply annoyed Mrs Heath," Maria affirmed.

Burns bowed. "Indeed, ma'am. And, regrettably, by the time Mrs Heath had silenced everyone and restored discipline, there was no sign of the letter. When eventually William recovered it, the loose wax had parted company with the paper it was meant to seal. I have rebuked William sternly, sir and ma'am, and I do not think he will ever be so negligent again. But the long and the short of it is that everyone knew the contents before it was delivered to His Lordship."

"Assuming that all the servants could read."

"Indeed so, Dr Campion. But one of them read the contents aloud to the others. You will understand that Lord Hasbury's staff will have been augmented by his guests' servants so one does not know whom to blame. It is a sad business, sir, and I can only offer my apologies for my part in it."

I got up to shake him by the hand. "The fault — the carelessness — is all mine, Burns. I put you to a great deal of trouble. More, I exposed poor William to ridicule from his peers. Let us go down to the servants' hall so that I may apologise in person."

Burns recoiled as if I had bitten him. "But, sir — remember the hour. Everyone will be completing preparations for dinner."

"In that case I will come down after dinner." From the tail of my eye I could see that Maria was minutely shaking her head. Of course, that was when the servants would rightly be taking their ease. "Or perhaps . . . perhaps you would send William forthwith to the library, where I may speak to him alone."

"Make a public apology to a servant? One of the lowliest of the servants? I could not believe my ears, my dear Campion," Toone drawled as I returned.

Thank goodness Jem had not yet arrived: there might have been fisticuffs in the Hansards' drawing room. On the other hand, Jem had a much stronger sense of the social hierarchy, so perhaps he would have surprised me by endorsing Toone's sentiments.

"In fact, I did rather more than apologise. I asked him to write down a list of people who were present when he was tormented and to recall if any left precipitately. He will hand it over to Burns to deliver with the tea tray."

Before any of my friends could comment, Burns announced the arrival of Jem, and also declared dinner to be ready; as usual, as long as he was in the room we kept our conversation general, though I did regale them with the story of my surprise visitor at matins. From there it seemed a short step to an account of Mrs Trent's aplomb in dealing with Jim Tump, and extended praise of the lady herself.

It was not, however, until Burns left us to our own devices that something of much more moment was raised: Maria's endeavours to make the damaged face of the dead man appear like that of a living being.

She shook her head in irritation. "I fear I raised our hopes in vain and wasted a great deal of Dr Toone's time. Had I been working at first hand, as it were, I might have done better, but I can see that that would have been quite ineligible." She glanced at Jem with a rueful grin. "If Tobias's enquiries find Mr Snowdon, then we may have more success — assuming that he has not already quit the area, of course."

"May I see what you have done?"

"All three of you may: Edmund arrived only minutes before you did. I should imagine Dr Toone is heartily sick of the originals and what I have done, so we will excuse him if he prefers. The sketches — I dare not call them likenesses — are under lock and key in Edmund's study."

"In a different light, perhaps they will be more illuminating," Toone conceded, rising as we did to adjourn. In other words, he wanted to be present if and when any startled recognition took place.

"I concentrated," Maria declared, as Hansard produced the drawings from his desk, "on trying to make acceptable to a bystander the damaged flesh that Mr Snowdon had depicted. Astonishingly he had been close enough to the poor corpse actually to take measurements, so I know that I have the outline of the face correct. And I know where in relation to the eyes and mouth the ears would be. So this is my most basic effort."

The face was round, rather than long, with two double chins. The ears were notably large. She had not attempted to include any features, hardly surprising given the mass of flesh and bone that had been all that remained of a human visage. The cheeks had met the forehead with no sign that there might be eyes beneath the swelling — though Toone had assured me that the crows would soon have found them.

The second sketch added some wispy hair, the third an old-fashioned wig — the sort a doctor or clergyman might have favoured before the powder tax.

Then, perhaps as her confidence increased, Maria had essayed adding a simple stock and the shoulders of a coat. She smiled apologetically.

"I was merely letting my pencil take charge," she said, tucking the drawing behind the others and tapping them all into a neat sheaf. "Without his eyes, nose and mouth, what sort of sense can I give of him? I might have made him a military man, but Dr Toone says that he had never had a hard life."

"There were no signs of wounds or other injuries — no scars at all," Toone explained. "My friends, Mrs Hansard has worked a minor miracle with very little to aid her. Even so, I know not what we are to do with her handiwork. Perhaps," he added less brusquely, "we should keep it safe until we have a suspect we can confront with them and observe his reaction."

"Meanwhile, I should imagine that Burns is ready to produce William's list," Hansard said, once again locking the sketches and Snowdon's originals in his desk. He rarely took such precautions, trusting his servants implicitly. When I caught his eye, he gave an apologetic shrug: he did not wish anyone to identify the second artist lest they react as Jem had done. But when I asked for one or two for my study, where I could glance at them from time to time to catch an image unawares, as it were, he obliged. He did not need add, as he rolled them carefully and tied them securely, that they were for my eyes only.

The writing on the list that Burns discreetly laid beside me was ill formed, but clearly William's memory was more finely tuned than his hand.

Now was not the time to scrutinise it, however: Maria was being importuned by Toone to sing again to his accompaniment. She offered me at first as a substitute and then as a fellow singer, an invitation swiftly seconded by Hansard, who freely admitted, rightly, to having a voice like a crow.

Just as we embarked on our second duet, however, Burns tapped on the door. It seemed that both Hansard and I were needed to attend an elderly parishioner's deathbed. Toone eyed the decanters and us. To my great pleasure, he asked for his coat too, and the three of us went into the chill spring night to do our duty, accompanied for part of the way by Jem. As we left, Maria thoughtfully picked up William's list.

The good doctors could offer no more than kind words and a quantity of laudanum to their patient, who was dying in agony of a disease that had rendered a giant of a man a virtual skeleton. He was alert enough to mouth some of my prayers with me, but then, with his family gathered around, he slipped into unconsciousness and quite soon into merciful death.

Toone fretted on our cold, dark ride home. "Until we can see exactly what happens inside the body to take it to that point, we have no chance of curing even common diseases. Our herbs, our simples, are no more than fleas biting an elephant — though neither Edmund nor I would dare admit that to ourselves, let alone our patients."

"You would cut open Farmer Smart?" I asked, disbelieving.

"Indeed. And why not? Surely you believe that the most important part of us is our soul? So when the soul departs to its Maker, a mere husk is left behind. All we do is inter the husk for the worms to do their work. I for one would like to be as useful after death as before. Pray remember that, both of you, if I predecease you. And I warn you," he added with a laugh, "that should either of you be in my care when you shuffle off your mortal coil, I shall certainly wish to find out what deprived me of your company."

"But this would be to treat the dead man as a criminal — a man hanged for his crime, moreover!"

"Neither you nor I nor the foulest murderer would feel any pain. My friends, now our legal system is, thank goodness, less keen on hanging people for trivial crimes, there is a terrible shortage of bodies for medical students — our doctors of tomorrow — to anatomise. Am I not right, Hansard? Exactly so. We must shed our prejudices."

Neither of us could think of an adequate response, so we completed the rest of the ride in silence. It was too late to ask for the results of Maria's thoughts about William's list, so I made my farewells. I had, after all, a home of my own, with Mrs Trent improving daily as my housekeeper. After her triumph today I did not wish to discourage her. In any case, tomorrow I would have to discuss with my churchwardens Farmer Smart's funeral.

Thank goodness they were decent, hardworking men, both the vicar's warden, George Tufnell, a miller, and the people's warden, Henry Mead. Once he had been a thatcher but a combination of a bad fall — he still walked with a pronounced limp — and a legacy from his godfather meant that he no longer plied his trade. Neither had been a warden long; afraid of making mistakes, they were perhaps overzealous, but if that was a fault I have certainly known far worse ones. Our meeting, assisted by Mrs Trent's ale and some surprisingly good cheese biscuits, went very pleasantly — a stark contrast to my encounters with Boddice and Lawton.

When they had departed, leaving me with a welcome sense that all would be well and unobtrusively organised, I wandered into the kitchen to ask Mrs Trent's advice.

"Visit Clavercote without me to lend you countenance? Dr Campion, if I might make so bold, I would not. Not to visit Sarey Tump." She eyed me as if I was mad.

"But there are some duties a priest must do: I cannot leave the sick or the dying on their own simply because some hungry and brutalised men resent a clean, well-fed man trying to do good."

"In that case, Dr Campion, my advice would be to ask Jem to go along with you: a fine, strong man as he would make anyone think twice before raising a hand against you. And don't go at night. You don't want to end up like that other gentleman, do you?"

"So I need to persuade the sick to die during daylight hours." I tried to sound rueful, not bitter. "Or I could get a very large, fierce dog. Perhaps if Matthew's Salmagundy sires a litter: he's very good at scaring away poachers, I gather."

"Go on with you, Dr Campion, do. Now," she said, looking at the clock, "I've some nice cold beef here, and some pickles. It's not often you take luncheon, but perhaps those cheese biscuits will have given you an appetite?"

I could not feel that they had, but she had her pride, just as I did. It dawned on me that each afternoon she must spend her time preparing a dinner I might or might not eat. Last night the smell of roasting beef must have filled her kitchen — and the only ones to appreciate it were her and young Robert. Even as conscientious a parson as I did not prepare sermons for weekdays when I only read the service to myself.

"There is nothing that I would like more," I declared.

But as I worked my way through the beef, I found another reason for acquiring a dog — an uncomplaining hungry dog, with a preference for tough meat.

CHAPTER
ELEVEN

William's list had clearly provided Mrs Hansard with food for thought. He had had the sense to indicate those who were household servants, separating them from those who had accompanied their visiting masters or mistresses, with a valiant stab at identifying who worked for whom — even if Lester and Bister might have more conventional spellings.

He had even noted the comings and goings as prompted by the dictatorial bells — Lady Tunstall had demanded more hot chocolate, Lord Brierley hotter shaving water. Each request had sent someone scurrying off. There was no mention of Lord Hartland's man. Only one young woman, Sally, a skivvy, had slipped out for no apparent purpose — William assumed she'd visited the privy, and had spent a long time there. More likely, Maria opined, she had a sweetheart on the outdoor staff. But she sent for William nonetheless, talking to him in Hansard's study rather than making him face a whole team of inquisitors.

She returned looking pensive. "Only Sally and Lord Brierley's man left the servants' hall after Tobias's note was read to the gathering. So one would assume that they are the only ones we should talk to at this stage.

Yet after all this I cannot but agree with Dr Toone that we are grasping at straws. Even if we locate Mr Snowdon, all we can do is ask him — I know not what." She spread her hands in despair. "Surely he can have had no part in the murder or crucifixion — no one capable of such violence could have been so meticulous in recording the effects."

"We have nothing but straws to grasp, my dear. Even if we were to send for the Bow Street Runners, they could do very little more."

"They could question with more authority, less delicacy than we do."

"In that case, perhaps we too should be more forceful. Tomorrow we speak to Brierley's man and to Sally. At least you do, my dear — if you would be so kind? And with Tobias to remind them of the importance of telling the truth?" He shot a look at me — I need not fear that the exalted Lord Hartland would venture so far backstairs.

Of course I did not fear that. But equally I did not wish to encounter my father's valet in such unusual circumstances.

Mrs Hansard had the forethought to send a note to Mrs Heath before we set out, requesting the presence of the two servants and the use of her private sitting room.

Lord Brierley's valet, known to his colleagues here simply by his master's name, was appalled that he was being accused of any indiscretion — predictably, and probably genuinely appalled. Of course he had heard about the contents of the note, as everyone had, but would such information be of any significance to a man of Lord Brierley's status, especially as he was attempting to tie his cravat?

Sally was equally shocked, stuttering and stumbling at the very idea. Spying Mrs Heath's Bible on a shelf, she seized it, swearing her innocence with tears streaming down her face. She had said not a word to anyone. Not her. To no one.

Mrs Hansard waved her less kindly than I had expected back to work, waiting till the door was firmly shut before turning to me to ask, "Well?"

To my surprise I found myself throwing open the door. No, no one was eavesdropping. Closing it again, I said, "I am sure she was telling the truth. But was she telling the whole truth?"

"I am glad you share my reservations, Tobias. I too believed that part of her story which she chose to tell us. But she was concealing something else. I will make it my business to find out what. But that will involve women's talk with Mrs Heath, and I will spare your blushes by leaving that till a time when you are not with me. Don't worry — I'm sure that Edmund will need to call on his patient here later this very day and will bring me with him." She looked at me sideways as we stepped into the corridor: "And you, Tobias?"

"I have work about the parish to do," I said, wilfully misunderstanding her.

Before she could reply, a figure stopped abruptly before me. "Master Tobias — can it really be you?"

"Walker!" It was fortunate the old man's hands were empty, as I clasped them with an affection I had forgotten I'd always felt for my father's valet. "How very good to see you! How are you? But I have forgotten my manners. Mrs Hansard, may I present Mr Walker, my father's valet, whose good advice has saved me many a beating? Mr Walker, this is my dear friend Mrs Hansard, whose husband has had the honour of treating my father for his gout."

Walker laughed grimly. "I fear your husband has had to endure some of His Lordship's worst — I was about to call them tantrums, Master Tobias! We are never at our best when beset with the gout," he continued in his more usual deferential tones.

"As if I could forget," I said. "How does he now, Walker? I have followed his progress through the good offices of Dr Hansard, but as for calling in myself —"

He shook his head sadly. "That was a sad business, Master Tobias, and we could all wish His Lordship's words unsaid. I would not advise, for a few more days, that you present your card and ask to be admitted. He is still tetchy with pain, but soon, very soon, he will be tetchy with boredom and grateful to listen even to the Ancient Mariner. If you permit, I will say nothing of this conversation. But when the time is ripe, I will speak to your husband, ma'am, about the best way of bringing it off." He looked me up and down and tweaked the shoulders of my coat. "Time for another visit to Weston for a new one, if I might make so bold. For preference before you see His Lordship. You have lost weight, My Lord, have you not?"

"I have indeed. But pray, Walker, call me Master Tobias — Mr Tobias, if you must."

"Forgive me: 'Tis now Dr Campion, is it not?"

"It is for only my new friends, however, not my old ones, Walker. But you must not keep my father waiting, or he will vent his spleen on you."

"Good day to you then, Master Tobias. And I promise to tell Dr Hansard when I think the moment is right. It will do my heart good to see you back in each other's favour."

"Thank you, Walker — and God bless you."

I believe we both had tears in our eyes as we parted.

Mrs Hansard soon joked me out of my reverie. "So when will you be going to London to visit your tailor?"

It was only when she repeated the question that I realised she was not joking after all.

"A trip to a tailor I must make, if you insist — but it will not be a London one, rather the best that Warwick or Coventry can provide. Yes, if the weather is fine I will ride over to Coventry on Monday. Meanwhile, if I may, when I have prepared tomorrow's sermon, I will wait on you and Edmund this evening in the hope that you and Mrs Heath have between you plumbed the depths of Sally's secret."

Most of the discussion over dinner involved my conversation from my encounter with Walker and my proposed errand to the lovely medieval town of Coventry, my vanity occasioning a good deal of amused laughter: "Imagine Tobias turning into a tulip of fashion!" Edmund declared affectionately

"He will not be a nonpareil if his tailor is provincial," Toone said truthfully.

"You wait — I shall put Brummell to the blush."

"But possibly for the wrong reasons." However, Toone, soon bored with the ribbing, volunteered to accompany me, claiming he needed to purchase reading matter even his host's excellent library could not satisfy, and offering, to my amazement, to undertake any minor commissions for Maria.

At last, Burns having brought the tea tray into the drawing room and been kindly dismissed for the rest of the evening, I asked about Maria's second visit to Orebury.

"There is very little to tell. Sally is a good little worker, but her efforts are very uneven — perfection one day, the opposite the next. Mrs Heath has had cause to speak to her more than once, and even threatened not to hire her next quarter day. But each time she redeems herself. There is no rhyme or reason to it. And she does have this very bad habit of taking herself off for far longer than she ought. Sometimes this heralds the wonderful Sally, sometimes the annoying one. Sometimes she is consistent for days at a time; sometimes she changes by the hour."

"I have often observed how young girls of her age can be *aux anges* one minute, and in the depths the next; sometimes it seems to be related to their monthly cycle," Toone said. "If so there is little that one can do about it — unless you have any remedies, Hansard?"

122

"Alas, there seems to be no cure for such attacks of the vapours. As for such an extreme case as Sally . . ." He shook his head. "Is she from a village family?"

Toone's laugh was almost offensive. "Ah, more of your family experiments. These are people, Hansard, not hyacinths."

"Mrs Heath will know," Maria said, riding over Toone's second sentence. She looked pointedly at the clock. "Now, Tobias, I believe tomorrow's service is eight o'clock Communion . . ."

After a calm and pensive Sabbath, we set out early on Monday morning. The day away from my parish, even in the acerbic company of Toone, by turns amusing and irritable, left me feeling like a schoolboy released for a half-holiday in the middle of a long hard term. I found I did not want to return early, even to Langley Park, and we drew the day out with a visit to every promising shop, buying this and that because we needed it and that and this because we didn't. We might have been children at a travelling fair. I enjoyed myself so much I resolved to put in a stern day's work on the morrow.

First, however, after a most pleasurable late dinner at Langley Park, we presented our friends with the trifles we had purchased for them. They exclaimed like children at Christmas. Just as I had found gifts for my household, Toone had made an especial effort, remembering the Langley Park servants. He presented an assortment of parcels to Burns when he brought in the tea tray. Burns was always far too much on his dignity to beam with joy, but the sight of new cricket balls brought a decided twinkle to his eye as he bowed himself out, far more swiftly than usual.

"Ah — I had almost forgotten with all this largesse before us," Maria said, passing Toone his tea, "that Mrs Heath tells me that Sally comes from Oxford way. She is an orphan, as far as Mrs Heath knows, but she does have a sister in service somewhere in this area. I hope she is less troublesome than Sally."

"Does Mrs Heath know where exactly?"

"She started with a respectable farmer but left a couple of quarter days back — first for Lambert Place, but then for somewhere else that Mrs Heath has forgotten. She has promised to question Sally when an occasion presents itself."

After our excursion, my life returned to its usual humdrum pattern. There was a great deal to do in Moreton St Jude's, but little of it worth the telling, which, Mrs Trent's cooking apart, was almost enough reason to spend my evenings, when invited, at Langley Park. I made a point, however, of taking luncheon on as many days as I could at the rectory. I was working, awaiting the inevitable summons to the dining room, when Susan showed Archdeacon Cornforth, who had presumably arrived in all his equestrian pomp, into my study. I had at my elbow Maria's sketches of the late traveller. In my clumsy efforts to cover them I merely drew attention to them, of course.

"I did not know that you had turned artist, Tobias," he said, so like Toone in his patronising delivery that I felt my hackles rise.

124

"When I have I will tell you," I said, more pointedly than politely, as I tucked them swiftly into the desk drawer where I kept them, turning the key automatically. For nothing would I expose Mrs Hansard to his disapproving derision.

For some reason his eyes repeatedly strayed to the drawer as our conversation continued. His visit, he said, was to tell me that neither curate had been happy with his reception at All Souls', and wished more experienced priests to replace them.

To my shame I snorted. "My dear, Archdeacon, we all have to be blooded, do we not? I often think that that is why rectors who should know better send naïve young men, still wet behind the ears, on the toughest missions. Or perhaps I misjudge them and they simply prefer to lead idle and self-indulgent lives while others do their work. You must have met many of that sort," I concluded, with a half-smile, as I proffered sherry.

His answer was at best non-committal. "I would ask you to reconsider your refusal to serve there."

"My answer would be the same regretful negative. My own star is so low that I travel there only with the bravest of companions — in particular, my admirable housekeeper, who keeps the unruly villagers at bay simply because her family are from the place. Every time I go I fear a lynching: nay, pray do not laugh. There is a hostility towards me I have never known before, and God knows I only go there to do His will."

"How have you managed to offend a whole village?"

"If I knew I could apologise —"

"To a mob?"

125

"A soft answer is supposed to turn away wrath, is it not? Indeed, Archdeacon, had the English a revolutionary turn of mind I would fear the construction of a guillotine."

"You jest."

"If I do it is the blackest of jests. No, Archdeacon, God has called me to serve, but not at the expense of my own parishioners — whose lives are hard enough, goodness knows. The neighbouring gentry are generosity itself, but someone has to distribute their alms. I have no curate. Both my churchwardens died during the winter. Their replacements are decent, hardworking men, but need to refer constantly to me."

"It is a different excuse from last time. Then you were dashing about the countryside as would-be Bow Street Runners. I take that problem has been resolved."

"By no means. It is very tempting to believe that there is nothing more to be done, and leave all to divine justice. But others would argue that without the rule of law there can be no civilisation, and that miscreants must be detected, apprehended and punished — particularly for *such* a crime."

He had the grace to flush. "Indeed. But are you truly no further forward in your enquiries?"

"We still know the identity of neither the victim nor the villain. Perhaps when bellies are full again, and people disposed to trust those who regularly have meals on their tables, then perhaps someone will come forward with information. Until then . . ."

"Are you suggesting that the murder was occasioned by jealousy? The poor envying the rich?"

"I cannot imagine the family of a rich man failing to raise a hue and cry if he disappeared." I felt I was being disingenuous — but in truth there had been no frantic enquiries, no appearance by the Runners the Archdeacon mocked me with. Why ever not? Even if a recluse like Lord Wychbold had disappeared, his servants would have raised the alarm. This was certainly a reflection to take with me to Langley Park this evening.

Although I was carefully enthusiastic with my invitation to the archdeacon to join me in some refreshment, with equal politeness he found himself forced to decline. He was certainly angry that I had not given ground, but without a direct instruction from the bishop himself I would not change my mind.

"Such determination is quite unlike you," Hansard declared later that evening, "and I honour you all the more for it."

"Will it have an adverse effect on your preferment?" Maria asked anxiously.

"What if it does? I have no wish as things stand for a bigger parish with a better stipend. I feel that God wants me to remain here. And I am certain He does not want me to become a prince of the church." Staring at the claret in my glass, I mused, "When I first met the archdeacon I thought he was deeply spiritual, a man to emulate. Then I saw his equipage: a man with that taste in horses is not one blessed with humility. And the more I am acquainted with him, the more I see him as a politician, trying to manipulate others, though whether for good or otherwise I am not in a position to judge."

"But you did not want him to see Maria's sketches," Hansard observed.

"They were not mine to show. They will be safer in your library than in my study, Edmund. It was wrong of me to leave them in full view, though I dare swear that neither Mrs Trent nor Susan has seen them."

Toone, hitherto quietly sipping his wine, looked me straight in the eye. "Yet you credit this man with having prompted you to wonder why no one has mounted a search for a missing relative or friend? — which, hitherto, to our absolute shame, we have collectively failed to generate between us. You are a generous man, Campion."

Jem nodded. "But no longer generous to a fault, thank God. Recollect, Toby, that when you do have to venture to Clavercote you may call on my company. I'm training up a puppy some children were trying to drown. He'll rival Matthew's Salmagundy in size the way he's eating. We'll guard you!"

"Thank you," I said, adding in parentheses to Toone, "Matthew prefers canine teeth to those on a man-trap to deter poachers."

Toone nodded curtly. "You've been keeping your ears open for useful gossip, Jem. Am I correct in assuming that since I arrived nothing at all of interest has happened in the village and its environs?"

"In the village, no," Jem declared cheerfully. "Nothing at all. Being so far from London we don't get all the latest news about which great lady has been found in a compromising position with which lord." With hardly a pause to enjoy Toone's amazement at his retort, he continued, "In the *environs*, however, we have news of a wicked bogeyman, sent specially to make bad children attend their betters. Since this apparition arrived less than a week ago, I suspect he might be too late for some hardened cases. And I also suspect he might indeed be human. Matthew has been keeping an eye open for someone who seems to have been helping himself to birds — even birds' eggs — and beasts and cooking them over a campfire. But each time Matthew locates the fire, the ashes are cold, and he finds signs of another bivouac elsewhere in the forest. He suspects he's harried him on to someone else's estate by now."

"A fugitive from justice? Could he be the killer?" Maria asked eagerly. "No," she answered herself, "not if the first sighting was only a few days ago."

"But the first part of your theory might be correct, in which case he might be a dangerous man," Toone agreed.

"Or he might be a pauper struggling not to be returned to his parish poorhouse. Or a deserter. We cannot know until he is found and questioned," Jem said flatly. "And it is hard to mount a manhunt for someone so skilled at not being caught."

"Pray God all our neighbours have obeyed Tobias's demands from the pulpit to remove mantraps from their land," Maria said.

It was obvious that when three villagers' cottages were broken into everyone would deduce that the man in the woods was the miscreant. In truth, since no one ever locked their houses in Moreton St Jude's, it was more the case that an uninvited guest walked in and made a mess. No one could discover that anything at all was missing, not even bread from the kitchen. Everyone was still talking about the drama — which would no doubt prove Toone's theory that nothing of note ever happened in the village — when Jem, out for a walk with his new dog late in the evening, experienced a similar invasion. He found his books left in disarray; someone had taken all his clothes from the press; but nothing was missing. Then it was Mr Tufnell's turn.

Together Mr Mead and Mr Tufnell visited me, and insisted, apologetically, that the church must be locked. Both sucked their teeth as their eyes took in my books and some of the ornaments my mother had pressed on me to remind me, somewhat equivocally, of my home.

"Pity you've not got a dog," Tufnell said. "That horse of yours would make enough fuss if anyone ventured into his stable: 'Tis a pity you can't keep him in here."

"What about the lad who looks after him? Young Robert? No," he answered himself, "he's too hen-hearted, poor little mite. Still not speaking?"

"Only to Titus, in general. Though he knows his letters now."

"You don't want him to write a letter to this here burglar — you want him to shout out loud!" Mead said, though his laugh was kinder than his words. "He'll be one like my grandson — says nothing till he's four and now you can't stop him."

"Excepting that Robert must be pushing ten," Tufnell mused. "Mind you, he's turning into a nice little batsman . . ."

Mrs Trent refused to countenance my asking Robert to sleep anywhere except where he chose. "The lad's coming on. Knows he has to say please and thank you for his food. But any argy-bargy about burglars and you know where he'll fetch up — sharing Titus's stable again. In any case, you can't break into a rector's house — it would be nigh-on blasphemy! Everyone says that Mr Tufnell is a warm man, and, apart from Jem, most of the others are rumoured to keep a well-filled sock under their beds. Don't you worry, Dr Campion. I shall keep my eyes and ears open, and lock up the silver without saying anything to Robert. And you might lock those bookshelves of yours: no one would know except you and me." She patted my arm. "If they try to steal any of your clothes I think people might just guess, don't you?"

CHAPTER
TWELVE

Blasphemy or not, one night when I was present at a deathbed in the village, I did become a victim. Whoever had entered my study had done it so silently that Mrs Trent, Susan and Robert, cosy in the kitchen, heard not a sound. The women were sewing, Robert practising forming his letters — both quiet enough occupations. So whoever broke open my book cupboards and forced my desk drawers must have worked like a cat. The china and porcelain remained intact. Nothing was removed, as far as I could tell. And of course no food left the house.

The Hansards had no qualms about taking stern precautions. As Edmund pointed out, his patients depended on his being able to lay his hands on their medicines, nor would they want the notes he kept on their conditions and the treatment he prescribed being bruited abroad. So he sent for a locksmith, despatching him to the rectory once he had secured Langley Park. To reassure Mrs Trent, who reminded me cheerfully that lightning never struck twice, and the less confident youngsters, I agreed to the man's expensive suggestions, though I cannot recall ever using the locks he fitted once the strange epidemic was over — which it very soon was. Someone tried to remove the few coins the innkeeper had taken one evening, but was dissuaded by a large but sadly flat-footed dog, which returned from its futile chase with its jaws clamped round a juicy marrow bone stolen, it later transpired, from an irate neighbour's kitchen.

Despatching Susan, who declared herself reluctant to be alone in the rectory, to an aunt in the village for the afternoon, Mrs Trent, Robert and I continued our visits to Clavercote with items for the Tump family. By now Sarey and Joseph were well enough to sit in the warm spring sun, so all the village could, if they wished, chaperone my visits, and more found themselves willing to share Mrs Trent's largesse. To families whose idea of a nourishing meal was dry toast soaked in cold tea, cuts of ham and slabs of cheese were luxury indeed. Fearing, however, that all would find its way on to the plate of the man of the house, we discussed, as we packed the once overflowing baskets prior to our return home, the possibility of ensuring that the children had a share. We agreed that a visit to Mr Lawton was called for, with the bonus that Mrs Trent was first cousin to his housekeeper and might be able to engage her co-operation in the plan.

"Curates? Waste of time. Stuttering and stumbling — can't put together a decent sermon like you, Parson Campion," Lawton declared.

"Could they teach children their Bible stories?" I asked.

Lawton snorted. "Those feckless brats? We can't even drag their parents to church."

"The children might be persuaded if they knew they would have a square meal there," I said, watching his face turn an alarming hue. "Very well, let us start on a small scale. Let us promise every child who presents itself for an hour before divine service a portion of bread and cheese. What you and your fellow warden cannot provide, and I fear you would not need much at the start, I will endeavour to supply. The rest is up to your curates. I will write to the bishop myself to tell him of your largesse."

It would be wrong to say I was delighted to be summoned to a deathbed in Clavercote, but I felt a certain satisfaction that at last I was trusted. So confident was I of my welcome, that I did not summon Jem and his dog, now known as Cribb, because of his habit of knocking down anyone with whom he had a chance encounter.

It was deep dusk when I left the village, having stayed with the old man until he went quietly and penitently to meet his Maker. Titus was inclined to flinch at every snap of a twig, and soon his nervousness conveyed itself to me, bringing home to me my folly. I strained my eyes against the darkness. But I sensed, rather than saw, a man lying by the side of the road. I approached cautiously.

My sense of smell returned first. I was lying under a coat that smelt of sweat and dirt. There was also the worrying odour of a suppurating wound. Nearby was a man who had clearly not washed for many a day. I forced my eyes open. Standing over me, cudgel raised, was a footpad. To my amazement, however, he had his back to me and was yelling at people I could not see. At last he bent down to me, using his cudgel as an old man might use a walking stick as a support.

"Cowards," he said, his breath as foul as the rest of him. "Three of them. Oldest trick in the book, Your Honour. One lies himself down, groans a bit, up turns a good Samaritan and the others lay about him and rob him. Only I spoils their game."

Was he telling the truth?

"Can you help me up?"

"Doubt if I should. You might have something broke. And, Lord love you, sir, it's all I can do to stand myself. Carry you I cannot."

"Did they take my horse?"

"Him? It'd take old Hookey's army to capture him. Made himself scarce, but I reckon he's over there — hear him cropping?"

I whistled. Over he came, wanting, it was clear, to nuzzle me but not keen on making the acquaintance of my rescuer.

"Nice bit of horseflesh," he said.

"Strong, too. He'll carry both of us back to his stable. Can you help me on to his back? Then I'll haul you up behind me."

Neither was achieved without a struggle, but at last Titus had us both safe and we were on our slow way. Dimly I realised that I should have had the man in front of me — had he been ill-inclined he could have cut my throat with ease. But he held on as if in genuine

135

fear of slipping off. As we entered Moreton St Jude's, we passed Jem and his Cribb. Jem was by our side in an instant.

"Would you come with us to the rectory?" I asked feebly. "I doubt if either of us can dismount without help. I was attacked — so stupid, to travel by night without a companion."

"Not to Clavercote — Toby, what a fool you are to be sure. Nearly there," he said reassuringly — though whether to me, the man clinging to me for dear life, to Titus or even Cribb I had no idea. "I'll run ahead and warn Mrs Trent. You'll need Hansard for sure. But how may I send for him?" he pondered.

"Send Robert. Yes, on Titus. They have an understanding." Possibly that was what I said. I tried harder with the next sentences. "Look after this man. He saved my life and needs Edmund far more than I do."

How I reached my bedchamber, I knew not — nor how I came to find myself clean and in my nightshirt. And in daylight? Maria was seated beside me, reading a leather-bound volume that provoked her to silent laughter from time to time. I must remember to ask her why. But then it dawned on me that there was something — someone! — I needed far more urgently to remember.

"The man who rescued me?" I asked, only to be surprised how hoarse and thin my voice sounded.

She put down her book and plied me with water. "Your throat is very bruised. Someone tried to strangle you. Was it that man?"

"The one I brought home? Far from it. He saved me. Titus carried us both."

"More than that — he let Robert ride him to Langley Park. And can you believe it — Robert told us you had been hurt and needed us urgently. A lot of words, Tobias, all at once! I think your sad injuries have occasioned a miracle."

"But what of the man who saved me?" I insisted. "Pray do not tell me he is dead."

"The word is that he is the man responsible for all the burglaries. The villagers want to haul him before a magistrate — he is threatened already with the noose or with transportation. Were Lord Chase at home I think his hours would be numbered but they are shy of approaching Lord Hasbury."

"You must not let them. Not till I have spoken to the man."

She pressed me firmly back on to my pillow. "He will speak to no one at the moment, rest assured. Admittedly he is guarded by two sturdy villagers, but Edmund tells me he is very ill. Far worse than you. The man is starving and has a very bad wound. He may not survive the day. Now what are you doing?"

"Pass me my dressing gown and slippers, I beg you. I must see him. I will pray for him — pray with him!"

He did indeed look very ill. They had installed him in the bedchamber intended for Robert, but hardly ever used. Kind hands had washed him and dressed him in what I recognised as my oldest nightshirt — it hung about him as if he was a child. His hair had been cut very short, so he almost looked like a convict. But they had shaved his face and trimmed his nails too. He was so still he might almost have been laid out. But someone had made a little cage over his legs, like those Edmund favoured for his gout patients. He was being treated like a living man, at least.

I found my legs too sore to kneel but could sit beside him, holding one of the poor thin hands as I prayed.

Edmund soon appeared, every inch the authoritative physician, to shoo me back to my chamber. "You need sleep, my friend — that's the best drug I can prescribe. And so does this poor starving creature. Damn it, there's not enough of him for me to risk bleeding him. I am relying on poultices for his leg. In a few moments I will endeavour to persuade him to sip a little milk mixed with water. No, not brandy — his constitution is too weak — but I have prepared a restorative draught. And Mrs Trent is preparing chicken broth even as we speak." We exchanged a grimace. "But Maria tells me no one can ruin chicken broth. Or thin gruel."

"I will wait here while you feed him — if only we knew his name, Edmund!"

"It may be several days before we do. Go back to bed to rest and pray: that is my advice both as your doctor and as your friend. And I promise you that should he be capable of speaking, I will summon you instanter." He smiled. "Toone is dealing with all my other patients — him and his coloured water . . ."

I was well enough to demand something other than gruel and chicken broth the following morning, and was greeted by the good news that my rescuer was still alive, with a much stronger pulse. I insisted on donning my day clothes, though I consented to being propped up in my rarely used drawing room in a chair by the window with a pile of my favourite volumes beside me. Truly my head felt as if it was stuffed with horsehair: I could not follow the words of a sermon or even a poem. It was hard to recall the name of a daffodil or of the robin that Robert had been training to take crumbs from his hands. Maria had told me something important about Robert: what was it? And what was the much more important thing that was hopping round my horsehair brain like a flea in the upholstery of a cheap hackney carriage?

My usual means of summoning things to my memory was to occupy my mind in other ways — even by taking a turn in the garden. However, I was by no means sure I could trust my legs. Then I believe I smiled: there was one thing I could always trust, the power of prayer — even if, to my shame, I verily believe I dozed before I had finished.

But as I slept, the question — and, more importantly, the answer — came to me. Where had I come across my rescuer before? The answer came like a beam of light: when I was daydreaming on the road to Radway Park — when he had signally failed to rob me. Then I had rescued him from a certain encounter with the hangman. Now he had amply repaid his debt.

Or so I hoped. What if it had been he who had attacked me but found himself too weak to sustain the attempt?

Even my quavering power of reason soon dismissed that idea: Titus was a strong animal, capable of outrunning most pursuers, and definitely not likely to dawdle along while some pedestrian tried to pull his master from the saddle. Someone must have been agile enough to climb a wayside tree and drop on top of me from it, thus dislodging me and bringing me down. Then — without a doubt — someone had tried to strangle me. Would this man have had the strength to do that?

To my surprise it was Toone who looked in on me in the early afternoon. He forbade me the wine I offered to him, but then relented, mixing it with a little water. When Mrs Trent, bobbing one of her deepest curtsies, came in to ask if he might fancy a nuncheon, he pleased her enormously by saying he would, if I could fancy a morsel too. Fearing gruel, I was inclined to demur, but it seemed that from somewhere had sprung a beautifully cooked chicken, which would go perfectly with some of Mrs Tufnell's best bread. It transpired that Mrs Mead had prepared the chicken. As if excusing herself, Mrs Trent said her neighbours had feared she would be too occupied with two invalids to spare time in her kitchen.

As we finished our repasts, his by far the more impressive, I glanced at Toone. "Might I ask you a favour? It concerns the attack."

He paused, the decanter over his glass. "Ask away."

"Toone, there will be those who wish to accuse and convict my fellow patient of assaulting me. What I would beg you to do is return to the place where he found me and see what you see there. Broken branches, hoof marks — anything."

He poured swiftly and drank with equal speed. "In other words, Tobias, you do not want that rapscallion to be your assailant. Well, we shall see. The only problem would be finding the exact place."

Stammering and starting, I tried without particular success to tell him where to go.

He threw his head back and laughed, not unkindly. "Look, the day is as fine as any in high summer. Hansard will not be pleased, but would you care for a spin in my curricle?"

CHAPTER
THIRTEEN

"There — over there, I think. Toone, this may be a fool's errand, for which I am truly sorry."

He overshot the site by some furlongs, and then turned his curricle beautifully before bringing his horses to a halt some twenty yards from the copse I had indicated. As he jumped down, he bade his groom stay and guard me.

"Guard?"

"My innocent young friend, do you believe that having been unable to kill you once, they will give up the notion? I think not. For that reason Binns will keep his pistol to hand, and you will find yourself provided with another if you can bend sufficiently — well done — to locate it. You will find it throws a little to the right. I am already armed." He put the reins in my hand as the groom hopped down and took the horses' heads. "Binns, if you hear me whistle, have Dr Campion spring the horses and come to my rescue."

What had seemed a pleasurable alternative to lying at the rectory feeling sorry for myself was rapidly assuming the seriousness of a military expedition. I felt unwontedly vulnerable, and grateful that Binns, standing at the horses' heads, should be gazing around him, his eyes wide and his head constantly on the move, reminding me of an owl on the lookout for a field-mouse.

Before my increasingly heavy eyes drifted me into sleep, Toone returned, pulling himself easily up beside me. Binns returned to his position and Toone set us briskly on our way. None of us spoke — Binns almost certainly acting on instructions and I because I was trying not to call out in pain each time the wheels hit a rut.

Binns helped me down — I cursed my invalidish ways in a most unecclesiastical way, much to Toones' amusement — and helped his master escort me back into the rectory. He established me in my window chair, poured his master some wine, and withdrew, closing the door very firmly. Only then did Toone speak, as he downed the wine. It seemed there was none for me this time.

"At least one horse besides Titus — a big one, probably more used to pulling a trap than carrying a rider. Several sets of hobnail boots. Your guest's boots were so worn it is a wonder they would carry him — they were bound about with twine of some sort in an effort to keep them together. One explanation is that he was part of the gang; another is that he did indeed risk life and limb to rescue you. Sadly I suspect he will be in no state to be questioned for a day or so yet." He paused to ring the bell, summoning Binns, who reappeared instantly. "Binns will see you back to your room and ensure that you are reposing in your bed in

143

time for Hansard's visit. Come: lean on Binns. This is no time for false pride."

I nodded wearily, but found enough energy to say, "We must not lose that evidence. Could you — I know not how I ask this — could you take some paper from my study and rescue some charcoal from the range and make crude rubbings of the boot prints?"

His eyes opened wide.

"A trick Jem taught me when I was a child."

"A trick worth trying, then. Very well. I will ride out, Binns, but since you will be occupied here, I will take young Robert. He needs some fresh air: did you know, Tobias, that the boy mounted a vigil outside your room these last nights, sleeping on the drugget as if it were the softest bed? No?" He smiled, but looked at me closely, feeling my wrist. "Indeed I should not have taken you out, but Mrs Trent assures me it will rain tonight and tomorrow and I did not wish to lose any evidence. Rubbing the marks with charcoal, eh? I would have liked to have sketches, of course, but Snowdon is not to hand and I fear that Mrs Hansard would positively revile me if she heard in detail of my doings. And I suspect that she is very much a woman for details . . ."

Assuredly she was. Though I am sure she registered Toone's absence and my extreme weariness, however, she said nothing. Binns had removed any trace of mud from my clothes and boots, and, after casting a disparaging glance at my bands and my neckcloths had seized the lot and decamped to the kitchen to discuss with Mrs Trent the best way to launder and iron them,

144

as if the poor woman did not have enough to worry about.

Maria seated herself beside me. "You are very pale."

"Indeed, I am much recovered. Were Mrs Trent able to cater for so many at such short notice, I would insist that I am well enough to come downstairs to dine with you. As it is, I am inured to the idea of remaining here in my bedchamber to consume more broth and more appalling gruel."

"I can tell her that Edmund has forbidden gruel, and that a little cold chicken would be more healthful. Binns, well on the way to driving her insane, has announced that he will remain here tonight and act as your valet, leaving Toone to the tender mercies of Edmund's saintly Marsh. No, no one has told him that in addition to dancing attendance on Edmund at all hours of the night, though of course he is expressly forbidden to do any such thing, he has a probably more exacting master to serve. Apparently he and Binns have had an exchange about the height of Edmund's collar points. As if a country gentleman ever gave such a thing a thought . . ." She broke off to smile up at Edmund, ominously carrying his medical bag. "I have exhausted him by my chatter, my love. Before we leave, I will just see if Mrs Trent is in need of any assistance."

I endured a few minutes' prodding and pulling from my good friend, who pronounced himself satisfied. On the other hand he submitted me to a long stare: "You seem surprisingly fatigued for one who has lain on a sofa all day — I had expected you to be arguing with me about my recommending you keep your room this

145

evening. And I have to observe that when I passed Toone, who was returning to Langley Park, he appeared to be filthy dirty. Black, like a sweep's boy. What the distinguished Binns would make of his cuffs goodness knows. It is a good thing that Marsh is more tolerant. And when I come here and find Robert in a similar state just about to submit to a session under the pump I am quite baffled."

I grinned. "If I tell you nothing you will not have to lie to Mrs Hansard. But I hope that you will tell me how your other patient here goes on."

"Perhaps the incident affected his brain: he positively relishes both broth and gruel. Mrs Trent is entirely charmed. Starvation is a wonderful condiment, of course. He would not have lasted much longer — he is yet at risk with that ugly wound I hope and pray will not turn gangrenous."

"Has he said anything yet?"

"He manages 'please' and 'thank you' but nothing by way of sustained conversation. Nor has he given his name yet. But he did ask one question — a reasonable enough one in the circumstances. He asked where he was. When I told him it was a rectory, he looked entirely bemused. But when I added that we were in the village of Moreton St Jude's he uttered two simple words. 'Thank God!' Now why should the name of our undistinguished if pleasant village inspire such relief?"

I gave a terse explanation.

"A footpad! My dear Tobias, this lends credence to the general theory that he is our housebreaker."

"If you were as hungry as he, would you make a mess with books and papers and ignore good food in kitchens and larders? Exactly so. So, please, I beg you, don't repeat those words to anyone."

"Or he will swing for sure. I promise to keep quiet until he is well enough to be questioned. But if I doubt him, if I catch him in a lie, then I must tell the magistrate — Lord Hasbury, in the absence of Lord Chase. What a strange system, to give a man like that responsibility for the legal welfare of others, poor soul. I wonder if he will ever recover more of his reason . . ."

"I told the man to come here. I urged him to. A dishonest man would have avoided the place like the plague."

He felt my wrist. "Your pulse becomes tumultuous, Tobias, and I do not want to bleed you again . . . If only we had better remedies . . ." He straightened. "If I can't give Robert good news I fear he will repeat his guard dog impersonation."

"Does he still speak? Or was it only fear that loosened his tongue?"

"He has returned to shyness and timidity — but now he greets me by name. I believe we have a true miracle, Tobias. I hope and pray we have a similar one for our other silent friend."

"Amen," I said fervently. "When should I visit him, Edmund?"

He looked at me ironically. "Were you not so unaccountably weary, I would say now. Very well, for five minutes only — for both your sakes. Tobias," he added, as I struggled out of bed, "take great care what

147

you say. You may be putting food on to his plate, but take care you do not put words into his mouth. He may be a hardened criminal, remember, and while you may forgive, justice must be done. Here, let me help you with that, though Binns will be deeply offended that I usurp him — what a splendid garment it is, quite befitting the scion of a noble house!" he added, as he settled my dressing gown on my shoulders.

I turned to him. "Have you seen my father recently?"

"As recently as two hours ago. The coloured water and reducing diet are slowly proving beneficial to his health, but not necessarily to his temper. He is sadly in need of entertainment other than railing at his medical man."

"He is still — his old self?"

"If by that I apprehend that he was always autocratic and curt to his inferiors, yes. Tobias," he said with a curious edge to his voice, "had your injuries been more severe, undoubtedly you would have wanted me to send for your mother. I would have done it without consulting you, to be honest. Would you have wanted your father to attend — to take this to an extreme — your deathbed?"

I sat heavily on the bed. "What a facer! Yes, Edmund, I believe I would. And by the same token, should his condition worsen for any reason, I would like to know. Would like you — well, it goes without saying that Mama would be there. Perhaps she would . . . negotiate . . . between us."

He pulled up a chair. "I have been at more deathbeds than I care to recall, and seen some touching reconciliations. Each time my main thought is of the waste — the waste of *time*, Tobias. The happy meetings, the family meals . . ."

"The opportunities, in short, for many more disagreements, for the throwing of plates, for stormings from the room!"

"Of course. Those too. Very well, are you ready to make a regal progress to see your guest?"

The room in which he was being nursed was small even by the usual standards of servants' accommodation. There was no fireplace, and the window high and small. The two men who had initially stood guard had disappeared, so at least its cell-like appearance was slightly lessened. Perhaps I should have insisted that he be carried to a guest bedchamber, but for once would bide my time.

"You have a visitor," Edmund announced.

The man, who had been lying back apparently drowsing, started up in quick apprehension. But as he saw me, his face was transformed. "'Tis a miracle. I have found you! Now let me kiss your hand and thank you."

"Let me shake yours instead," I said, alarmed at such excesses. "Because I am glad to see you again. What brought you here?"

"Why you did, Your Honour! You said if I ever made my way to Moreton St Jude's, you might put work my way. And there's nothing Dan Strudd needs more than work: begging, finding food where I may — it's no life for a soldier, Your Honour. Ex-soldier, I should say."

I looked at him sternly. "Are you a deserter, Dan?"

"I was sent home — that good doctor of yours will tell you I took a ball to my ribs, and I was like to die."

"He has certainly suffered a bad injury, which has healed leaving an ugly scar."

"But my family was gone from my village I know not where, and who could I turn to? What I did to you was the worst, though, master, and I'm truly sorry."

"I forgive you unreservedly. But tell me, what happened the other night? At some point I must have banged my head, for I have no recollection at all . . ." I was being disingenuous, of course.

"I was just settling down in a copse for the night," he said. "Heard voices. Thought I'd best scarper, because maybe I'd taken a rabbit or pigeon I shouldn't and who was I to know if it was a gamekeeper and some friends. But then one climbed a tree and the others — two of them — hid themselves in the ditches, I thought to myself. 'They don't mean any good to anyone.' So I lurked down the lane a bit. And this horseman came along. With white bands, not a neckcloth. And I said to myself, 'Buggered if I'll let them rob a clergyman.' I didn't have time to warn the man — you, as it turns out. I thought I might scare that great horse into shying, so the rider'd have been as badly burnt as he would scalded. Then this man jumped and another had his great hands throttling the life out of you, so I could bear it no longer. And then somehow I helped you on your horse and you helped me up too." A spasm of pain overcame him.

Edmund held a glass to his lips. "This will ease the pain and help you back to sleep. As it takes effect I will dress your leg again. I fear you may always walk with a limp —"

"Who will employ a cripple?" he cried. "A man who doesn't even know his letters?"

"There are many round here who will find work for a man who saved their rector. A little more? Excellent. Now, Tobias, I suggest you return to your bedchamber. Be so good, if you should see Binns, to ask him to assist me."

CHAPTER
FOURTEEN

The visit from Archdeacon Giles Cornforth was an honour I found I could have done without. Susan showed him into the drawing room, where Maria, waiting for Edmund to finish his rounds in the village, was sitting with me. Perhaps his sensibilities were offended when he found me alone with a lady, but since we were chaperoned by her sewing basket and some articles she was making for Mrs Trent's next maternal box, he could hardly demur. More as if it was due to his standing than to hers, he greeted her as if she were at least a duchess, but then almost literally turned his back on her and devoted himself to me. She raised an eyebrow: should she withdraw? The shake of my head was minuscule, but she responded with a brief smile and applied herself to her stitchery.

"You are unwell?" he asked, indicating the table of potions beside me.

"Indeed, sir, were it not for the skills of Mrs Hansard's husband, I doubt if I would be receiving you. Rather you would be receiving me, in my coffin."

"You joke!"

Determined that he acknowledge my kind friend properly, I said faintly, "Indeed, my recollection of events is so shadowy that Mrs Hansard can probably give a more coherent account than I can."

His eyes widened at the suggestion, and even more during her succinct narrative. Nonetheless he addressed his question to me. "But you have no idea who these assailants might be?"

"It was dark. I was thinking more of the scene I had left behind than of my journey."

He said nothing. Mrs Hansard caught my eye: I should ring for refreshment.

Equipped with a glass of wine, the archdeacon found he could address Maria directly. "The man who rescued Dr Campion: did he recognise no one?"

"He is a stranger to the area, sir, and is so ill that my husband fears for his life. He has as little memory as Dr Campion of the events," she declared.

"Perhaps I should visit this hero and express my thanks," Cornforth said, setting down his glass.

She shook her head gently but firmly. "Such is his condition, Archdeacon, that even Tobias is permitted the shortest of visits once or twice a day. The poor man sleeps or lies unconscious the rest of the time."

I noticed, as perhaps the archdeacon did not, that neither of us mentioned him by name.

Cornforth's nod was supremely gracious. "I will remember him — and you too, Campion — in my prayers. Now, tell me, how do you while away your hours? May I perhaps send you some books? A selection of sermons? Or — what was that hobby of yours? — a sketchpad?"

"I fear, Archdeacon, you are misled. I did have some sketches on my desk, but they were not mine. I was merely keeping them for sentimental reasons — a friend, you understand, who is far away." I hoped a note of unrequited love crept into my voice as my head drooped in melancholy reflection. Straightening my shoulders, I continued, "But there is no place in a clergyman's life for false hopes." Almost I added that Mrs Trent had started the fire with the drawings, but that would have been an arrant lie rather than a half-truth.

"Quite so." He coughed with embarrassment. "Now, I hear," he began, in quite a different tone, "that you have suggested that the curates doing Mr Coates's work should effectively start a Sunday school in the village."

"I understand that they are very successful in the great towns and cities," I said. "And there is such great need we should embrace the opportunity to feed the children's bodies in addition to their minds and spirits."

"But you yourself would not be party to this venture?"

"I have my own responsibilities here in Moreton. We have a tiny village school here, of course, kindly endowed by a local family," I said, unwilling to enter another wearisome discussion. "And indeed," I added plaintively but accurately, "I know not how long it will be before I am fit to read Divine Service for my own flock, let alone someone else's."

Suddenly but silently Maria was on her feet beside me, holding my wrist. "Your pulse is tumultuous once

154

more, I fear. Pray let me give you a measure of the restorative draught my husband prescribed. If you do not improve, I will have to summon Binns to carry you to your chamber."

As hints went it was pretty broad. It was also effective. Within two minutes Cornforth was asking for his hat and gloves and being curtsied from the room. I did not attempt to rise and bow, waving instead a languidly apologetic hand.

Maria had no sooner watched his departure from the window than she said flatly, "The moment Edmund or Toone returns we must remove Dan from here to a place of greater safety."

"Such a move would put the man's life at grave risk," Toone declared. "And on what grounds, pray, Mrs Hansard? The fact that you do not like the archdeacon? I dislike churchmen as a matter of principle — Tobias is an honourable exception — but that does not sway my medical judgement, and I am convinced that Hansard will share my view. In any case, Dan is guarded, is he not?"

"Intermittently," she snapped.

"I will ensure that their presence is constant, day and night," I said swiftly.

"To be honest," Toone said, adopting a more conciliatory tone, "I have been wondering if we should not send for a colleague with military experience. Army surgeons have far greater experience than either of us in speedy amputations."

"Amputations?" we echoed as one.

"That is why I called back in earlier than you perhaps expected me. I did not like the look of that leg this morning. I want to be here when Hansard examines it. Amputation is not something one undertakes lightly. But that does not mean it should never be done. For all our knowledge of herbs and poultices and fomentations, we simply have nothing in our pharmacopeia to fight against an infection like that, especially when the patient is too weak to put up a fight." He produced a crooked smile. "This is a case where your profession may have more power than mine, Tobias, but bruit that not abroad. Excuse me — I must visit Strudd."

Maria and Hansard himself, as dour as I'd seen him, decided that I would be much happier away from the rectory when Dr Keble, Toone's military acquaintance, arrived, and that an afternoon tooling in Maria's new gig round the burgeoning countryside would be beneficial in my recovery. My rebellion was brief but sincere: if I could not be praying for Dan in his room, I should be on my knees in church. Not to be was a dereliction of duty.

Hansard's rebuke was stern. "I have a very sick patient whose condition needs all my concentration. Dear as you are, Tobias, I cannot be worrying about you having an attack of the vapours because of the sounds you may or may not hear, or feeling faint at the very thought in church. Go with Maria: let the countryside be your nurse."

156

Indeed, nothing other than the beauty of the newly greening fields, with their promise of crops, would have taken my mind off what might be happening. Maria took us on byways the far side of Langley Park, towards Orebury House and beyond my usual sphere. Amazed that even in so short a distance the countryside should change so much, from largely arable to wilder wooded areas, I looked around me as if I were an artist indeed.

Soon we realised we were not the only ones taking our leisure on such a lovely day. A young man on horseback was riding towards us on a handsome roan, which probably deserved a better rider; though he was dressed to perfection, from the brim of his modish hat to the toes of his glassily polished Hessians, his seat was awkward, and it was with some difficulty that he persuaded his mount to come to a halt beside us. Though I hoped for a moment he was the young man whom I'd seen riding hell for leather from Clavercote, his horsemanship suggested otherwise. When the horse was sufficiently calm, he doffed his hat to reveal an array of golden curls a debutante might envy; many would covet his periwinkle blue eyes too. Instead of a girlish lisp, however, he spoke with a pleasant baritone, with an accent suggestive of Harrow.

"Julius Longstaff," he declared, "at your service."

"The poet!" I hoped I sounded impressed rather than sceptical.

"I do my best. Alas, I fear that my mount will not permit me to offer you my card." He certainly needed both hands to steady it.

Having introduced Mrs Hansard, who responded with her open smile, I at least was able to produce mine, which, as his horse sidled nearer the gig, I was able to proffer.

To my surprise, his eyebrows shot up. "Dr Campion!"

"You recognise my name, sir?" I said.

His smile was disarming. "You have a certain reputation amongst the local gentry. Personally I would be honoured to be referred to by certain of the more antediluvian landowners as a *turbulent priest*."

"Provided," said Maria dryly, "that no one sent their knights to be rid of you."

"Indeed. However, I have no intentions of that sort, so pray, let me offer you hospitality. My wife and I are currently rusticating here at Taunton Lodge. The lodge is but five minutes up the lane, and I would be honoured to welcome you."

Being turned by his horse, keener on returning to his stable than quitting it, Mr Longstaff led the way. His formal education had not made him bound by formal etiquette, to be sure. Maria shot me a sideways glance, full of amusement and mischief, mouthing the words *turbulent priest* clearly accompanied by a plethora of exclamation marks. My only reply was a conspiratorial smile: I was sure that both of us were interested in what he might say, if we questioned him about local gossip, of our anonymous corpse. The very thought of his hideous death, coupled with the thought of what Dan might even at that moment be undergoing, brought bile to my throat.

Without so much as tweaking the reins, Maria passed me her vinaigrette. "So this is our romantic poet," she observed. "But very much the gentleman, even if I perceive you do not admire his horsemanship."

We could certainly admire Longstaff's hospitality, which was disconcertingly generous considering that we were complete strangers — even if he had assuredly heard of me. He introduced us to his wife, a pale rabbit of a child, terribly young to be expecting an imminent confinement. Mrs Hansard oozed sympathy from every pore, her kindness enabling our hostess to speak, though in a dazed whisper, as she pressed us to more cakes and more wine.

Longstaff tried to quiz me on my reputation, but seemed happy to take me at my own word. We spoke, as anyone with eyes must, of the poverty in the villages and the need to ameliorate the lot of the workers. He was passionate at the injustice: looking around me at the luxury in which he lived, it was hard not to smile wryly at this champagne revolutionary. Only when he had railed at the government for a full five minutes did he change the subject, with some violence, and mention, without any prompting, my role in finding the crucified corpse.

"We have still failed to identify him, despite enquiries in our more immediate neighbourhood," I admitted. "But indeed, Mr Longstaff, I cannot think that this is a conversation that should be overheard by Mrs Longstaff, in her present condition at least." I glanced at Maria, whose minute nod spoke volumes. Prompted by the older woman, within moments Mrs Longstaff had recalled that her London *accoucheur* had indeed recommended gentle exercise as well as rest, and soon Maria was tying the bow of her bonnet for her and easing a light shawl across her wilting shoulders.

"A doctor's wife?" Longstaff said, watching Maria tuck Mrs Longstaff's arm within hers and set her in motion along the terrace.

At a sign from his master, the butler closed the French window and then bowed himself out, leaving us to our conversation.

"Indeed. She and her husband are my dearest friends. She will let your wife come to no harm."

"But what about him? They say he is an admirable physician, treating Lord Hasbury's guests with some success. But is he the sort of man to whom I could entrust my wife's welfare?"

"I would trust him with my life. Indeed, it is on his advice that I am enjoying the balmy air." I gave the tersest of explanations. After all, I wanted any information he might be able to give, not to sidetrack him into sympathy for me.

"I cannot believe that a man of the cloth, known for his charitable work, should be so assaulted!" He took a quick turn about the room. "Surely it is obvious that this means your enquiries into the anonymous body have irritated someone, who wants you silenced. Whom have you questioned?"

"My dear sir, whom have my friends and I not questioned?" But perhaps there was something I should reflect on. They could have attacked — heaven forbid! — Edmund many a time as he rode home alone. Why

160

had I been picked out for such treatment? I asked this not in any sense of self-pity, but my interest was far from academic: if, as the philosophers tell us, every effect has a cause, what had I in particular done to cause this attack? Or was I merely being sucked in by my new acquaintance's zeal and I had coincidentally been on the same stretch of road as some unpleasant footpads? If there were more attacks in the same area, it did not make their attentions appear quite so particular. Not that I ill-wished any travellers, of course — but I suspect no one would want to be singled out with no explanation.

"One person I would very much like to speak to is Mr Snowdon. I understand that he was a house-guest in this area. He has amazing skill with a pencil," I continued, puzzled by my host's lack of reaction — so strong a negative it almost seemed to be a positive one, "and I need his help again." I was sure Longstaff knew how I might obtain it here.

But he was very firm in his denials. "Indeed, I know of no one of that name. But we live very privately here, not simply because of my wife's interesting condition. I am trying to complete a drama — in verse, you know — on the subject of Boadicea and her rebellion against the Romans. My friend Byron has seen fit to make some judicious revisions, and now speaks of the first two cantos with great enthusiasm. Are you a poet, Dr Campion? I am having such trouble rhyming Camulodunum."

I smiled. "I doubt if Colchester is any easier. But the ladies return." And indeed I was feeling far more fatigued than I cared to admit even to myself.

Our mutual farewells were warm and expansive: Longstaff insisted on scribbling a note to Edmund entreating him to visit with a view to taking on his wife as a patient. Then Maria resumed the ribbons again, taking us not to the rectory but to Langley Park.

"Burns wants to talk to you about the cricket team," she said. "And indeed we could not ask poor Mrs Trent to feed quite so many medical men. But we will keep town hours, and it may be that you want to withdraw to your bedchamber here for a few minutes' rest."

I did indeed. And fell asleep so quickly that I was hardly aware of the admirable Marsh pulling off my boots.

CHAPTER
FIFTEEN

The news that greeted me as I awoke remarkably refreshed from my doze was that Dan still possessed both legs. According to Marsh, whom Edmund had despatched to help me dress, Captain Keble, now retired from active service following the death of his father and the need to take over the family estates, had brought more than a sharp saw with him; he and his former batman, a bustling little man called Wells, had engaged to try some new fomentations and would stay the night at the rectory to ensure that they were regularly replaced. Binns could therefore return to Toone. Such was their devotion to duty that they were even prepared to endure Mrs Trent's cooking, Keble averring that the cuisine he'd experienced during his early years in the army had inured him to tough meat and rough wine. At least my cellar would need no apologies.

When I made my way down to the drawing room, there was no Burns to announce me. In what was effectively my second home, however, I did not wait on ceremony, letting myself in quietly, to find Jem, of whom I seemed to have seen remarkably little during my short illness, and Burns himself in deep discussion.

Cricket. So Mrs Hansard had not been telling a kindly untruth. We still lacked a couple of men, Hansard having declared himself too old for the game. Jem was keen to push young Robert's claims, but Burns insisted he was too young to be blooded in a full eleven. Our host and hostess entered before the matter had been satisfactorily resolved.

Before long, Toone appeared, and Burns, resuming with aplomb his more usual duties, served us all to sherry. My great desire was to press Jem to reveal the local news he must have gleaned from the schoolchildren. But in line with our unspoken convention I waited until dinner was over and Burns had withdrawn from the dining room.

As one we looked at my oldest friend, who rewarded us with a smile. "If I have neglected you all while Toby was ill," he said, "it is because I have been talking to my young charges and to their parents. But they hail if not from Moreton St Jude's itself then from Moreton Episcopi. A lot of folk admit to knowing that there's trouble in Clavercote, but none speaks openly of it."

"Is there any way we — you! — can probe further? It would be good to know whom I have offended — and how, of course."

"I tell you, I've not heard of anything precise — they're not complaining about your doctrine, for instance," he added with a dry smile.

"Hardly surprising since so few of them attend Divine Service," I said more tartly than I intended. "It seems to me that it was my visit to Sarey Tump that has provoked a response I simply do not understand. Surely it is not unusual for a man of the cloth to visit a woman caring for — adopting! — another's babe? But without Mrs Trent's admirable sangfroid, I fear that matters would have turned ugly. Truly ugly. Alas, the poor woman had been so busy I have not had a chance to discuss it with her."

"Not to mention your being otherwise engaged," Toone agreed. "So is this Clavercote a village of misanthropists? Or are they so inbred they regard any interloper with hostility?"

"There is one way to find out," I declared. "I will write to tell Boddice and Lawton to summon all the villagers to a meeting at one tomorrow on the village green, where I will address them. I cannot believe that Squire Lawton did not set up a hue and cry once he heard what had happened to me. Men do not spring from nowhere only to disappear God knows where. If I appear before them with my bruises still vivid, perhaps it will touch someone's conscience."

There was a stunned silence.

At last Jem said, "If Edmund thinks you are well enough, I cannot think of a better plan."

"But the risks!" Maria cried.

"Fewer risks if you are accompanied by the militia," Toone said.

"On the contrary, far more! Those men are ready to riot — what do they have to lose? Death by shooting would be more honourable and much quicker than death by starvation. Some might even see the horrors of transportation to Australia as the chance to start a better life in a new land once their sentence is served."

165

"Tobias is right. There must be no provocation," Jem said. "My only recommendation is that Toby leaves off his clerical bands and isn't tempted to wear his fancy new coat."

"Which the carrier has yet to deliver," I pointed out. "You want me, Jem, to stand as an ordinary human being, not a man of God?"

"I do indeed. And I fear you had best go on your own — with only me to drive you."

Maria spoke first. "I fear that Jem is right that an additional trio of us might well be a provocation. But I beg you to reconsider. A soft answer might turn away the wrath of an angry man, but an angry mob is like an animal with several heads. You have to persuade each one. And you are very far from well — look how exhausted you were after even the minor exertions of today. Edmund!" she appealed, in the face of his silence.

"I cannot be stronger in my medical opposition to the scheme — all that blood I took from you! You will be as weak as a kitten! — but I can see its advantages as a means of getting information. Surely the mob would not turn on a man on his own. No, I know not what to say." He left the room abruptly.

"Very well. So it is decided. Let us talk of this no more. I will write notes to the wardens, with your permission, Maria, and would ask Burns to ensure their delivery first thing in the morning. That done, Toone, there is nothing I would like better than to hear some music."

166

Two songs were enough to draw my friend back into the room. I could no more have made him happy by giving up what even I could see might be a foolhardy enterprise than I could have given up my vocation to suit my father's notions.

Toone and Jem made an extraordinary effort to introduce some light conversation into the charged room, but even with Maria's efforts and my own the venture was a failure in the face of Edmund's obvious distress.

"I suppose I must give my blessing to this crazy expedition, Tobias. But I have a question to raise first. It has been agreed that you present yourself as a common man. This is to imply that there is something about your profession that has provoked wrath. Is there anything to suggest that the two curates that the archdeacon despatched suffered similar antagonism?"

"Not to my knowledge. All I heard was that the churchwardens were not impressed by the preaching of either of them. But neither did they argue when I suggested that the curates instituted a form of Sunday school, even though the cost of the food I suggested as an enticement would be paid for by the wardens themselves." I paused. "It begins to sound as if I am the cause of their resentment."

"Or just the focus of it?" Toone put in. "How did the real incumbent get on with his obstreperous flock?"

"Who knows? I cannot imagine the archdeacon giving me an undiplomatically straight answer, can you,

Mrs Hansard?" I smiled at her, as she stared into her glass, apparently preoccupied by the bubbles.

"That toad! Indeed I am so glad of the presence of not one but two military men at the rectory tonight." She gasped. "I fear that was a very undiplomatic observation. Forgive me, my friends. But indeed I cannot warm to the man, right-hand man to the bishop though he be."

With a sour laugh, Toone made a slight circular movement with his index finger as if to take us back a step in the conversation. "How on earth can a rector, such a vital figure in a small community, simply absent himself?" Toone demanded.

Jem laughed. "Not all rectors are like Toby, believe me. You wouldn't notice if some of them flit the coop."

"What neither the archdeacon nor I could understand is why Coates should eschew safe English spas in favour of one on the Continent," I said. "But that was what he told the bishop — by letter, I gather, without even the courtesy of a personal request."

"And no one knows which spa? Not even the bishop?"

"I have not spoken to the bishop personally, of course. The archdeacon has told me all I know — and it seemed all that he knew. And there was no reason for me to be informed. All I was asked to do was take his place for two or three services."

"Has the archdeacon said anything about trying to summon him back?"

"Nothing. Edmund, you look very pensive."

He nodded slowly. "Toone, you move in more distinguished circles than I — do you have acquaintances who might frequent fashionable watering places abroad?"

"Of course. But they have the common sense to remain in England until Napoleon is finally defeated."

Edmund and I looked each other straight in the eye. I nodded as reluctantly as if he had asked a terrible question — which in a sense he had.

"My father," I began, "my father has friends and acquaintances in the Diplomatic Corps — from lowly consuls to senior ambassadors. He would ask on your behalf, Edmund."

"I think he would rather ask on your behalf," he said firmly. He added with an impish smile, "The sooner your new clothes arrive the better, even if you do not wear them to Clavercote."

The following morning, back at the rectory, it seemed that Dan was slightly improved, though still feverish. Keble and Wells would not leave until a crisis had arisen — either of healing or one calling for their skills with knife and saw. They withdrew to a respectful distance when, kneeling beside Dan's bed, I asked the Almighty for His assistance, but did not join me. Perhaps the contents of my study, which they told me they had established as their headquarters, had more than satisfied their taste for prayer.

Mrs Trent learnt of my proposed trip to Clavercote with alarm in her eyes but no verbal protest, other than to say that she would prefer me not to take Robert with me. Indeed, she was remarkably phlegmatic, merely asking if I would as usual be dining at Langley Park.

"I should imagine that the Clavercote churchwardens will invite me to share a nuncheon to discuss what was revealed this morning — after all, I have asked them to organise everything. And I cannot imagine I could fail to report back to the Hansards. So I fear the earliest you can look for me is tomorrow, after matins. How would you feel if I were to invite Mr Mead and Mr Tufnell and their wives to join me for breakfast?"

"Give over, Master Tobias, do — it's neither here nor there what I think and feel."

"But you are already cooking for an invalid and his doctors, and have all the extra responsibility for Dan's bedlinen too, since his sheets have to be changed so often."

"Dan eats like a fly and I've taken the liberty of asking the laundrywoman to come here every other day, Sundays excepted, of course."

"Excellent. Remind me when you come to settle her account: this is something for which you had not budgeted."

Feeling strangely as if I was about to start a long journey and wanted to bid my church farewell, I made my way to St Jude's, to look at each well-loved cranny before spending time in prayer. The striking of the clock came unnaturally loud.

It was time I asked Robert to bring round the gig.

Jem insisted on bringing his new dog with him, though I could not feel that Cribb would bring any dignity to the event. We trotted gently through the hedgerows, and kept conversation to the following week's cricket match with Abbots Maine. We even spoke about the likely origin of the name — perhaps Maine was a corruption of demesne. But I had an untoward heaviness about my heart. When Jem pointed out that I could still cry off I felt as if I were Hamlet talking to Horatio before the fateful fight. I dismissed the analogy instantly, and concentrated on looking ahead to see the churchwardens, who would surely be waiting to greet me.

They were not. Just a straggling group of villagers, arms folded implacably across their bodies and eyes full of resentment. This did not look like a gathering of people who would exchange information in a free and friendly way. Mentally I revised what I was going to say and how I might better say it. In the end I admitted I was sorely afraid and did what I ought to have done at the start: I implored God to give me wisdom. And strength.

All would be well, and all manner of things would be well.

CHAPTER
SIXTEEN

I had expected sullenness, even anger — but I had not expected to see a rope, quickly joined by another, slung over a branch of the oak tree on the edge of the green. Nor had I predicted that the horse should be seized, and the whole equipage, Jem and me still aboard, would be dragged towards them. Jem clamped his hand over Cribb's mouth, and glanced at me. It was many years since I'd seen this rock of calm look frightened. He did no more than mirror my own expression.

Should I whip the horse into action to try to free us that way? The attempt would almost certainly be futile, and an accidental slash across the face of our captors would rightly enrage them.

Second by second, they inched us closer. Jem's life depended on me. Somehow I must save him.

By now we were directly under the tree.

Somewhere my brain registered that my hands were still unbound, Jem's too. Jem would not submit to that without a struggle, any more than I would. If only the accident had not left me so weak. I couldn't have hit the head off a dandelion.

"Leave it to me," Jem muttered. "Cribb and I can create a bit of a diversion and you can slip away."

"If you knocked five down, ten more would spring up. And how far would I get? Two paces?"

"Damn it, we can't just sit here and wait for them all polite and helpful!"

"Of course we can't. But we do have Someone on our side."

"You think we can wait for divine intervention?"

"I can't think of anything else." Even if I couldn't frame a prayer, assuredly he knew my need. If it was His will that I die, then so be it. Not Jem, though. He had always got me out of scrapes. Now I must make a push to save him. *Dear Lord, be at my right hand now!*

I felt impelled to stand up, as if to make it easier for them to fit the noose round my neck. But then I found my voice. "Brothers and sisters," I said, as if I was in the safety of St Jude's, and trying to ensure that all heard the collect, "why this anger? Why this threat of violence? And why, for goodness' sake, if you hate me, do you hate Jem too? A decent working man, if ever there was one! For your conscience' sake, let Jem walk free, I pray you."

There was silence, then a rumble of conversation. Women's voices grew louder. I heard words like *ashamed of yourselves* and *cowards*. Under cover of the noise I hissed, "Do not argue, but go. Run. Save yourself. Promise me. Promise me."

He did not speak, but looked me in the eye. He gave an infinitesimal nod. Soon he was manhandled down, Cribb still secure in his arms, and pushed through the crowd to safety.

It was time to speak again. "Thank you, my friends. That was both generous and just. Now accord me the same justice. If I am to die, at least let me know why. What in God's name have I ever done to harm you? I swear to you that I have only ever striven to do you good."

Because of the thudding of my heart, re-echoing through my ears, I could not tell what people at the edge of the crowd were saying. Were they baying for my blood, or protesting that I should continue to speak?

Two men leapt up beside me, twine at the ready to bind my wrists. I could smell their sweat — their fear, their hunger, their poor rotting teeth.

I did not proffer my wrists but stood as tall as I might. I did not fear death. We all had to come before the Judgement Seat, where I trusted my Saviour to speak on my behalf, sooner or later. Yes, I had hoped it would be later — I still had so much work to do. But I did not relish the physical indignities of death — would I scream? Would I void my bladder, my bowels?

There was movement in the crowd.

I thought I picked out a woman's voice. Surely it was Sarey's? She would testify for me if she wasn't shouted down. But what was one voice against those calling for revenge for Molly? Why Molly? Why me?

I spread my hands. "Brothers and sisters, how can my death avenge Molly's? I never met the poor maid. Never in my life. Though she was driven to take her own life, I would have given her a Christian burial here in your churchyard. Has not our Master told us, *Judge not that ye be not judged!*" Suddenly I was tempted: I wanted to accuse Mr Snowdon in my stead. Should I? Dare I? I had no grounds apart from one fleeting glimpse. Surely it was the devil whispering in my ear! No, I would say nothing that I did not know to be true. "Surely you know that I would give anything to bring her vile seducer to justice? Surely you know that I am here to serve you in whatever ways I can? Had I not been visiting one of your own friends on his deathbed would I have been set on by footpads and nearly done to death?" In a horribly theatrical gesture, I tore off my neckcloth and showed them my bruises. "Even now a poor stranger who came to my rescue lies at death's door."

There was more murmuring, still not wholly friendly. But then a woman's voice called out strongly, and everyone turned to look at her because she was riding a splendid horse. Astride it. Clutching a small boy to keep her in place.

Robert halted Titus long enough for her to sit tall and speak. "You've all had your say, and not much of it sense either, from what I hear. Where are you, Sarey Tump? And that wastrel husband of yours? Jim? Show your faces if you dare. And hold up young Joseph, who would assuredly be dead if it hadn't been for that good young man."

Robert nudged Titus nearer. Mrs Trent could not decently dismount without help. Titus was beside me. My gig was to be her mounting block, I her groom. Robert remained glued to Titus's back, Titus pressing himself to me. Robert flashed me a smile that in anyone else I would have thought encouraging. Perhaps it was. I smiled back.

"Thought we'd best come," he said. "Just in case."

Mrs Trent smoothed her skirts and adjusted her bonnet. "That's better." She turned again to the crowd. "Now, get rid of those damned nooses, before anyone thinks to tell the militia about it. Go on: both of them." Arms akimbo she looked about her. "And where is the squire, may I ask? And Farmer Boddice? Humph!" As if she were saving that topic up for later, she continued, "What children you all are, picking on an innocent man just because you can't find the guilty one. You owe Dr Campion more than you'll ever know because he's a man who does good by stealth, like the Bible tells us. Now, he came to talk to you all particular — suppose you get him a glass of that rubbishy stuff that passes for ale at the Dun Cow and when he's wet his whistle, you can all stand still and listen."

The first sip tasted like nectar. Only then did I realise that the ale was indeed thin and sour and I left the rest untouched.

This time the silence was expectant.

"Thank you, my friends, and may God in His mercy remember you in all your troubles. Mrs Trent has spoken kindly but truthfully: I am trying to improve your lot, which heaven knows is bad enough. But I fear that I have indeed done something that has caused you great offence, and if you do not want to shout it out, perhaps you will speak to me in private and I will do my best to put it right. But I also need your help. As you know, a man was killed horribly just before Easter.

Sooner or later it will not just be me and my friends trying to apprehend the murderer — the full force of the law will descend on Clavercote, and you know what will happen then: many secrets best kept hidden will be exposed. And, whether I wanted it or not, someone would be brought to justice for the attack on me. I am prepared to forgive and forget if my assailants are men enough to ask my pardon. But the Bow Street Runners would not understand that. If my rescuer, a homeless soldier, dies, the Runners may consider that he was murdered. Consider that. Remember: if someone confesses, I will do my best to protect him. Otherwise the best I can do is pray with him as he ascends the gallows." I could say no more. Indeed, I could do no more. Weariness washed over me in a great tide. My body folding of its own accord, I sank to my knees.

Perhaps the crowd thought I was praying. I ought to have been. And soon was, as I heard braver voices than some reciting the Lord's Prayer. I managed to add my amen before a roaring tide filled my ears and a swirling mist closed my eyes and I was no more.

I knew I ought to recognise the face swimming before me, but could place neither it nor the sunny room where I lay. Soon I sneezed horribly — someone was waving burnt feathers under my nose while another hand proffered a vinaigrette.

"There you are, Master Toby: you'll be as right as ninepence in a moment."

"Mrs Trent?"

"Now just you lie still. You're here in Taunton Lodge, on account of Mr Longstaff's rescuing you."

"Rescuing me?"

"Aye. Jem ran all the way to Taunton Lodge, that being the nearest dwelling, and begged for help. Mr Longstaff sent straight off for Dr Hansard. He and Jem were already riding hell for leather down the road towards Clavercote when they came across young Robert and Titus heading straight towards them. As for me, Master Toby, it's some time since I drove a gig, specially one as fine as yours, but there's some things you don't forget, and I was heading that way too. Only more slowly," she added.

"That's three times you've saved my life," I whispered.

"Get along with you, do. Dr Hansard will look in when he's not so occupied. It seems Mrs Longstaff's pains started with the upset. Such a to-do you've created. And nothing to show for it all," she added, with the sort of reproving look my mother used to give me when I came home in all my dirt after a youthful adventure.

I managed to laugh. "At least I learnt to trust your judgement in the matter of that beer. Vile, bitter stuff. But perhaps strong enough to go straight to my head since I was imbibing on an empty stomach? I cannot imagine why else I should have collapsed as I did — unless it was the memory of you galloping in like Boadicea. Mrs Trent — you, riding astride Titus!"

"Robert riding Titus, and me clinging on for dear life. Now, Master Toby, will you do the sensible thing and sleep a little more?"

178

I looked at her quizzically. "I'd rather have a mouthful of tea and a slice of toast. If Longstaff's household isn't in too much chaos with the baby on its way?"

"If it is, you may trust me to set it back in order again."

Within minutes she reappeared. My paragon of a saviour had somehow contrived to burn the toast, but it tasted like manna from heaven.

Before I felt strong enough to find Jem and bid farewell to my kind host and would-be rescuer, the screams from upstairs became more frequent and more urgent. Longstaff's heir would surely not be long in coming. Hansard, looking unwontedly anxious, despatched Jem in my gig to recruit a midwife whose services he could trust; until she arrived, both Mrs Trent and Maria were with the poor mother-to-be. Longstaff meanwhile paced about wringing his hands, telling anyone within earshot that he should have stayed in London where he would have commanded the services of Sir William Knighton, not some country sawbones.

I pushed him into his study, strewn with sheet upon sheet of scrawled-on and screwed-up paper. My intention was to give him a bear-garden jaw for undermining my friend's efforts and for alarming his servants who might carry his opinions to his wife. Then I would invite him to join me in prayer. However, he no sooner saw the mess than he fell upon one of the sheets with a cry of triumph. Sitting at his desk, he was soon absorbed in his rhymes; it was not long before more sheets accrued on the floor.

With time obviously on my hands — I could not suggest that I leave for home if a difficult birth was in train and I might be needed, even if I could offer no more than prayers, my emergency case being still at the rectory, of course — I asked if I might have paper and ink, taking his grunt as an affirmative. This time my letters to Lawton and Boddice were couched in less friendly terms. They were to present themselves to me at two-thirty the following afternoon, it being the Sabbath notwithstanding. Robert could take Titus for a little more exercise, returning home via Clavercote where he would deliver my missives.

"Ride Titus again?" His face was transformed.

"Of course. But this is not an emergency, so I want you to have more care for your neck and for his. Robert, will you and Susan be able to fend for yourselves this evening? Those two military men will still be there, and of course Mrs Trent is with Mrs Longstaff, and I feel I must stay. Just in case."

He looked around, sucking his teeth in the way Jem occasionally did. "I dare say this 'un will have an ivory teething ring?"

"Probably two. But none more precious than the one you whittled. Off you go. And say a prayer."

"Just in case, eh, sir?"

"Just in case."

The baby made its appearance before Jem returned with the midwife, and was pronounced by Hansard to be a pretty, taking little girl. Mrs Longstaff was tired, but perhaps not as exhausted as her husband, who had completed another seven lines almost to his satisfaction. Mrs Trent, no longer needed as a nurse, was already anxious about returning home, being unused to driving at night, particularly when there was no moon. Jem, clasping my hand with unusual fervour, offered to lead the way, if Longstaff could lend him one of his hacks. I declared myself fit to handle the ribbons and so the three of us made a decorous return to the rectory, Cribb providing a rather fidgety warmer for our feet.

Cribb at his heels, Jem led Longstaff's hack and the gig pony straight to the stables while I handed down Mrs Trent. Almost before her feet touched terra firma, Jem returned, dragging both Robert and Susan with him.

"Look who I found bedded down together in there!" he thundered, furious that his special charge should have let him down. "You should be ashamed, the pair of you, taking advantage while Mrs Trent's back is turned. Toby, I'll be giving this young whelp of yours the benefit of my belt."

Mrs Trent, pointed, brooking no argument. "Get indoors, do, Susan: I'll speak to you later! You too, Robert — I'll have my say and then Mr Jem will have his."

But Robert dawdled, even as her hand fell on his shoulder. I thought I heard him whisper, "Please, Dr Campion, sir, it was just in case."

CHAPTER
SEVENTEEN

The last thing I wanted after all the drama of the day was a loud and hysterical scene in the kitchen, but I followed, unwilling to undermine Mrs Trent's authority. I also wanted to hear what Robert obviously wished to impart. However, in the presence of three adults, Robert unsurprisingly lost all power of speech. Susan was hardly better, covering her face with her apron, and sobbing so hard that her whole body shook. "I didn't . . . we thought . . . that man," was all I could make out.

I drew the ashen Robert to the quietest corner. "Just in case, Robert? In case of what? Quietly, now — pretend you're talking to Titus."

But he would not or he could not.

Mrs Trent, equally frustrated, shook Susan not quite gently. "If you carry on like this I shall have to slap your face just to quieten you." She looked at Jem and me. "With your permission I suggest we deal with this in the morning. There's no sense to be got from them. Go you to your room, young woman, and be thankful you're not out on your ear without a character."

Susan stood stock-still, shaking her head dumbly. At last she managed, "Please, please Mrs Trent — let me stay down here until you go up. Please!" The girl fell to her knees, hands raised.

I expected her to receive a flat negative, but something — some sort of understanding — softened the tired lines of the older woman's face. "Very well. Light our candles, there's a good girl, and we'll go up together. As for you, Robert, I shall expect to see a bright fire burning in here tomorrow."

The boy went rigid.

I shot an apologetic glance at Jem, knowing he would feel that I should have let him discipline the child, and said to him, "Titus has had a difficult day — it's left him very nervy. He'd like some familiar company, I have no doubt, but you and I have a lot to discuss, Jem. What would you advise?"

"I'd advise . . . but that can wait till the morning." At last he seemed to understand me. "I suppose you're right: that horse needs a bit of a fuss. Robert, look to it, will you?"

To my shame I had almost forgotten about Dan and the decisions the medical men had to make. While Jem found us bread, cheese and beer, I hauled myself upstairs to the room — once nominally Robert's, of course — to enquire how he did. There was no one to ask but the patient himself.

He appeared to be asleep, but opened his eyes as a board creaked under my foot. "Still got both my legs," he said tersely. "But such a to-do there's been, master. Such squawking and carrying on. I think Captain Keble and that man of his are blowing a cloud downstairs to calm their nerves." He shifted uncomfortably.

"I'll send Wells up to you, shall I?"

"I'd be obliged, master."

The temptation to head straight to my room and close the door on everyone was almost overwhelming, but I made my way down to my study. Before I even entered I gasped at the smell: someone was smoking pungent cigarillos in my private room! I could not approve such want of consideration. My study might be their headquarters, but it was not ultimately their territory, and I allowed myself to feel offended. I opened the door. Their back to me, both men lounged at their leisure, neckcloths undone, and both had their booted feet on my desk. Neither showed any inclination to turn round, a fact that perhaps owed something to the presence of three empty bottles, which had once held my finest claret.

Silently I reached across my desk and picked them up. They had left wet rings, which were already bleaching the mahogany.

"Gentlemen," I began quietly, having the satisfaction of seeing them struggle into a more vertical position, "you are here as my valued guests, but I fear that this is an abuse of my hospitality. Mr Wells, your patient needs you. Captain Keble, I am happy for my guests to smoke, but not indoors, and certainly not in my sanctum sanctorum."

He threw the butt — and the one that Wells had left smouldering on the edge of my desk — into the fire, and straightened his clothes.

"We told you that we had made this our headquarters," he said. "They never bleat like that when we commandeer properties abroad."

"I'm sure they don't," I agreed affably, throwing open the windows despite the cold night air. Suddenly I found my brain clicking together things that people had said or done earlier this evening. What had Dan called it? A to-do? I felt anger burn within my breast. "Your smoking apart, is there any other trivial cause for me or my servants to *bleat?*"

"Oh, you heard about that silly wench, did you? Couldn't take a bit of friendliness? Tried to give her a guinea to stop her crying, stupid bitch. There it is." He pointed to the coin as if it made all well.

"I will pass it on to her when I see her in the morning," I said coldly. "I take it that Wells will sit up with your patient tonight? In that case, sir, I suggest it is time you retired to your bedchamber. I would suggest that you do not smoke your cigarillos there but limit yourself to snuff, if tobacco you must have." I held the door open for him.

Jem was waiting in the hall, arms folded. He waited until Keble had made his unsteady way upstairs before steering me by the shoulder into the kitchen, where Cribb, dealing with a bone, barely looked up as I collapsed on to a chair, needing the table to support me. "Well done, Toby. I was ready to wade in and offer a little assistance if necessary, but you handled that beautifully, if you don't mind my saying so — and after all today's heroics, too. Come, tell me all — what happened when I scooted off?" He poured beer for us both and pushed a tankard towards me.

"In a moment. I want to see that Titus is all right." I struggled to my feet.

He pushed his chair away from the table, apparently determined to accompany me. "What was all that about nerves? That horse would walk through cannon fire without turning a hair."

"I have a hunch. Shh."

Together we walked on tiptoe to the stable. When our eyes got used to the dark we could pick out horse and stable lad curled up together. Robert was still whispering in the great soft ears. In a moment he would talk himself to sleep — infinitely better than crying himself to sleep. "Just in case, Titus. That's what it was. Nothing soppy. Just in case . . ."

I pressed Jem's shoulder — we were to return without waking either of them. In fact we were seated again at the kitchen table before either of us spoke.

"We may have misjudged him and Susan," I said mildly, topping up his tankard. "According to Dan, there was some trouble — a to-do — earlier. Keble says he offered 'the wench' a guinea to stop her crying. And Susan wouldn't go upstairs on her own — in fact I'll wager she is sharing Mrs Trent's room even now. As for that romp in the hay, my guess is that Robert took Susan to the stables "just in case" the men — whichever of them or both — misbehaved again. He is but a child, surely, and you will remember that her affections were rather embarrassingly engaged elsewhere."

"Indeed they were." He laughed sadly at the hopeless passions of first love. "But surely by now she must be looking for a beau in the village — which I would be the first to agree that young Robert is not."

Cribb, now asleep, twitched and turned, as if chasing a dream butterfly.

"You are nine-tenths asleep yourself, Toby. I am, too. Go to your chamber; I will use young Robert's bedroll down here beside Cribb. If anything untoward happens, call me."

I was too weary to argue. If I thought anything as I dragged my way upstairs it was a vague wish that the immaculate Binns might have been at hand to drag off my boots. But I had used a bootjack before and could do so again. And before I slept I must plan the next day's sermon.

To my amazement it was Binns himself who brought my shaving water the next morning. "And I must respectfully suggest, Dr Campion, that speed is of the essence if you are to be ready to take the morning service at St Jude's. Pray allow me to assist."

"Indeed — great heavens, is that the time?"

"It is indeed. If you will be still, sir, I will endeavour to apprise you of this morning's activities while I shave you. Your stable lad arrived at Langley Park betimes, I gather, with a letter for Dr Hansard, the contents of which he shared with my master, still in his bedchamber. The gist was that the village schoolmaster considered that Dr Keble and his colleague Mr Wells were too inebriated to take proper care of their patient, whose groans they had failed to hear and whose medicine they failed to administer. Dr Hansard and Dr Toone were invited to come here to give their professional opinion. Naturally, knowing that you lack a valet, I offered my services, and here we all are. Dr Hansard has warned your churchwardens that Divine Service may start a few minutes late, but you can hear that the bells are already ringing. One moment, sir! You need two boots . . ."

". . . You obviously know, my friends, why I cannot insult you by offering a half-considered sermon this morning," I said with an apologetic smile, as the last member of my congregation settled down. To my amazement, as I had scurried into church, my surplice like a sail behind me, all my flock raised their hands in applause. One or two had actually called out a blessing on me. I was very near to tears. "But let us worship God with joy in our hearts as we sing our first hymn . . ."

Mrs Trent's breakfasts were second to none, whatever else defeated her. Today she had to feed a small army — though fortunately without any actual military men, who had resentfully slunk off, still full of righteous indignation over what they saw as their Turkish treatment. The only thing that made her baulk was being required to sit down with us, so that we might thank her for her heroism the day before. Maria had warned us that the good lady would find it excruciatingly embarrassing, so we kept our meal short

— my excuse being that there must be enough left over for Susan, waiting on us with unusual dexterity, and Robert to share. Jem, Mrs Trent and I had apologised for ever having doubted them, and I had passed over Keble's guinea. Since I found a half-guinea to reward Robert for work well outside his remit, they were both happy, but, on Robert's advice, both handed over their new-found wealth to Mrs Trent — "Just in case," Robert said solemnly, but with a glance in my direction that was almost impish.

The news of Dan cheered us; for all their personal faults, Captain Keble and Wells and their fomentation had apparently saved his leg. Now there was a question of what should happen next. Maria suggested once again that he should be removed. She was tactful enough not to mention her previous apprehensions and her insistence that he should be guarded, simply pointing out the rectory was not a hospital, and that as soon as he was deemed well enough to travel, he should be taken to somewhere where he could recover his strength without burdening Mrs Trent.

To my surprise, Mrs Trent did not protest that she did not mind the extra work. She and Maria exchanged a glance that suggested that the matter might have been discussed in private beforehand, and that Maria might have been more explicit. In fact, Mrs Trent suggested that Dan might find a safe haven on a farm in Worcestershire run by a second cousin who would find some extra income useful. With our approval she would write to him tomorrow to see how much he would charge for bed and board — and also to ask if he might be able to offer Dan work as he got stronger.

To my surprise Toone, who had been very quiet, drawled that he would pay the piper, by way of apology for the behaviour of a man he had once thought a gentleman. No one argued.

Predictably my appointment with the two Clavercote wardens was far from satisfactory.

I would have much preferred to interview them in my study, but it still bore more relation to a soldier's billet than a gentleman's reading room, and I had expressly forbidden Mrs Trent and Susan to set foot in it till the morrow. Considering the dining room the most formal alternative, I sat with my back to the window, the bright sun playing on their resentful faces. Jem sat almost invisibly in the furthest corner, taking notes.

"I was amazed that you were absent from yesterday's gathering — amazed, disappointed and indeed insulted," I began. "And horrified that, suspecting violence might occur, you did nothing to prevent it. I hesitate to ask if in fact you hoped for a violent outcome — that you hoped to be rid of your troublesome priest." I suspected that they might not immediately place Longstaff's version of the quotation. Indeed, I doubt if they recognised this. "Indeed, I wonder what has already happened to the curates whom Archdeacon Cornforth asked to replace Mr Coates. Let that be my first question. The curates, gentlemen — are they leading a nascent Sunday school or are they dead, hanged by an angry mob?"

190

Boddice looked at Lawton; as squire he should do the talking. Lawton fidgeted at the unwelcome honour.

"Well?" My father could not have spoken more coldly.

"As we told you, they weren't satisfactory. They couldn't preach, couldn't —"

"I am less concerned with the negatives than with the positives. Are they still alive?"

"Lord bless you, yes, sir. As far as we know," Boddice added with a sudden rush of honesty. "We just told them not to come back — paid their fees till the end of the quarter, too."

"How uncommonly generous. So how do you propose to fulfil your legal obligation to hold regular worship? After all," I added dryly, "had things gone as someone planned, I might have been otherwise engaged." I leant forward, pointing from one to the other. "Very well, gentlemen, which of you planned my death? First of all as I quitted your village by night, secondly, when that venture failed, by lynch mob yesterday?"

They stared, twin gargoyles of terror.

"Answers, gentlemen!" I counted silently to twenty. "Very well, I have no alternative but to ask Lord Hasbury, in his capacity as magistrate, to question you." I half-rose. Fully rose. "You may go. You may expect to face me in a court of law."

Boddice broke first. "Please, sir — it weren't like that. We were shocked as you by that dreadful attack — and then you go and care for the man what did it. Even the Good Samaritan didn't do that, did he?" he added ingratiatingly. Staring down at him from my full height,

191

I said, "I fear you are misinformed. But let that pass. Yesterday's outrage. Tell me about that, if you please."

They exchanged furtive glances. I did not dare let my eyes stray to Jem, lest we both succumb to a fit of unseemly giggles: how many times had my father spoken to us like that when we had been caught in some boyish escapade?

"We had this note, sir. Just a piece of scribble. It said we weren't to be there under pain of death."

"Pain of death," Boddice echoed solemnly. "And our crops razed and cattle killed if we told anyone."

"Of course you recognised the handwriting? No? So where is the note?"

"Burnt, sir." Lawton's eyes opened wide as if the question were stupid. "Like it said to do."

"So you are alleging that some evil person is giving you orders to do things which you suspect are illegal. And I suppose that if you had not paid off the curates the fate that nearly befell me would have befallen them. Yes or no?"

"They were more persuadable than you."

"How very convenient. Now, you have no doubt heard of the offer I made when I was about to be hanged. If any of the malefactors — any who conspired to kill me — is brave enough to step forward and confess to me, then I will be as merciful as I can. That does not necessarily mean," I added, as I had failed to do the previous day, "that they will get off scot-free. But I suspect I would be kinder than a magistrate, do not you?" I looked them up and down. "Very well, gentlemen — you may go."

CHAPTER
EIGHTEEN

It was good to wake in my own bedchamber, even though it was less grand than the one at Langley Park. When she brought my hot water, Susan was bright and cheerful, telling me that Dan continued to improve. She pulled back the curtains with vigour, with a slightly disparaging look at what was obviously a grey day. It seemed an omen: today was the day I had to do what I dreaded. No, there was no argument.

No one said anything to shake my unspoken resolution: "If you want your breakfast in peace, sir, you should make haste. Today's the day Mrs Trent and I are going to clean your study and make everything right and tight again. Mrs Trent says Robert must help too — she says if the rugs aren't beaten properly the smell of those ciggirillows will linger."

Naturally I did as I was told.

Soon after ten, however, the carrier's waggon drew up outside, draining all my optimism. He would be delivering my new clothes — I had ordered buckskins as well as a coat to go with the boots and other essentials I had bought when I was gadding about the shops with Toone. Surely this was an omen.

Binns, who had remained at the rectory to care for Dan, materialised beside me as I regarded the packages with disfavour and laid them unopened on my bed.

"If you would permit me, Dr Campion, I can have the creases out of these in a trice. You bought a new hat and boots, I understand? Perhaps I might cast my professional eye over those too. It would not do to visit Orebury House looking anything other than your best. Your hair . . . I have not mentioned it before, sir, but the cut has lost its shape somewhat. Oh, and not your bands, sir, not for Lord Hasbury, if you are to pay him a morning visit today. Nor even a simple stock. A neckcloth it must be."

Willy-nilly, then, I was to be turned from my humble self into a man fit to greet a duke. Clearly the day I had been dreading had chosen itself. I told myself that in any case I needed to speak to Lord Hasbury, keeping him abreast of the activities in Clavercote: I did not want him to use all his judicial might yet, but he should not be kept in the dark, lest the coroner, Mr Vernon, question him about the background to the murder. As far as I knew no date had yet been set for the inquest, nor a location requisitioned.

Within an hour, I was mounted on Titus, who was the picture of equine health. My father would have disdained as unmanly anyone who presented himself in a workaday gig, in the absence of a curricle or phaeton, neither, of course, a suitable vehicle for the life I had chosen.

The venture felt momentous, but all around me people went about their workaday lives. Mrs Trent was chivvying Susan over some fancied omission; Robert, the mat-beating apparently over, was polishing horse brasses; the gardener whistled as he tied netting over the peas. As I rode past the village school I could hear childish voices repeating parrot-fashion the words Jem had said a moment before. The blacksmith swore as a horse fidgeted. At Langley Park I would have had support and encouragement aplenty, but to seek it would have felt wrong. Bearding my father in his temporary den was like facing down the mob two days before. It was a matter for me and me alone.

My Lord Hasbury was still in his chamber, his butler told me, his voice reprimanding me for seeking a man of his tastes before noon. As for My Lord Hartland, he would summon Walker to take up my card.

"You could not have come at a more opportune moment," my old friend declared quietly as he led me upstairs. "His Lordship is not sleeping well. Dr Hansard says that it is because he is unable to take any exercise — a strange notion, but one the doctor clings to. He says that any day now he may take the air, and that soon he may be able to ride a little, but in the meantime he wants something to occupy him." He stopped at the first landing to look me up and down. "I see there is no Stultz or Weston round here, sir, but there is nothing wrong with that waistcoat." His eyes took in my buckskins and boots.

"Nor is there a bootmaker to match Hoby's," I agreed with a laugh. "All one may do here is look the gentleman."

"Which I have to say you do, Master Toby. Or will do in a moment, if I may make so bold." He gave two delicate tweaks to my neckcloth, and left me to inspect some morally improving paintings, huge and ugly, which had clearly been relegated from more public locations in the house, while he told my father of my desire to see him. Never had the concupiscence of the elders seemed less attractive.

Although I had resolved to make no more than a formal bow as I entered the room, I found myself on my knee at my father's side, kissing his hand. For a moment I fancied his hand rested on my head, as if in blessing. But he growled, "Is this how the clergy are supposed to greet people? Take a seat. No, that one, so I can see you better." He pointed with his walking stick.

Tongue-tied, I obeyed. It was hard not to stare at the man before me, resplendent in a magnificent frogged brocade dressing gown. He had aged a great deal in the six — no, seven — years since we had last met, and he had lost weight — something which he could afford to do, though he had never been fleshy. I was sure, however, that as soon as Edmund declared him well enough to travel, he would head for London and his tailor. His gouty foot, swathed in bandages, was propped up on a stool. Beside him, on a delicate mahogany table, were a newly ironed copy of the *Times* and a carafe of what I suspected was some of Toone's coloured water.

To my chagrin I still could not speak. But I asked myself how many sickbeds I had attended. All I had to do was employ some of what Edmund occasionally disparaged as professional patter. Even so, I had to swallow hard; if I had to force the words out, they had to be reasonably intelligent words. My father would not wish to be patronised simply because he was an invalid.

"I am sorry to hear that you have been so unwell, sir," I said. "Hear — and now see," I added, in a foolish gabble. "Has the gout spread beyond your foot?"

"Not as far as my brain — though it sounds as if the bang on the head that sawbones friend of yours tells me about addled yours."

"Indeed, it probably did. And being bled left me as weak as a kitten — probably as stupid, too."

He glared at me under eyebrows that had grown greyer and bushier. If anything his eyes were more piercing. They were always cold. "So why are you here?"

The truth came out unbidden. "To make my peace with you, sir. And to ask for your help in a matter of some moment."

"My help! Can you not see that I am crippled? Dear God!"

"Your foot may be diseased, sir, but your brain and hands are not. Between them, they can accomplish what no one else in my acquaintance can. No one," I added firmly.

"Hasbury is awake on every suit: ask him."

"Hasbury was remarkably helpful when I found the corpse on Wychbold's land, but has shown no interest in any of the strange goings-on round here since. He is hosting a houseful of guests, sir, and can hardly spare the time to assist a mere country priest. Even if that priest is your son, sir."

"Hmph. He has a secretary — of sorts. Burford, or something like that. Would not he be of assistance in whatever you are doing, which I tell you to your face is not the sort of business in which a man of the cloth should be meddling. No, nor a gentleman either. Even in this benighted part of the world."

"Alas, sir, we are so benighted that we lack even a parish constable. And the man to whom I would have turned, the rector of Clavercote, in whose parish these distressing events took place, has taken himself to the Continent, to take the cure."

"With Napoleon . . . Dear God, he is more foolish than you, sir! Has no one bid him return?"

"No one can. It seems that not even the bishop knows his direction."

"You are trying to tell me a man can simply — but surely he has left behind him his curate?"

"He never had one, sir."

"Is he under the hatches? A gambler, perhaps?"

"I know nothing of his financial affairs. Indeed, sir, to my shame I never met the man."

"Never met —!"

"He never responded to the card I left and never made me a welcoming morning call. There have been church functions to which we were both summoned, but I never knowingly encountered him there. Certainly we were never introduced."

"Sounds a damned havey-cavey business to me. And next time I see that bishop of yours in the House so I

198

shall tell him." Reaching for his stick he tried to struggle to his feet.

"Sir?" I gave him my arm. He had never leant on it so heavily before.

He steered me to the window. The grey day had turned to the sort of thick, mizzling rain that never knows how to stop. The drenched view gave him no pleasure, but he stared out like a prisoner gasping for any view but the bars of his cell. "So what did you want me to do?"

"As I said, sir, I know of no one else with your wide range of acquaintances in the *ton*. And I know of no one whose request for information would be responded to with such alacrity. Whichever spa Mr Coates — my absent colleague — has taken himself to, the British consul or better still ambassador there will know. Might I ask you, might I beg you, to use your good offices to find any information about him?"

He reeled off a list of names — those of his cronies and the cities where they represented His Majesty. "Any one of those would oblige you if you mentioned my name . . . No, we were known to be at odds, were we not . . . Damn me if I do not write to them myself. Hasbury's secretary shall assist me. Just jot down a little memorandum for Brentford or whatever he calls himself. Everything you know about the man. Excellent. Now, my boy, you'll join me in a little wine?"

"Only if the wine comes from that carafe," I assured him, pointing at Toone's coloured water. "How might I imbibe if you may not?"

Supporting himself on his stick, he turned to face me, nodding slowly. "You may come and visit me again soon. When your parish work permits, of course," he added with a mocking inclination of the head. "As I recall, you play a halfway decent game of chess . . ."

This was not the time to protest that he was mistaken, and that my eyebrow still bore the scar from when he had thrown the board at me in his rage at my stupidity. "I should be honoured, sir, and will send you word." But I must make sure that Edmund was at hand to interrupt the game.

My father consulted his watch. "I'd best set that good-for-nothing secretary of Hasbury's to work. Burntwood. Ring the bell for him, if you please."

Walker, a conspiratorial smile on his discreet face, was at hand as I left the room, going so far as to invite me to join him for a mug of ale in the servants' hall. I gladly accepted his invitation, happy to reminisce with him if not for my own particular pleasure, certainly for his.

Silence fell as we sat at the broad, scrubbed table. No doubt many of the servants were disconcerted to see a fellow servant, even one as distinguished as valet to a duke, entertaining a gentleman in their midst. Mrs Heath was almost outraged, bustling up to offer the use of her sitting room, but as she recognised me in my new guise her curtsy was more amused than obsequious. She herself brought us a jug of ale, but, summoned elsewhere, she had to beckon a maid to bring us tankards. She happened to pick on Sally, the girl I had cross-questioned and caused to be further interrogated. Perhaps she had reason to be sullen, but she was bright and happy, responding to our thanks with a smile and toss of her head as I slipped her a coin. What she did not do, I would swear, was recognise me. Even though she could see my full face, and I was facing the window, not a glimmer of acknowledgement entered her eyes. Even when I spoke to her by name, her expression was blank, though she responded politely as she bobbed another curtsy and resumed her usual duties.

It would be wrong to interrupt Walker's stream of recollections by mentioning it, and soon we were laughing at yet another of my childhood follies.

Soon, however, his bell rang, and he prepared, with some haste, to part. However, I followed him, asking him to hand me over, as it were, to Hasbury's butler. I needed to be conveyed to his master.

I had had some fifteen minutes to make a further exploration of his underused library when my host appeared. Hasbury's coat, exquisitely cut, fitted him so well that his valet must have had to ease him into it inch by inch. His snowy neckcloth fell into such intricate folds that I was grateful that Binns and then Walker had taken such pains with mine. Even so I was a country bumpkin alongside a master, a comparison he did nothing to allay in his manner.

"You have put me to a great deal of trouble," he said, playing with his quizzing glass, "you and that damned corpse. That self-important man Vernon is insisting on holding the inquest here" — he waved a letter before me — "despite all Beresford's letters representing how inconvenient it is. What do you pay a secretary for, if not to persuade people of the rightness of your opinion, eh? And moreover, Vernon wants me to bring witnesses to the inquest. Holds me responsible, he says! What is any of this to do with me? A bit of poaching, I can deal with that, or someone pilfering someone's chicken. But this is beyond reasonable!"

"Indeed, I understand your anger, Hasbury. But imagine the chaos if Vernon had asked Wychbold to provide a suitable room."

He laughed, to the imminent danger of those neckcloth folds. "But surely an inn is the usual location — surely there is one in Clavercote?"

"My experience of the Dun Cow is limited to the worst ale it has ever been my misfortune to taste. If the accommodation resembles that in any way, then I cannot think it would be remotely suitable: more a byre than a place for humans to assemble. I believe your excellent housekeeper, Mrs Heath, and her team will transform whichever room here is selected to host the occasion to a courtroom and back again in the twinkling of an eye, with minimum inconvenience to you. As for any hoi polloi wishing or required to attend, they can surely be directed via a backstairs route," I added ironically. Why should the Sareys of this world go through their brief lives without ever seeing the first-class works of art hung on walls or standing on tables like those in Orebury's entrance hall?

Despite his penchant for using irony himself, this morning Hasbury was not a man for subtlety. "Quite

202

right. I suppose I must tell Beresford to convey my gracious permission." He reached for the bell pull.

"I fancy you will find Mr Beresford is heavily engaged with my father just now."

"Your father?" Taking me by the arm he spun me round to face the window. "Great heavens, you're Hartland's son! Hardly recognised you in that rig." He did not intend a compliment. "First you turn up looking like a tramp that had seen a ghost and now you're masquerading as a small-town lawyer. What does your father say? A man of the *ton*, always such a stickler for . . . No wonder he cast you off without a penny."

"If he cast me off, sir, it was not because I patronised a provincial tailor." I would have taken my leave had I not recalled that it was I who had wanted to speak to him. "Now, My Lord, has your steward had sightings of any miscreants on your land? Because there have been further . . . disturbances . . . in Clavercote. Not once but twice my life has been in jeopardy. I have put enquiries in train, as you may imagine, but I lack your authority, of course."

He sighed, an action to which his waistcoat took exception. "I suppose you want me to press once again for the appointment of a parish constable. Well, I tell you straight, sir, that my steward informs me that there is no man in Clavercote reliable enough to take on the task, not a man whom he would pay in beans, let alone shillings and pence. Such was your man Coates's view too, I gather. I suppose I could send for the man from Claverbourne. But he has no great reputation. Best you carry on yourself."

"But I am a clergyman, sir, not a man in need of a shilling a day. Furthermore, and possibly more germane, though I beg you not to mention this to anyone else, I am currently most reluctant to return to the village where a determined attempt to lynch me occurred but two days ago. Perhaps I have won them over — but it is not something I would wish to put to the test." And I would certainly not make the attempt without Mrs Trent at my side — though I cannot think Lord Hasbury would appreciate my taking my housekeeper as a bodyguard.

"Lynch you? Campion, the details if you please. Let me summon Beresford to write everything down. He would probably rather serve the son than the father, especially one as Friday-faced as yours."

"He has much cause to be in a fit of the blue-devils: he comes here expecting the hospitality for which you are famed, sir, and is confined to his room in great pain with none of the diversions he expected." Had I ever defended my father before? If so I could not recall it. "I understand that Dr Hansard will permit him a little exercise in the fresh air very soon."

His eyes narrowed. "For a duke's son you keep some strange company. Look at Hansard, a man who gambled his fortune away twice or even thrice and is now reduced to being a country quack. And Toone, with his predilection for cutting up cadavers. Where on earth did you find him, Campion?"

"He found me at Eton, sir. And were you to have the deepest purse in the country, I warrant you would not find a physician more able than my two good friends."

He brought the quizzing glass into play. "No need to fly into the boughs, sir."

Yes, there was — every reason. But I contented myself with an imitation of my father's chill hauteur. "Indeed not, sir. I will trouble you no longer. But I will be visiting my father within the next few days to play chess, a game at which I am sadly inadequate. Perhaps in the meantime one of your other guests might find it in their hearts to challenge him. It would be a kindness. And now, if you will excuse me, I have work to do."

As he pulled the bell rope, he stared. "Work?"

"My Father's work, sir." Next time I visited, the clothes I wore would make it quite clear to which father I alluded.

CHAPTER
NINETEEN

What Maria had said to Toone I know not, but to my amazement he was far more sanguine than Edmund about Dan's ability to travel into Worcestershire. However, equally to my surprise, he offered to accompany in his curricle the farm cart carrying his patient. No doubt such a handsome vehicle would draw many eyes en route. Good, kind Binns would go too, of course, both to keep horse and master looking respectable and, should a crisis arise, be at hand as a nurse.

Mrs Trent, whose second cousin was providing the accommodation, begged the favour of being allowed to spend a few days with him and his family in a village a few miles from Pershore, provided that I promised not to venture anywhere near Clavercote or its environs while she was absent. I did not want to give such an undertaking. However, Jem and Robert promised on my behalf, and she felt able to leave me. When Toone, all courtesy, offered her a place in his curricle, her cup was clearly ready to overflow.

As Mrs Trent told me, the problem arose of what to do with Susan and Robert. Clearly the Hansards expected me to take advantage of my chamber at

Langley Park, and were more than happy to offer hospitality to them and to my horses too. But emphatically they did not want me to leave my home unattended — "Remember that outbreak of housebreaking," Maria said, with some exaggeration.

To my surprise, Jem dealt with the problem without even referring to me. Meeting my churchwardens on the village green as they practised for the new season, he asked to borrow some of their strongest outdoor servants, all twice the size of my poor Abel, who was so afflicted with rheumatism I dare swear a snail might outrun him. Young and ripe for an adventure, but so far prevented by the earnest prayers of their parents not to take the King's shilling, apparently the young men had been delighted to prove their excellence at something other than hitting a cricket ball out of sight. Four of them would act as guards, patrolling the gardens, checking on the stables and, if the weather were inclement, setting up their camp in the hallway itself. Mrs Trent, who had admitted to last-minute qualms, pronounced herself delighted with the scheme, donned her newest clothes and finest bonnet, and set off like a queen.

My heart as light as on my extravagant trip to Coventry, I let Robert lead my little entourage on Titus, with Susan pink with pride as any villagers we passed doffed their hats or tugged their forelocks to us — to her, I rather think, because Mrs Trent had mysteriously found a length of apple-green cambric, very much Susan's colour, and together they had sewn it in time for her visit to what she called the great house. I did not mention another young woman who might be patiently waiting for largesse from Mrs Trent: Sarey would have to wait until her kind patron's return.

But some things would not wait. The chess game with my father was one of them. In my vanity, I was thinking of asking Marsh to cast a critical eye over my apparel, though this time I would prefer to look like a member of my calling than a provincial lawyer. I was on the point of asking for a note to Papa to be sent warning him of my imminent arrival when Burns appeared, looking uncommonly grim.

"'Tis a message from Clavercote, sir," he told Hansard, with a sideways glance at me. "Seems there's someone there needs your help. Dying, his friend said. And to be honest, his friend — that's Ethan Downs — doesn't seem to have much longer for this life either. Sir, forgive me if I speak out of turn, but what if it's a trap, like the one for Mr Toby?"

"Mr Toby will no doubt be finding out," I said grimly. "If a man is dying he needs his parish priest — and in the absence of Mr Coates and the rejected curates, who else is there but me?" How fortunate I had not fixed a date for the chess game.

"You have a desire for premature martyrdom?" Maria asked, so crisply that I suspected she might be trying to stop her voice shaking.

I touched her hand lightly. "Not at all. I should imagine that all our minds are pondering how this can be accomplished with no loss of life." I looked at Burns's broad shoulders — he would be handy in a mill. But he was no stronger than Jem, who had been powerless in the face of the lynch mob. At length I smiled. "Edmund, why do we not put this conundrum to the man asking us to help his friend?"

"He's out in the scullery, sir, on account of he — to be honest, he stinks, sir," Burns told Hansard.

"Maria, my dear, will you excuse us while we speak to this man?"

Her lip trembled. "I know you have your callings — but for God's sake do not put yourself in harm's way — or you, Tobias. Please!" She turned from us, dashing tears from her eyes.

Leaving Edmund to comfort her, I motioned Burns from the room and followed him to the scullery, the door of which someone had hopefully propped ajar. He had not exaggerated when he said that the messenger looked ill.

Nonetheless, I kept my voice stern when I addressed him. "Ethan Downs, when I came to Clavercote the other day, my friend and I were nearly lynched. By rights I should have summoned the militia and had the ringleaders executed for their pains on the tree meant for me. I am a charitable man, Ethan, a man of God — but I will not put my head into another noose of your making, and I will do all I can to keep my friend Dr Hansard safe too, even if this means refusing your request to visit a dying man. So tell me, as you hope to be saved, if you can guarantee our safety if we come. If, and how, please."

"It was them young hotheads — and they'll all be in the fields today."

"Not good enough. One breath of a whisper that I am about my work and I give not a click of my fingers for our safety." How dared I vent all my anger on this helpless old man? But I could not back down and take Edmund to his probable death. For a wild moment I thought of taking our pistols and shooting our way out of trouble, but I could not conceive such an act. I stared at him — all skin and bone. "How did you manage to get here, Ethan? Did you walk?"

He mumbled something about a lift from a carter.

"And how do you propose to get back? It is a good three miles, maybe more." Despite myself, I was so overcome by pity for the poor old man that I softened my voice.

"May I make a suggestion, Dr Campion?" Edmund had stepped up behind me. "Let us send for the worthy churchwardens, and ask them to guarantee our safety. And one of them could return our friend here to the village. I dare swear you could manage some bread and cheese while you wait? But I think," he added tactfully, registering the foul odour and holding open the scullery door even wider, "that you might be warmer in the herb garden — it gets all the morning sun, and as you see there is a seat and table there. Our maid prefers to sit there to shell peas. I'm afraid the crops will be very late this year, will they not?"

He joined Maria and me some minutes later, smelling strongly of the lavender water he and Toone had such regular recourse to in the sickroom. "Ethan has less than six weeks, I'd say — it must have taken a huge effort of will for him to get here. I have told

William to return with Boddice or Lawton — both, for preference. They will convey him back." He added with a half-smile, "I have given him a verbal message, which I think he would die sooner than forget — or pass on to anyone else. Now, Tobias, do you have all you need?"

"When I decamped here I thought of every eventuality," I assured him. Less blithely I added, "But I am anxious, I will not deny it. I fear betrayal." I found my fingers creeping to my neck, where the assailants' bruises were now yellowing reminders of the first attack on me. "I cannot carry a pistol," I said. "But is there any reason why you should not?"

He exchanged a long glance with his wife. "I have promised Maria that if I sense danger, I will turn back. And so, my friend, should you." In a different voice, he continued, "Where is the best place to receive these wardens of yours? My study? Or here, with Maria as a witness?"

"I don't know why you wanted us, and I don't know why you wanted us to come in a gig, not on horseback like any Christian," Lawton said truculently. His eyes fell on the pistol that Edmund had been cleaning, lying on his desk. He mouthed something, then stopped.

"Ethan Downs is not well enough to walk back to Clavercote: we rely on you to get him there," Edmund said firmly. "More than that, we require you to guarantee our safety should we agree to visit Mr Downs' sick friend. I repeat, guarantee. There shall be no repetition of Saturday's unfortunate events, for

211

instance — and no one to ambush us as we return home. Is this clear? No bluster, please, gentlemen."

Red-faced and gobbling, Lawton, the squire out-squired, looked likely to have a seizure. Edmund's expression might have been unkindly described as appraising. I suspect, however, he was not calculating a possible fee, but working out a diagnosis and possible prognosis for the future when the man must needs become his patient.

"I always said we needed a parish constable," Boddice observed. "Always. I'd have been glad to put myself forward. Glad. But that Lord Hasbury was always keener on wining and dining those harum-scarum friends of his than paying me a fee. I told him, I said —"

"Shut your mouth," Lawton suggested without particular animus.

"Do we have your word? Will you escort us everywhere we go?"

"Look here," Lawton said, "we had a warning. We told you. Threats. Dire threats."

"Contained in a note I never saw because you had thoughtfully burnt it," I said, scathing as my father would have been. "Perhaps you wrote it yourself — *if* it ever existed."

The result of that chance piece of sarcasm was amazing: both men turned colour, Boddice pale and Lawton purple. Lawton was already talking, suddenly co-operative. "We'll go with you as far as Sarey Tump's. Talk to her. See if she'll walk with you."

"Assuredly she shall not," I said, perhaps stung at the thought of relying once again on a woman for protection. "Can you imagine taking a young babe to a deathbed? Use the sense God gave you, man! Indeed it is you two or no one. And I suggest you make up your minds soon, lest the poor man dies before we get there. Ethan, too — he is a very sick man and should be in his bed, not on his feet."

Boddice looked at Lawton and then at Edmund. "And who will be paying for these here medical visits?"

Before Edmund could assure them that his services would be free, I stepped in again, my voice icily reasonable. "The village owes me reparation for my injuries. The village will pay — presumably, gentlemen, you, inasmuch as you represent the village. So are we ready to set out? Dr Hansard and I are ready as soon as our horses are brought round from the stable."

Edmund left me to speak to his wife, while Marsh located our boots and our bags. We both fell silent as Edmund joined us.

"Has Maria accepted your decision?"

"Without enthusiasm, shall we say? I would hardly be surprised to find her in the stables, directing Tom to fasten kitchen knives to the wheels of the gig so she can ride like Boadicea to our aid. She suggested, in fact, that we might ask Burns to abandon his usual peaceable duties and accompany us. I concurred. He might be the epitome of restraint, but his size has a certain abstract value, especially if he wears everyday clothes. And he is an excellent shot. Yes, against all my

213

instincts, and — you may shake your head all you like — I have pistols for two in my bag."

There was little Edmund could do for poor Luke Stokes except give him some draughts to ease the pain. But he assured me, almost sadly, that though the old man was suffering, he too still had a long way to go before his death. We prayed together before some of Edmund's laudanum drops eased him into a merciful sleep. As his eyes fluttered, he squeezed my hand. "Should have told you — but I know not what. I was to say I was sorry." Whatever it was he regretted, I was not this time to learn.

Despite the presence outside of the reluctant churchwardens, we were both braced for perhaps an attack, or at the very least unpleasantness, as we left Luke's dwelling, stolidly guarded by Burns. There was nothing to raise our pulses. The village seemed as deserted as our next patient had predicted, with all the men and probably all the children in the fields. Then I waited in the sun with Burns, talking about the developments in the cricket team, and in particular Robert's still pleasing progress, while Edmund did what he could for Ethan, now stretched on the rags that made up his bed. This was, as he explained, little more than to provide a quantity of sweet-smelling dressings for his awful lesions. Then I entered and offered him Communion, but he lay face averted, with his eyes tightly closed. So I asked for God's blessing upon him, and retreated, quickly, to the spring air.

Boddice and Lawton accompanied us to the village boundary, and showed signs of quitting us there, until Lawton suddenly bethought himself of his manners, inviting us to join him in a glass of sherry. Surprised, indeed, nonplussed, we accepted, despatching Burns back to the Park to assure Maria of our safety. When he dragged his feet, Hansard asked blithely, "What on earth can go wrong?"

Burns was too disciplined to reply, but his darkling glance spoke volumes.

"Don't forget, Burns, we rely on you to reassure Mrs Hansard with as much fervour and sincerity as if she were your mother, not your employer," I said.

He bowed his assent. "Rest assured," he said, solemn as if he was in the drawing room, "I shall do no less."

CHAPTER
TWENTY

It was very hard to make small talk with men for whom we felt little liking and less respect, but we both sensed that behind the talk of the weather and the state of the fields lay another topic that the men were reluctant to broach. At last Hansard pulled out his watch, setting down his glass with a tiny but perceptible rap: he was ready to be on his way. I took this as a signal to get to my feet. If anyone had reason to wish to shake the dust of this village from his feet it was I.

Lawton half-rose before sitting again. "This bit of bother the other day," he began.

"The ambush or the lynching?" I asked pleasantly. I did not resume my seat.

Perhaps the airy movement of his hands suggested both. "You said that if people confessed to you, you could forgive them. Did you mean properly forgive? Shake hands and let them go about their business?"

"What would you do, Mr Lawton?"

"Hang them and be damned! But you're a parson, aren't you? You're supposed to be good."

"Even if people try two separate ways of throttling me? And there is another crime to which these two may well be connected — the hideous murder of that poor unidentified man. Even if I do not claim justice for my own injuries, I cannot legally or morally forgive the crime committed against him. His killers must and shall face justice. As the most important laymen in the village, you would not want anything else, surely. If there is no connection between the cases, then if I am convinced of the sincerity of my assailants' penitence, then forgiveness must and will be forthcoming. If and only if," I added sternly. "And now, since I have my own parish to care for, I most strongly recommend that you summon the curates whom you so rudely disdained and implement the Sunday school I understood we had agreed upon. I shall write to the bishop to tell him my views. Dr Hansard, shall we ride back together?"

"So these people confessing might still be hanged?"

"Not for their attack on me."

"Even so . . ." Boddice's wheedling tone reminded me of my younger sister when, still in the schoolroom, she was determined to persuade her long-suffering governess into a course of action she had already declined.

Like dear Miss Buttridge, I found a short answer. "I am no lawyer, no magistrate. I cannot therefore negotiate. Do you understand? Good day, gentlemen. My advice is to do what I have already recommended. Meanwhile," I added, "there is the small matter of no church services. What arrangements are you making? I suggest you contact the archdeacon instantly to ask for advice. Obviously a speedy decision is required."

Edmund set our horses in motion, congratulating me, the moment we were out of earshot, on my stance. "I was proud of you, my friend. You said the right thing. And before you start agonising, I have to tell you that your own people need you alive, not dead in some vendetta you don't even understand. Now, is Titus up for a bit of a gallop?"

"Watch him!"

At last, when the horses had enjoyed themselves, we slowed them to a gentle walk.

"It occurs to me that this is just the sort of day when your father would benefit from some fresh air," Edmund remarked, stopping to admire the verdant fields and woods before us.

"He would benefit from many things, not least a visit from my mother. I have been a coward not to put the notion to him before. Or to write to Mama and suggest it to her."

"Even with a man as easy-going as Hasbury it is a mite awkward to wish another visitor on him — especially a lady who might not appreciate the entertainments on offer. Maria and I would be delighted to offer her accommodation if she is not too high in the instep to accept the hospitality of a man required to work for his living. Maria suspects, however, that she would welcome an invitation to your rectory, once all signs of its use as a hospital have been removed and it is returned to its usual tranquil state."

I shot a sideways glance at him. "So long as the standing invitation for me to dine with you is extended to her!"

"Can you imagine that it would not be? Very well, let us take a light nuncheon with Maria and then tool over to Orebury to suggest your father takes the air."

"It is too late, Edmund. Look yonder!" I pointed with my whip. "Surely that is he — though I do not recognise the equipage. And I do not believe he ever travelled in a governess cart before in his life."

We cantered gently down the hill towards the governess cart, where my father sat with his bad foot supported on a regal stool quite at odds with the humble vehicle, which was driven by no less a person than Thompson, the groom who had saved me many a beating. Strangely he looked as if he feared the overweight and rheumatic old pony might take it into his head to bolt. More likely my father had just vented his spleen at some trivial mishap.

Titus whinnied in delight and fretted for the sugar he knew should be in Thompson's right-hand pocket. "Turned into a beauty, hasn't he, Master Toby — I mean, My Lord."

"Master Toby, please."

"Dear God — that excrescence of a hat!" my father, who had been visibly seething, greeted me. "I thought you at least dressed like a gentleman. And whatever happened to your neckcloth?"

Raising the offending headgear I bowed as low as Titus would let me. "I am but just come from attending a sickbed, sir. How else should I dress, but as a clergyman?"

Thompson's eyes rounded in horror, but Edmund, eyes a-twinkle, spoke before my father could: "I am delighted that you have taken my advice, My Lord. Has the exertion caused any pain apart from to your groom's pride? The footstool is an excellent notion."

I caught Thompson's eye, mouthing, "Walker's?" His nod was almost infinitesimal.

"Are you returning to Orebury, My Lord? If so, we could ride beside you. I would welcome the chance to see that the exercise has done you no harm, and I am sure that Titus would enjoy renewing his acquaintance with what seems an old friend. Now, my good friend and colleague Dr Toone has just written to me concerning a new treatment for your condition, by the way. Ginger. Do you enjoy curries, sir, as I do? After my years in the East . . ."

"Her Ladyship visit His Lordship here?" Walker repeated in what I might only describe as a discreet squawk. I glanced in alarm at the door connecting the dressing room to my father's bedchamber, but Walker had assured me that our quiet conversation could not be overheard, which considering what he said next was fortunate. "Mr Tobias, this is no household for a lady. The only reason it is so quiet now is that many of the guests are still abed."

It was my turn to express subdued horror. "At this hour?"

"If you do not retire till daylight, you are unlikely to rise before the better part of the day is past," he said. "And, to make no bones about it, many are not in their own beds, if you take my meaning. The young persons are not necessarily Paphians, sir, but assuredly they are not the sort of lady one would wish to propose to one's parents as a future bride. *Chères amies*, opera dancers, actresses — that class of young person, sir. And for gamblers, like His Lordship, the tables are open throughout the night, with the highest stakes. Some are quite rolled up and are living on their IOUs. One young sprig had to be dissuaded from staking his whole estate on the progress of a raindrop down a window."

"What on earth can have possessed my father to come here?"

"He clings to his youth, Mr Toby, in a manner not altogether becoming. But I have said too much. All I beg is that you will not encourage Lady Hartland to venture here."

"I had hoped to invite her to the rectory."

"My advice would be to write one of the letters she so much enjoys, telling her of your adventures about the parish, Master Toby."

I could not suppress a shout of laughter. "My dear Walker, if she heard of my recent mishaps, I could not stop her posting here to nurse me! It would have to be a very carefully edited letter." Serious again, I reduced my voice to barely more than a whisper: "Does my father have any other more — more respectable —

acquaintance in the area? Lord Wychbold lives but a stone's throw away."

"Lord Wychbold? Here? They say he rarely stirs from his house except to make trouble. In any case, Master Toby, I can't see him improving the situation."

"You are right — a scholar amongst all these hedonists — though I have yet to discover his area of expertise. Walker, you are awake on every suit: keep your ears and eyes open and find out just what he reads all day, can you?"

He bowed, a smile lighting his tired features. "I will indeed, Master Toby. It will be good to have something to talk about in the servants' hall, and your average servant is a great purveyor of low gossip."

"In that case you might launch another topic for your colleagues to chew over — Mr William Snowdon. I would give much to know his whereabouts." My explanation was brief, but I could not forbear asking rhetorically how he came to know with such speed of our need for an artist. "My interrogations of the servants came to nought," I added.

"I will see what I can achieve. But that is My Lord's bell. Shall I see if he will receive you?"

Fortunately the fresh air had indeed inclined my father to sleep, so our game of chess was mercifully postponed till another day. On the other hand, there was one thing that I must do before nightfall — I must write an entirely fictitious account of my recent days in Moreton St Jude's for my mother's delectation. That done, if not entirely to my satisfaction, I wrote another letter, this

222

one to the archdeacon, formally expressing my lively concern over the lack of services and pastoral care at Clavercote, and asking him to communicate my views to the bishop. I had an idea I was throwing a lighted spill into a heap of kindling.

Despite Hasbury's reluctance to provide a room for the inquest, it was held at Orebury House. Mr Vernon's proceedings were short and to the point. Assuring us that at the moment the only possible verdict the jury could return was murder of an unknown person by person or persons unknown, a very unsatisfactory result, he sent us all on our way within ten minutes to find out at least the identity of the victim, assuring us that the rest would soon fall into place. He added a tart observation that it was more than time that even hamlets like Clavercote had a village constable. Since I had expressed identical sentiments I could not be surprised. The surprisingly few people come to view the proceedings as opposed to a surly and reluctant jury trooped out without audible comment.

One person I did not expect to see was Sarey Tump, clasping Joseph, who was also supported by what I recognised as one of Susan's shawls. She hung back in the darkest corner, almost wincing when I caught her eye but then defiantly raising her chin and making the tiniest of gestures with her head to the outside world. With others of the gentry, I was ushered out before the villagers and servants, but I dawdled on the gravel path, warning Edmund swiftly that I must talk to her alone.

223

Nodding, he withdrew to the shade, but still, I noted, within earshot.

"What on earth are you doing here, Sarey?"

"Came to thank you for seeing Ethan Downs, sir," she said.

Really? Why should she walk all this way with the weight of a baby in her arms? "Thank you. But I was truly just doing what any parson would do." Perhaps I expected her to bob a curtsy and back away. But her face was troubled, as if she had something still to say but did not know how to begin.

"Does Joseph thrive?" I stroked his velvety cheek with my index finger. "I hardly need to ask — he is by far the healthiest person I have met in Clavercote."

"I wanted to ask, sir — all that food and these clothes . . . Are they really for me? Do I have to do anything to . . . to pay for them?"

Dear God, what sort of payment did she mean? "They are all gifts freely given, with no expectation of anything in return."

"Really? Truly? So I don't have to . . . you know . . ."

"Are you asking me if you have to prostitute yourself with me to pay? Can you really imagine that? I am a man of God, Sarey."

Flushing a painful scarlet she muttered something I strained to catch.

"Are you saying that other parsons might demand that? Has anyone asked you?" I had a sudden fear, so great it gripped my stomach and bowel and it was all I could do to stand upright.

"Not me. Not me."

"But other women? Other girls? Tell me, please, Sarey, so that something may be done to punish this fiend!"

She shook her head.

"Is there anyone you could talk to? Dr Hansard? He is a wise and understanding man, as you know." She shook her head slightly, whispering something. "Would you feel able to confide in my housekeeper, Mrs Trent, who has been such a friend to you?" Did she nod slightly? "Sarey, she is not here at the moment but staying with friends. The instant she returns I will bring her to you. I promise." I added, not quite joking, "Provided that you undertake to stop anyone trying to hang me. I was very frightened."

To my astonishment she put out her hand as if to stroke my face. Reassurance? Or something else? I leapt back as if she had threatened me with a white-hot brand.

Edmund stepped briskly forward. Joseph was soon in his capable arms, and he shot a series of questions at Sarey, none of which made sense to me but which she answered to his satisfaction. At last he asked, "Did you walk here, Mrs Tump? Let my wife and I set you back on the road to Clavercote. Have you ever ridden in a gig, young man? No, I thought not. You will have to lie quiet and still in your mama's lap . . ."

"Another sickbed, Tobias?" my father drawled, as he set out the chess pieces.

"News of one," I said, refusing to rise to the bait. "And there will be more, I fear. This winter has been

225

very harsh and the late spring means crops have been slow. I anticipate even more losses before summer arrives. Starting with that pawn," I concluded, as my father embarked on his habitual slaughter.

No matter how hard I tried to concentrate, nor how hard I tried to engage him in conversation that could enrage neither of us, the next hour was a disaster.

I think we were both glad when he finally administered the *coup de grâce*.

CHAPTER
TWENTY-ONE

"You put yourself in grave danger there, Tobias, I have to tell you."

Edmund had summoned me to the privacy of his study, and amazingly kept me standing before his desk, before he recollected himself and settled us down in the deep armchairs either side of the now empty fireplace.

"Danger?"

"With Sarey."

"Sarey? I have cut my eye teeth, Edmund!"

"You may think so. Toby, you are a handsome young man, you know, and it will not do for you to be seen alone with a young woman, even a parishioner, in public. Think of the poor child who killed herself and her illegitimate babe. No one knows who the father was. That village is a sewer of gossip: what if the conclusion is that the father is you? Think, man — the men of the village already loathe you enough to want to hang you — how much happier will they be if you are seen tête-à-tête with another young woman? Your reputation! Your very life! You must and shall be accompanied by a respectable woman next time you go to Clavercote, or who will be answerable for the consequences? Not I!" He flung his hands wide in exasperation. "We need to find you a wife, my friend."

For a moment I sparked up. "I would never marry simply to provide myself with a chaperone — only for love." Then I saw the funny side. "In fact, Edmund, my mother is already hunting a suitable bride. What did she say I needed? An heiress? Yes — provided that she would not mind giving up her life in the *ton* and her ten thousand a year so that her new husband might feed the poor. Mama said I must have a lady light on her feet, but equally quick-witted, if slow to anger. A great reader: but though the lady loved books, she would rarely sit in my library, since she must constantly devote herself to good works amongst my flock."

He joined in with glee. "A lady with musical accomplishments? So that she might join us round the fortepiano?"

"She might bring her own harp," I suggested. "But she would have very little time to practise because she would be too busy learning to play the church organ."

He threw his head back and laughed. The lecture was well and truly over. "Between us, your mama and I have things pretty well worked out. Tobias, I have never asked you before, lest it chafed old wounds — but do you have a lady in mind? Or better still, in your heart?"

"There is a young lady to whom I found myself much attracted when I was staying with one of my mother's bosom bows. Lady Julia Pendragon." It felt very strange to say her name aloud. "We were friends as children, forever getting into scrapes together. She is still unwed — some would say on the shelf — and the evening we spent in each other's company was very pleasant. I have no doubt that had I lingered longer, we would have many equally enjoyable conversations. But since then . . ." I spread my hands.

There was a gentle tap at the door. Hansard leapt from his chair to open it, to be rewarded by Maria's smile. "Have you finished giving him his bear-garden jaw, husband? If so, shall we adjourn to the drawing room? Though it is so lovely in here this evening, so warm, that it is tempting to stay a while." She sat in the seat Edmund had vacated.

"There is one thing you may not have heard — something Sarey offered me."

Maria stared. "*She* offered *you*, Tobias? What can a woman of her means — oh, no. Dear me, no!"

"Yes, she has something. Her body. She appeared to think Mrs Trent's largesse came from me and that I would require payment — carnally. I assured her I did not, but I think she tried to stroke my face. Thank goodness Edmund was at hand. But the deeper implication worries me more. Where in God's name did she get the idea that a clergyman expects sexual favours? A clergyman, my dear friends!"

Edmund's face became as sombre as when he had to admit he could not save a patient. "When I diagnose an illness, Toby, I put together all the symptoms that I can see. Let us take the same approach here. Firstly, let us cast our minds back to events in Clavercote. Would you say that you have felt — how shall I put it? — a little unwelcome in the village?" He paused as Maria and I laughed dryly. "There is a good deal of reluctance from the very start when the archdeacon tells them that you are to take the Easter services there. They obey eventually. They banish two perfectly decent curates — at least, I assume that they were — and make efforts to deter you each time you return."

Maria walked to the window, closing it as she gave a sudden shiver. "The body was found on Easter Day. Do you think that is significant? Was it meant to be found then?"

"In general local people do not frequent Wychbold's estate," I said, "so I would think that unlikely."

Edmund nodded. "True. Nonetheless, my inference — one I would much rather not make — is that in view of the way he was nailed to the tree the victim of that terrible killing was one of your colleagues.

"But he is abroad for his health! The archdeacon told Tobias he was."

"Perhaps that was what the archdeacon believes, my love. Perhaps Coates thought that Clavercote had had enough of him and it politic to leave for a while. Yes, this is pure speculation, but I shall be decidedly relieved if Lord Hartland can report conclusively that Mr Coates is having a wonderful time in Baden."

Maria bit her lip. "The sketches . . . the recreations . . . of the poor corpse's face . . . Do you recall that in one of them I added a stock? You locked it in this drawer, Husband."

Edmund met my eye. "As you can imagine, the only thing I ever lock in this house is my medical room: I do not want my records of patients' ailments and treatments or, of course, the medicines I use to go astray. Why I thought it necessary to protect these sketches I am not quite sure."

"The little spate of housebreaking, Edmund," Maria prompted him. "And your fears that the artist might be identified."

"Of course. Well, here they are. If only we knew what Mr Coates looked like. Was — is! — he the sort of man to have a portrait taken for his own pleasure? Is there one in his rectory, Tobias?"

"I have never once set foot within its walls, remember."

"Of course. And now the place is locked up. We would need the express authority of a magistrate to break into it. I suppose Hasbury might grant it though his legal duties do not appear to ride high in his priorities."

"I wonder if those two delightful churchwardens have a key, or know who would have one. It might be hard to convince them."

"Especially," Maria said dryly, "if they are aware of what we suspect may have happened. Or they might be genuinely nervous of retribution."

Edmund raised his hand. "All this is speculation. Let us wait a few days for your father's missives to bear fruit, Tobias. Now, before we adjourn for supper I want your solemn word that on no circumstances will you venture to Clavercote alone. No circumstances at all. If there is any basis for our theory, then it would not be impossible for you to be sent for on a false mission of mercy, one that will simply lure you to your death."

"Very well."

"That, Tobias, is not an oath. As your friend and as your medical adviser, I require one."

Half-reluctant, half-relieved, I gave him my word. "But what about when poor Ethan and his friend die? I must conduct their obsequies."

"We must in that case ensure that you are protected. Even if it means summoning the militia," he added, intending, perhaps, a jest.

I actually felt the blood drain from my face. I was sure my friends noticed. However, before they could question me, there came an urgent interruption.

"Beg pardon, sir, but Mr Jem needs you!" Burns gasped, bolting the moment he had delivered his message.

All three of us followed him through the house to the kitchen garden. By chance, Jem was in the same sheltered spot where Ethan Downs had rested. Looking almost exasperated, Edmund halted, hands on hips.

"A dog! Jem, I know nothing of dogs!" But he squatted beside them both, stroking Cribb's head.

"I'm sure he's picked up some poison," Jem said. "Surely you can make him sick?"

"I have an emetic I use for humans — but it may just cause him more suffering, Jem. A gun might be kinder."

"For an old dog, yes. But Cribb's hardly more than a pup. He's strong. And if . . . then I will use the gun."

Maria, who had knelt beside Jem, took his hand and looked up at me. "Does God listen to prayers for animals, Toby?"

Joining them on my knees, I said firmly, "He certainly listens to those for their owners. So I suggest we pray for Jem, and also for Edmund, as he chooses the medicine Cribb needs . . ."

Whether it was the Hand of God or mere coincidence I do not know, but within the quarter-hour Toone's curricle swept into the yard. Any doubts I had about his personality and his dedication to healing were swept aside as he flung off his many-caped cloak and joined his colleague with Cribb. He waved Maria and me aside, urging us to take ourselves inside out of the way. I believe that he would have preferred Jem himself to withdraw, but a look at his suffering face would have stopped anyone trying to persuade him.

Burns had already taken it upon himself, as he told Maria when she rang for him, to tell Cook to put back dinner indefinitely, and to be prepared to change the number of covers she prepared for. He laid a tray of biscuits beside her, and served us both sherry. He withdrew, promising to apprise us of any development.

"Tobias, may I ask you why, when Edmund spoke of your needing a guard if you took a funeral in the village, you went so pale? I have noticed it before. If it is something you would rather not explain to me, perhaps it would help to tell Edmund."

I could have blustered that I was merely tired after a difficult day, but it was easier to tell the simple truth. "It is nothing to do with conducting a funeral, Maria. It is the notion of bringing armed men against unarmed people. When I was young, my father had me destined for a military career."

"You, Tobias!"

"A poor soldier I would have made, indeed." I managed the ghost of a smile. "But that was his dream. I think he was all too aware of the pointlessness of his own existence. So he took me along with him to see the militia deal with a riot in Sheffield — to make a man of me by making me watch armed men slaughter their sick and hungry brethren. Any thoughts I might have had were killed as instantly as a child who ran across the street at the wrong moment. Perhaps he would have forgiven me for declining a military career, but I went further, and turned to the Church. The day I told him that I was to be ordained, he kicked me down the stairs."

"And now you are playing chess with him?"

"He is a lonely sick man. Hasbury's other guests are far too busy indulging themselves to give him any of their valuable time. Sad to say, though they are a worthless bunch, ritual murder is hardly the sort of pastime you associate with sexual promiscuity and gambling, which seem to be the chief items on Hasbury's *menu du jour*."

"Have you forgiven your father? At least you seem sorry for him," she prompted.

"Indeed, I am trying to see him as a man with the misfortune to be ill who has had a big disappointment in his life. But if I am a disappointment to him, how much greater a disappointment must he be to my mother? How can she love him? They are never together — his life is that of a fribble, hers — she might as well be a widow."

234

"They are of an age, are they not, to have been contracted into a dynastic marriage almost without being consulted. They produced their heir, a spare and a spare spare, and then — how many sisters do you have? Two? They have done as well as many people expect. Sometimes it is better to go your separate ways than spend your lives tormenting each other — at least that is my judgement, based on all the discord and pretence and hypocrisy I saw before I married Edmund." He preferred her to use that euphemism for being a housekeeper in the homes of people of rank, and it seemed to have become a happy habit.

"My mother appears still to love him — it always brings tears to her eyes when she refers to our final quarrel. Or perhaps it will turn out to be our penultimate quarrel — though I have no stomach for another fight yet. He can resume his old ways, riding roughshod over me until, from time to time, I simply dig my heels in and we have another battle." I laughed dryly. "My current tactics are less confrontational but more stubborn — my silent insistence on wearing attire suited to my calling, for instance."

"Which hitherto I have to say you have honoured more in the breach than the observance. And I also have to say that that round hat truly does not suit you. A man may surely be both a man of God and a gentleman in appearance? I dare swear that when you first helped Dan, you were dressed much more like your father's son than a poor priest, yet the deed was just as virtuous."

"I am tempted to agree — but does it not mark me out in the eyes of the poor as not being one of them?"

"You are not one of them, Tobias: you are fortunate enough to have a roof over your head and food on your table. But instinctively everyone recognises your good intent —"

"— and may, of course, try to exploit it," I concluded for her, to spare myself a continuation of the earlier lecture. "I hear voices, Maria — I pray that Cribb lives!"

Leaving Toone and Hansard deep in dinner-table discussion about the difficulties of treating a dog with human medicines, I took myself off to join Jem in the stables, where he was watching the sleeping Cribb as if he were a baby. Jem had claimed he had no appetite, but when Burns appeared bearing a tray on which were balanced tankards of ale, a pile of chicken patties and a fat slice of leek and bacon pie, he was obviously tempted. Burns also produced a hot towel soaked in Hansard's beloved lavender water, which he presented to Jem as if there were to be no argument.

"In case of poison lingering on your hands, Jem." His work done, Burns settled himself beside us, stretching long legs in front of him and putting his hands behind his head in a manner I was sure the servants' hall never witnessed. He only moved to reach for his tankard, as the three of us talked about rumours of a new bowler playing for Moreton-sub-Edge. Apparently he was proving devastatingly successful, and Burns was eager to learn the secret of his success.

But the idle chatter did not entirely calm Jem. He started every time Cribb stirred, feeling him again and again to make sure he was still alive. Each time, Burns proffered the towel, increasingly to Jem's irritation.

"If you take the same poison as Cribb," Burns demanded, "who will be blamed? Not you. Not Dr Campion. Me. Look," he continued, accepting the towel back and hanging it tidily over a rail, "I get to hear all these conversations, begging your pardon, Dr Campion —"

"Toby, if you please," I said, draining my tankard.

"All these conversations about who might have done what, so it's almost second nature for me to wonder about things too. And what I am wondering now, Jem, is who might have tried to kill your dog, there — a harmless enough mutt, nothing special, I'd say. Has he been rabbiting where he shouldn't? Or disturbing coverts? Or have you given the cane to the son of someone who didn't like his lad being punished? Or is it something to do with all the other goings on, those that Mr and Mrs Hansard and their guests are worrying about? Trying to kill . . . Toby . . . here, for instance — you two being friends, of course."

CHAPTER
TWENTY-TWO

The arrival of Toone and Edmund in the stable forestalled any speculation. Burns suddenly recalled that he had other, much more formal duties, and, seeing that the doctors were about to examine the dog, I allowed myself to drift away, bidding Maria goodnight before adjourning to my bedchamber, where I intended to spend a great deal of time in prayer. However, my flesh was as weak as that of others before me, and before I knew anything I was being awoken by Binns with my shaving water.

"The dog lives, sir, and my master, having watched with Jem for much of the night, sleeps. So I am here to offer my services. I understand that there is a summons to Orebury House, though in what connection I could not say. Your formal wear, sir, or your — er — canonicals?"

"A stock, but not my bands."

"An excellent compromise, if I might make so bold. And the more recent coat?"

"The one that makes me look like a country lawyer? Why not?"

My visit to my father brought yet another defeat on the chessboard, though I fought a rearguard action that delayed the inevitable for half an hour longer than the previous debacle. My father celebrated his victory by taking a stroll with Hansard on the terrace. Since the peacocks were in full voice it cannot have been altogether pleasant.

Meanwhile I had an enjoyable conversation with Walker in a quiet corner of the servants' hall. "I have heard two snippets that intrigued me but may signify nothing. One concerns a tiny cottage on an adjoining estate: I overheard a visiting lady's maid making a foolish assignation with one of the grooms, and he suggested it would be a prime place. Abel March, I believe, Mr Toby. And there has been continued speculation about the erratic behaviour of one of the wenches here — young Sally. One of her fellow skivvies said it was as if there were two Sallys — a remark that drew the deepest blush from the girl concerned. Mr Toby — could there be two girls looking alike?"

I thought back to my encounters with her — with them. "Of course: that would explain much."

"Such as, Mr Toby?"

"Do you know, I am not quite sure. But it will make something fall into place . . . Let us assume that both girls have positions, ones that give them little pleasure, so they vary otherwise tedious lives by changing places. For them to do that without detection, the other Sally must live fairly close by. Say, within a twenty minutes' run. I will make enquiries."

"As will I, Mr Toby, you may rest assured. And regarding our putative lovers, I am sure that Thompson will keep his ears open."

239

Ludicrously pleased with myself for finding — at
second hand — two nuggets of information, I made my
way home to Langley Park, only to find the household
in a flutter. It appeared that Mrs Trent had written to
Mrs Hansard.

"She begs me to journey to Fladbury," Maria
declared, "where she has found a person whom it is in
our interest to interview. At least that is what I think
she says."

She passed me the note. To save us money, Mrs
Trent had crossed and recrossed the lines, so the whole
was only decipherable with patience.

"Does this say the Chequers?" I pointed.

"I think so. Can it be that she recommends us to take
rooms at the inn while we conduct our business with
this person? Alas, nowhere can I find anything that
might be a name. But she is certainly asking for my
presence, so I surmise that the person is a woman.
Edmund suggests that the three of us leave early tomorrow
morning, returning in the evening, when the moon will
be bright enough to light our way. Toone has offered to
care for any of his patients should an emergency arise."

Such generosity surprised me but I did not remark
on it. "Edmund does not think it necessary to make
provision for an overnight stay? At this inn?"

"You are both busy men: he reasons that there can be
little need for all three of us to linger there."

"He would not leave without you, Maria," I pointed
out. "But I suggest that I ride alongside the curricle, so
that we act according to circumstances."

* * *

It might have been a cold wet spring in Moreton, but compared with Fladbury we had suffered not at all. It was still possible to see wet tidemarks on the bridge and other low-lying buildings where recent floods had reached, and the Avon was still running full. Despite this there was a pleasant air of prosperity about the village, and we were greeted by a warm burst of sunshine. Leaving Edmund to oversee the stabling of the horses, I summoned the landlord of the Chequers Inn to bespeak a private parlour. He was inclined to be slow and awkward — I was only a country parson, after all — but I had not recently been in my father's company for nothing and he was soon obligation itself, bowing gratifyingly low as the Hansards entered. Almost before we could think of it a pot of good coffee arrived, accompanied by some honey-flavoured cakes.

If Maria had wanted to open the conversation, she could not have been provided with a better opportunity: she was quick to pronounce the cakes delicious, and to ask who had cooked them. Soon she was able to enquire after another mistress of bakery, Mrs Trent. Soon a stable boy was despatched to fetch her from the farm at which she was staying.

Her pleasure in seeing us was infectious: one would have thought we had all been apart for a month. But she was big with secret, and could hardly wait until the by now almost over-attentive landlord had withdrawn to speak. Even then she looked anxiously at the door: she did not wish to be overheard.

"It is the most beautiful day," I observed, "and though it may be dirty underfoot, I for one would relish a quiet stroll to see the river."

And so it was agreed. When we were in the open, we gathered round a fingerpost as if discussing which way to take.

"I have found Mr Coates's housekeeper," she announced in a stage whisper. "Mrs Eliza Paten. She has come here to look after her niece until her confinement. I think she wants to stay."

"Did she say anything about Mr Coates?" Edmund asked.

"Nothing that she would say in front of a man," she replied awkwardly, "which is why I wrote to you, Mrs Hansard, begging your pardon, gentlemen."

"Not even another clergyman?" I ventured.

Her grimace was answer enough. "The water meadows are far too wet for us to walk to the farm. We would need to hire the landlord's gig; his horse is slow but very reliable."

Edmund and I found the wait uncommonly tedious: this must be how so many women felt, when required to wait at home while their menfolk had adventures. Assured that they would be absent at least one and possibly two hours, we continued the walk round the village that we had abandoned earlier. There were some attractive shops, but neither of us wanted to purchase a new bonnet or a frieze waistcoat. A handsome house, perhaps twenty years old, attracted the eye. The blacksmith toiled rebuilding some gates. At the centre stood a fine old church, though we both feared, as we entered, that it might need some restoration. Edmund was taken by the memorial to the Throckmorton family, one I chiefly associated with the Throckmorton Plot against Elizabeth, the anointed queen.

Neither of us, however, could be absorbed for long by either history or architecture. After several minutes kneeling in prayer side by side we were ready to return to the Chequers to temper the irritation of waiting with a glass of the landlord's finest and a tasty nuncheon.

Mrs Hansard and Mrs Trent returned as the landlord laid the first plate of food on the table, every inch of their demeanour indicating a successful foray, but they appeared to have agreed to tantalise us for a few more minutes by readily accepting glasses of wine, which they sipped with infuriating genteelness.

"Mrs Hansard was able to write down everything Mrs Paten told us," Mrs Trent announced at last. Then, as if ashamed at having spoken first, she ducked her head and said nothing.

Maria was more assured. "It is not necessary for a housekeeper actually to like the person she works for, but Mrs Paten appears to have held Mr Coates in positive loathing. She stayed because he paid her well above what she might expect, and because she was afraid of the consequences of quitting. At other times he was improbably kind, not to her but to some of the villagers, and she liked to believe that that was what he was really like. She insisted that he was regular and punctilious in the way he carried out his church and parish duties."

"Did she tell you what ailment might have sent him abroad to take a spa cure?"

"Not at all. She didn't even know he was going anywhere until he failed to return home one night. The next evening, when it was already dark, some clergyman she'd never seen before called round with the news that her master had left the country. It was he who told her to quit the place first thing the following morning."

Edmund stared. "So Coates goes on a journey of some length and duration without so much as asking her to sew a button on a shirt! Was this normal in him?"

Maria nodded. "Apparently all his comings and goings were erratic. She learnt from bitter experience — the threat of dismissal without a character — not to ask where he had been for the days or nights he was absent. Days and nights," she repeated meaningfully. She produced a sheaf of closely written papers from her reticule. "Everything she said is written down, as Mrs Trent says."

"She gave a great deal of information," Edmund observed dryly.

"And something else besides!" Now Mrs Trent patted her reticule. For the first time I noticed how bulky it was, with what an irregular outline. "The keys to Clavercote Rectory, Mr Toby, sir."

Much as we wanted to return home forthwith, it was incumbent on us, in all humanity, to call in to see how

Dan progressed. He was still weak and pale, but beginning to hobble about. Edmund inspected his wound, pronouncing himself satisfied thus far but insisting that he continue to apply fomentations and liberal applications of the ointment Toone had provided. Mrs Trent's cousin personified kindness.

"Kind nursing and good fresh food have helped him turn the corner. And the sun is to my mind a great healer," said Hansard. "Though I do not expect you to need it, here is the name of one of my colleagues who will provide immediate assistance. I will pay the fee myself."

Happy that Mrs Trent was content to be with her family, I promised her that I would come myself — with Robert as my tiger — to collect her when she was ready to return. "But do not leave it too long," I added. "Now I cannot spend time at the rectory I find I miss it and my good friends there."

"Next week at the very latest," she said, firmly, "now I'm no longer needed."

"It was meant to be a holiday for you!"

"So it was. But I don't think we women take holidays, sir. Now, you keep away from those folk from Clavercote till I come back."

"How can I make use of these keys without going to the village?" I joked.

Her face was a study. "Are you riding Titus, Mr Toby? In that case give me five minutes to gather my things and I swear I will ride pillion!"

It was all too clear that she was serious.

In fact our journey was altogether more decorous. Back at the Chequers I was able to hire a hack for Edmund, and the ladies travelled in the curricle, Mrs Hansard and Mrs Trent taking it in turns to handle the ribbons.

We found the Morton St Jude's rectory still guarded by the cricket team, who reassured us jovially that all was right and tight. But for once even Mrs Trent quailed at the thought of starting fires and airing beds, and doing all without the assistance of Susan, no doubt fast asleep at Langley Park. The Hansards insisted that we both postpone our return till the morrow.

A stop at the schoolmaster's house was rewarded by a volley of barks and from Jem a peremptory call for silence. Cribb slobbered all over us, his tail flaying any leg within range. Jem confined himself to a handshake, kissing the ladies' hands with some aplomb and, I suspected, much affection.

CHAPTER
TWENTY-THREE

There could be no housebreaking on the Sabbath, I decreed, and no one argued. Accordingly my little family and I returned first thing to the rectory, where I could hear all the bustle of fires being lit and water drawn. Meanwhile I got ready for the eleven o'clock service, praying that though my preparation had been scant, the sermon would nonetheless move hearts.

We all arrived at the church door with rather more haste than dignity. Mrs Trent led her charges in first, leaving me to catch my breath and assume a more reverent demeanour. I sensed, as I walked into the church, that there was a slight frisson: not the welcoming applause of the previous week, but a murmur of what felt like apprehension.

It was not until I was turning on the chancel steps to greet my flock that I realised why. Seated right in the middle of the nave was none other than the archdeacon. He did not look as if he was full of the joy of God.

I hoped the sermon would be better than I thought it was.

All the hymns were sung with enormous gusto: I must take courage from that. My wardens gave the

247

readings in good clear voices, with only the occasional nervous stutter. I suspect that Mr Mead winked at me as he concluded his, which had been the parable of the Good Samaritan. It was almost like a divine prompt. Putting aside my notes, I spoke extempore, speaking of the villagers' constant kindness to each other and to wayfarers. I held up a furiously blushing Mrs Trent, Susan and Robert as shining examples of people with little being generous in giving to strangers with less. But, I pointed out, sometimes being kind to one person meant having less time for another. I had neglected them of late, as I was trying to help people in great trouble in a village without a pastor, and I was very sorry. As soon as I could, I promised I would devote myself to all the needs of my own flock — even if, I ended, that meant opening the batting against the fiercest bowler the neighbouring villages could put up against our team. The demon bowler, I added.

The faces showed kindly amusement. We declared our faith in the Creed, and then, standing to one side, I asked Archdeacon Cornforth to preside over Communion.

The service over, I saw Mrs Trent in urgent conversation with Maria Hansard, who was accompanied by Edmund, but not by Toone. Maria appeared to calm and reassure her. But, collecting Susan and Robert like a frantic mother hen, she sped off home as quickly as she could. As I shook hands with the remainder of the villagers, Mead and Tufnell literally stood shoulder to shoulder with me, a phalanx of protection against any vicarious episcopal rebukes.

Accordingly, when I invited the archdeacon to join me in a glass of sherry, I invited them too and also their wives, blushing with pleasure under the brims of their best bonnets. Suspecting that there had not been time to light a fire in my parlour, I suggested we sit outside on the terrace, the gardener's efforts glowing in the spring sun. Perhaps Mrs Trent's cakes were fewer in number than usual, but I could explain that for her — she had been visiting a sick friend.

Archdeacon Cornforth was not a man to be confused by a smokescreen of idle chatter. "Did you not have a sick man living with you? A man some feared had attacked you but whom you were adamant had in fact saved your life?"

"I did indeed, sir, but from nowhere some relatives appeared in response to a letter he dictated to one of those nursing him and they took him away to recuperate with them."

"So he has evaded justice!"

"Begging your pardon, there is one Justice none of us can evade, Archdeacon," put in Mrs Tufnell, sherry-brave. She flushed to her ears and subsided.

"Indeed so." He raised his eyeglass to depress any further pretensions. "And how have you all fared while your rector has been gallivanting around the countryside?" His tone was regrettably patronising.

Stung, Mead pulled himself up as straight as a military man. "We have been praying for his safety, sir, hoping he would be saved from the lion's den like Daniel before him. People setting on a decent man while he rides home from a deathbed; people trying to hang him and his friend — men who only ever try to do good, sir."

"And you know this for a fact, not just as an overheated rumour?" asked Cornforth with forensic precision.

As if he did not know exactly what I had told the bishop! So my word was an overheated rumour, was it?

"I know it because my nephew's intended saw it — the lynch mob, sir, not the attack." He set down his glass on a stool Robert had conjured from somewhere in lieu of a table. "You know who saved Dr Campion, sir — the good woman who made these cakes. And yet he goes back again to tend another old gaffer. He ought to be made a saint, saving your presence, sir."

It was clear that unless Cornforth was prepared to outstay the wardens, we would not have the conversation he wanted. My father would have dismissed them with an arrogant wave of the hand. So, I suspect, would Cornforth, on his own territory. For a while I worried that they meant to make a day of it, but as if by common consent the wardens and wives got to their feet and made polite farewells. Then I recalled that they took their meals at country times, and did not want their lamb to roast to death.

I took the initiative the moment Cornforth and I resumed our seats. "There is something that you need to see, Archdeacon — a deposition by Mr Coates's housekeeper, Mrs Paten, regarding his behaviour while she was in his employ. Given its incendiary nature, it is currently locked away for safe-keeping."

"Indeed. I do not take kindly your direct appeal to the bishop, Campion — there are procedures to follow, hierarchies to honour. They are there for a reason. To be honest, it is a matter not under your jurisdiction. The churchwardens of Clavercote are the ones who should, if necessary, request assistance. In fact, I have half a mind to go and speak to them now." He dusted an imaginary speck from his coat sleeve. "I left my curricle at the inn I saw across the green. It looks a prosperous enough place."

"It was ready to fall down. But some of the local farmers joined together to repair it. There is a new landlord, and as you can see, a brand-new sign: the Lost Cause. After St Jude's," I added.

He might have been stung by an early wasp. "The patron saint of — Campion, I am appalled you should encourage such papism."

"It was a *fait accompli* by the time they told me — a pleasant village joke, Archdeacon. But what my wardens told you then was no joke. I truly believe that if you appear in Clavercote in your fine clerical clothes, with a pair of horses many aristocrats could not afford, you will be putting yourself in danger. If you wish to talk to the wardens, send for them and speak to them here: I will vacate my study so that you may do so in privacy. Or of course," I added, with what felt regrettably akin to malice, "you might ask my housekeeper to travel with you to ensure your safety."

He was spared the necessity of replying by the arrival of Will, with a message from the Hansards. Although it was addressed to me, it contained an invitation to

Cornforth to dinner, with a rider that he and his groom would be most welcome to stay overnight at Langley Park. I rubbed mental hands at the thought of an encounter between him and Toone. Who would come off better?

"If I might trouble you for pen and paper I will write to accept," he said at last — scarcely with spontaneous effusions of joy. "And perhaps I might avail myself of your study to speak to the churchwardens, if someone is prepared to deliver a message, that is."

"I believe Will has an aunt living in Clavercote — let us see if he is prepared to extend his journey. And I promise you that a verbal acceptance is all that the Hansards will require."

"In that case I am obliged to them for their invitation to dinner, but I will return to my home afterwards, given the fullness of the moon."

I had the doubtful pleasure of escorting Cornforth on a walking tour of the village until it was reasonable to suppose that the Clavercote wardens would have responded to their summons. Before he entered my study, on the pretext of tidying away the chaos of my desk, I checked that all the drawers and cupboards were locked. "Just in case," as Robert might have said.

Did Mrs Trent still need the lad's assistance? No? In that case we could spend a few minutes not exactly playing cricket, given the holiness of the day, but discussing ways he might improve his game. Then he sped off to the Lost Cause to assist the archdeacon's tiger harness his horses.

It weighed on my conscience that I had not told Cornforth about the keys to the Clavercote rectory. Should I? Would it be wise to invite him to join me in my proposed expedition — with Mrs Trent, of course — to investigate there? Or would his princely presence inflame anyone who saw him to the extent that even Mrs Trent would be unable to protect him — and us?

Knocking on the study door, something that felt decidedly odd in my own domain, I waited, just as, awaiting punishment, I was used to do outside my father's study. It seemed that several minutes passed before Cornforth called to admit me.

I nodded to the three men, and took a seat uninvited. "Your discussions have been private — but is there anything you wish to tell me?"

"What about?" Boddice was not known for his subtlety, of course.

I became my father's son in the face of his truculence. "Since I am not in the habit of listening at my own keyhole, I will have to leave that to you."

Even Cornforth blinked. No one offered to respond to me.

I had the floor to myself. "We have an intolerable situation, do we not? No clergyman dare venture alone within the bounds of an ordinary English village. Surely that situation cannot prevail. But to stop any recurrence, do you not need to find out the cause of such disaffection? Mr Lawton, Mr Boddice — I suspect you know far more about the goings on than you have so far cared to reveal, to me at least."

"And what might you mean by that?" Boddice demanded.

"Not to wrap it up in clean linen, why are the villagers so angry? What will appease them, other than a brigade of the militia hanging a few of the menfolk as examples?" There, I had said the word, even as I hoped and prayed such a solution might never be considered. I drew a breath. "More precisely, why did they hate Mr Coates?"

"That is a strange assumption," the archdeacon said.

"And you have another explanation?"

Lawton shifted. "'Tis true: he wasn't well liked. Lived high on the hog, even in times of hardship for the rest of us."

I noted his use of the past tense, and kept to it. "Did he never share his good fortune? Or if he did, was it with some families but not with others?" That question certainly hit home. "And for any particular reason? Perhaps a member of the family was owed a particular debt? A daughter or a wife?"

Cornforth was on his feet, but not quickly enough to suggest the movement was spontaneous. "You are speaking of a clergyman, sir."

"As a fellow priest who has been caring for Coates's flock, I am entitled to speak thus. How many weeks is it since a poor village girl drowned herself and her newborn babe? And since her own mother died of a broken heart?"

"These are slanders, sir!"

"But Mr Coates is not present to hear them, is he? No wonder he skipped abroad without warning anyone.

It would have been he who faced the lynch mob, not me." It was as if I took a step back from myself and watched words emerging from my mouth unbidden. Because even as I uttered them a terrible thought was forming in my head. I dared not express it, even to myself. I must change the subject quickly. More quietly I asked, "Have either of you wardens chanced to visit the rectory since Mr Coates left for the Continent? No? Archdeacon, have you?"

"Why should I?"

"Why indeed?" Belatedly I thought of Mrs Paten, and wished we had thought to suggest she took precautions for her safety. "I would have expected someone from the diocese to check the rectory from time to time to see that all was well — and that duty would probably have fallen in the first instance to the wardens. Do you have the keys to the rectory?"

"Mr Coates would have taken them with him, sir. Wouldn't he?"

"Of course. Now, gentlemen, I see Mr Cornforth's curricle is waiting for him and it would never do to let the horses get cold. Our dinner at Langley Park awaits, Archdeacon." I glued myself to the trio as I saw them off my premises, affording them no opportunity to speak to each other in private.

His hat and gloves in his hand, the archdeacon paused on the threshold. "I have just recalled that I have a previous engagement this evening. Present my compliments to Dr Hazard or whatever he calls himself and offer my apologies." Without a backward glance he strode to his curricle and set off at a spanking pace —

only, to my delight and no doubt his chagrin, to have to find a convenient space to turn and head in the opposite direction.

Before I could go indoors and comment on this, with an unseemly chuckle, to Mrs Trent, I became aware that I was not alone. Mr Boddice was sidling up to me. "You are a good man, Mr Campion. I mean that. You will be safe in Clavercote: we will see to it." He shook my hand quickly, and returned to where Lawton was waiting with his horse.

In the expectation of entertaining the archdeacon, Mrs Hansard's household had produced an elegant repast, not ostentatious, but certainly not frugal, one that Jem was delighted to partake of in lieu of Cornforth. Cribb had refused to be parted from him, trotting stubbornly after our horses as we left the village. It took a particularly meaty bone to stop him howling after Jem as he was confined to the scullery.

Our welcome was warm, and my account of the archdeacon's visit occasioned a great deal of sardonic hilarity, particularly when I gave his version of our hosts' name. My decision to reveal nothing of our plans was applauded, as was Boddice's curious declaration — the only problem was whether I should believe him.

Edmund, too, had had visitors: Mr and Mrs Longstaff, of Taunton Lodge. Edmund liked new mothers to get out and about as soon as they were able, opining that a change of scene would do much to combat the blue devils that afflicted so many ladies who had been confined. They had brought with them an invitation to dine, with another enclosed for me, since the poet did not recall my address: if only it had rhymed. The good news was that mother and babe flourished. They had remained no more than five minutes, which would have met with Edmund's medical if not social approval had not the inspiration for another canto precipitated their retreat.

I had already promised Mrs Trent that I would return betimes: I did not want my household to be on their own. Jem, approving the notion, invited himself and Cribb along too, to the huge delight of Robert, who thought he would make a wonderful guard dog — "Just in case, sir."

Once again Cribb was quick to resent relegation to the scullery, howling and whining until Jem and I, enjoying a glass of ale before a welcome fire, were ready to curse him. But the noise stopped abruptly: this brought us both swiftly to our feet. Then I bethought myself: sure enough, the reason lay in Robert, now firmly wrapped round the animal, and asleep with an expression of bliss on his face. "I have an idea we shall be adding to our household," I whispered. "Perhaps if he had a dog to call his own we could persuade him to sleep indoors."

CHAPTER
TWENTY-FOUR

His schoolmaster's duties calling him, Jem left early next morning, accompanied by Cribb, whose loyalties were now clearly divided. A hint of frost dusted the grass, although the day promised fair. To Mrs Trent's embarrassment, I lingered in the warmth of the kitchen, helping myself to one of her newly baked rolls.

"I do not want to put you in any danger," I said. "And I am unhappy that you may be breaking the law."

"Lord bless you, as if I cared for that."

"But I do. And accordingly I am going to speak to Lord Hasbury, as our local Justice, to tell him what I plan. But I will keep your name from him. All he will know is that I am still trying to discover Coates's whereabouts and believe the rectory will yield evidence. Pray do not argue." I added with a smile, "I do not wish to give the archdeacon an excuse to have me defrocked."

"He will if he sees you eating those rolls in here like any heathen. Get into the breakfast room, Master Toby, do, like a decent Christian."

Dressed, to my shame, in my gentleman's finery, I naturally arrived far too early at Orebury House. But I sent word to Walker to announce my presence and to crave a word. He greeted me in the servants' hall with the news that my father was closeted with Lord Hasbury's secretary, Mr Beresford. Walker himself would be required shortly, as my father planned to take another airing.

"Excellent! I could accompany him."

Walker shook his head delicately. "I think not, Master Toby. There is a . . . a lady . . . involved. I tell myself a little light flirtation will improve his spirits, which are sadly low. But I am sure that he will wish to see you first."

"I would not wish to incommode the young lady by keeping her waiting!"

"Do you suppose that would weigh with His Lordship? If it is you he wants to speak to, wait she must. And, to be fair, if it was her company preferred, you might, to use the common parlance, go hang."

"Quite. Now, my old friend, before my father rings for you, tell me — did you pick up any useful gossip?"

"I was not wholly successful. As to the matter of the servant, Sally, I have observed her as closely as one might, without appearing particular in one's attentions, and I suspect that she is in fact two girls. At a given time — it is the same time, but by no means every day — they change clothes and they change roles. So one of the Sallys has to be working not too far away — too far to walk, perhaps, but not too far if she is given a ride on a farm cart, for example." Encouraged by my appreciative smile, he continued, "The nearest house big enough to require a maid is Coryton Place. The

259

lady living there is said to enjoy but poor health, and does not venture into society, so you are probably not acquainted. Perhaps the second Sally finds life tedious there."

"Have you discovered the name of this lady?"

"A Miss Witheridge. I heard tell that she is very quiet and ladylike in her ways. She has a young relative to stay from time to time."

"I may have met him." Mr Will Snowdon!

"Beg pardon, but when you spoke of her reputation, to what were you alluding?"

"There is a rumour — I was wrong even to repeat it. Forgive me." My smile was penitent but my heart sang in triumph. At last I might face Mr Snowdon with my accusations. "And did you discover our lovers' trysting place?"

"Not yet, but — ah, that is my master's bell, Master Toby. Do you care to accompany me?"

I nodded. "I will await his pleasure in the dressing room."

"Dashed waste of everyone's time!" my father greeted me, throwing a pile of letters into the air. It would not be he who had to bend to pick them up. "No one's ever heard of the fellow. Not a single ambassador, not a single consul. Whatever were you thinking of?"

"I was thinking, sir, of getting exactly this response." While he spluttered his disapproval, I gathered up half a dozen of the offending letters. Having toyed with the notion of putting them on a convenient table, I decided to keep them in my hands. "I came to disbelieve the

260

rumour that Mr Coates was on the Continent. I now believe that the corpse we found — this was when you were unwell, sir, so you may not recollect — is his. May I show these to Hasbury, in his capacity as Justice?" I gathered a few more. With his stick he guided the rest towards me. "I am very grateful for your help, sir: thank you." More to the point I was grateful to Beresford for his undoubted industry — he must have despatched upwards of a score of beautifully written enquiries.

He nodded absently. "Properly dressed, I see. All the same, my boy, next time you're in Town, take yourself to my tailor, will you? And get Walker to see to those boots, for goodness' sake!" He turned to the looking glass, touching his cravat with apparent irritation. Any moment now he would rip it off and demand Walker bring another fresh neckcloth.

It was time to make my escape.

"Search the rectory?" Hasbury repeated in disbelief.

"Thanks to the efforts of Mr Beresford, it is clear that Mr Coates never reached any of the destinations to which he might have been heading. My contention is that, in fact, Mr Coates never left Clavercote but was slain there. He might even have been hurt within the rectory itself. That is why I wish to look round. I propose to take with me Dr Hansard, and, as an impartial witness, Dr Toone." Should I have mentioned Mrs Trent?

"What about the churchwardens?" Hasbury was capable of surprising me. "Would they not have an interest?"

"If we find anything of note, be assured, sir, that they will be informed immediately."

My plan went awry the moment we approached Clavercote. Mr Lawton, taking the air in an old-fashioned gig pulled by a fat cob, hailed us. I made the introductions with as much aplomb as I could manage.

"I reckon I know what you're up to — and I'm minded to join you. In fact, I might make it easier for you. I could see that archdeacon would fly up into the boughs if I said a word out of place, so I said nothing. I — I happen to have a set of keys to the rectory, sir."

I coughed. "It happens that we do not need them, Mr Lawton." I gave the briefest of explanations.

He raised an eyebrow but did not appear to disapprove. "I can see why you men might want to look, but why the devil is Mrs Trent here?"

She faced him, arms akimbo. "You reckon a man would know anything about a house being left in a hurry, Thomas Lawton? You ask your wife about that."

Toone said smoothly, "Mrs Trent is here, you see, as I am, as an expert witness."

We all made our way to the rectory, the grounds of which were already showing signs of neglect.

"He should have kept his gardener on," Lawton muttered, as I unlocked the front door. "And what about that housekeeper of his? Telling her to leave? She'd not have let the place smell damp and miserable like this."

262

No one argued. At first using the candle ready on the hall table, then opening blinds and curtains as we progressed, we found nothing to indicate that the house had been put to bed, as Mrs Trent put it, for its master's prolonged absence. A book lay here, a pen lay beside an inkwell there. A bundle of dirty laundry in the scullery awaited the laundrywoman. The kitchen was clean and tidy but not, as Mrs Trent said, properly scrubbed down.

The upstairs smelt of stale clothes: someone, Mrs Paten no doubt, had stripped the bed and left the blankets neatly folded, but no airing was possible with the windows and shutters tightly closed. Mrs Trent flung them open. Then she turned her attention to the clothes presses.

She turned to us. "Gentlemen, how many clothes would you take for a long stay abroad? And which ones? Here are all his smalls, his shirts . . . Here his evening clothes. All his shoes. I wonder where he kept his valises . . . In a box room or in the attic?"

Toone drifted off, and summoned us within a moment. "Here — a whole row of cases, from small grips to trunks, in ascending order. No gaps in the row at all."

"In other words, had Coates been intending to take a journey, he meant to buy absolutely all his necessities en route," Hansard said.

"Would a man even buy shaving things? Tooth powder?" Mrs Trent asked rhetorically. "They are still on his dressing stand."

For a moment, we all stood in silence. It was Lawton who broke it. "Looks bad, doesn't it?" He asked casually, "Did Mrs Paten happen to describe the clergyman who brought her the news."

"No," came my emphatic reply. "It was quite dark, remember. Now, before we report to Lord Hasbury, I would like to see if Mr Coates ever had his likeness done. Did anyone notice one?"

"Yes. It's over the fireplace in the dining room," Mrs Trent said, leading the way downstairs. "And a very fine thing it is. It makes him look very grand."

"So it does," Toone agreed, striding across the room and reaching it down. "I think Lord Hasbury might be interested in this — do you not, Hansard?" He added, very quietly, with a meaningful smile, "But not perhaps as interested as my distinguished colleague."

That, as two of us knew, was Maria, who had caught Coates in a very similar pose. Her portrait, of course, lacked a face.

"Did you mean what you said, Dr Campion, about being alongside the killers — provided they confessed their crime and were penitent — all the way to the scaffold?" Lawton asked, drawing me on one side as the others made their way out of the building. As if he expected me to need time to reflect, he turned the key in the rusting lock, pushing against the door to make sure it was secure.

"I did. God loves us all, remember, whatever sins we have committed." I hoped I sounded calmer than I felt. I had never seen a man die except naturally, in his bed.

To accompany one to the moment of death, no doubt a young man in his prime, probably with a wife and children — did I really have the moral strength to do that?

"Thank you, Parson. Like Boddice said, you're a good man and you'll be safe here whenever you come. You have my word." He extended his hand. For the first time in the whole of our acquaintance I was happy to shake it.

CHAPTER
TWENTY-FIVE

By common but not enthusiastic consent, we returned to Orebury House to report to Hasbury. Mrs Trent found an urgent reason to confer with Mrs Heath — there was no persuading her otherwise — and would have scuttled round to the servants' entrance on her own. However, before I could insist on accompanying her, Toone stepped forward, proffering his arm in the most courtly of gestures.

"You'll be like to lose her, if you're not careful," observed Lawton as we watched them walk away together, deep in apparently very agreeable conversation. "And good housekeepers are like hens' teeth."

I was careful not to look at Hansard, but, since a reply was clearly called for, I said, "So they are. Especially when they are good, brave human beings too. Do not forget I owe my life to her."

Hansard had barely rung the front doorbell when Toone returned, wiping a smile from his face: the four of us were a deadly serious quartet as we waited for our pleasure-loving magistrate to quit whatever pastime currently engaged him. Seated in the library, we were happy to accept refreshment: it would provide each man with an excuse not to have to share his private emotions. I looked up to find Edmund regarding me with concern. I hoped he was reassured by my smile.

It was Lawton who was the most incommoded by the delay, which grew quite unconscionably long.

"Grand folk are always like this, are they?" The question seemed to burst from him. Then he stared at me. "Dr Campion, they say you're grand too, but I always disbelieved it. But the way you sit there, it's as if you belong. So I reckon they're right, after all."

"My father is a duke," I said quietly, deciding against telling him he was staying under this very roof. "But I am plain Dr Campion. And I have to tell you, between ourselves, that I do not think that keeping people waiting is the sign of a gentleman."

"Do we ring that bell again to remind His Lordship?"

"If we did, I suspect that we would find that the butler had lately discovered that His Lordship was not in fact at home today," Edmund said sourly. He after all had often enough been referred by top-lofty butlers to the tradesman's entrance, though these days his reputation was generally sufficient for the front door to be opened for him before he even knocked.

"These men who want to confess," Lawton said. "Would they come here or what?"

"To be charged, yes, and asked how they pleaded — guilty or not guilty — and then they'd be taken to gaol in Warwick to await a trial and their punishment," I said.

"And would they be questioned and all?"

"They might be asked why they should commit such a heinous crime. After all, Squire, they did more than kill a man. They treated his dead body with, let us say, the greatest disrespect."

He opened his mouth to say something, but the butler flung open the doors to announce Lord Hasbury. To a man we stood. Bows were exchanged.

Hasbury sat, but did not invite us to. He crossed his legs, idly regarding a highly polished boot. "You are becoming a dead bore in all this, Campion. Inquests, enquiries — good God, man, haven't you got a church somewhere to go and preach in?"

My bow was as chilly as ever one of my father's could be. "Sir, we believe that Mr Coates was the man who was found crucified. And we have a man ready to confess to his murder —"

"Three men, begging Your Honour's pardon," Lawton chipped in. "Do I bring them here, or do I take them straight to gaol to await the Assizes, seeing as Your Honour is so busy?" There was nothing about his tone or his expression to indicate irony.

There was everything about Hasbury's to indicate insolence. "I'm sure one or more of these good gentlemen will write down their statements, assuming as I do that the men are not literate."

"They can sign their names, Your Honour, even if it is with just a cross."

"I am impressed. Very well, let me have their statements, with names or with a cross, and I will ensure that they are despatched betimes — I rely on you, gentlemen, to convey them to Warwick. Excellent."

268

I had to clench my fists behind my back lest I hit him for his insolence to us all. "Indeed, My Lord, this is not our work. It is not suitable that gentlemen caring for the bodies and the souls of men should be involved in their incarceration," I said. "In the absence of a regular constable, may I suggest that you make a temporary appointment? Certainly I for one will have no part in this scheme."

"Dr Campion speaks for us all," Toone said promptly. "Mr Lawton must know a reliable villager who will act."

"I do, sir," Lawton said bravely, "and will send him to you to be sworn in. Then he can take their statements, if it please you, and will arrange for a closed carriage to transport them."

"Dear God, how tedious this whole business is!" Without taking his leave, Hasbury swept from the room.

"Sometimes," Edmund said, as a footman closed the grand front doors behind us, "I can understand the French predilection for tumbrils and guillotines."

Mrs Longstaff was almost unrecognisable: from a pale and wispy shadow of a woman, she was as radiant a young mother as one would wish to see, in no small part, I suspect, as a result of Edmund's insistence on fresh air and gentle exercise. Her daughter, brought down by her nurse for a few minutes to acknowledge our appreciative coos, slept soundly. To my great pleasure, I was invited to church the mother and baptise the child. Edmund and Maria were to be

Emma's godparents, alongside Mrs Trent, who had been such a tower of strength during the birth.

A bustle in the hallway proclaimed the arrival of more guests, the butler almost immediately announcing Lady Blaenavon. This! Lady Blaenavon! This elegant and genteel-looking lady! I could feel my mother's hand on my shoulder, her breath in my ear: *I told you not to be a prig.*

She was, of course, accompanied by Miss Witheridge, who was a short buxom lady in her thirties, with pretty nut-brown hair; her features were good, her eyes especially being wide and expressive. In no way did she fit the verbal caricature my friends and I had drawn of her as a thuggish, strident cross between a man and a woman, for all she dressed very simply, with none of the laces and flounces that made our hostess's attire so attractive. Her hair was drawn into a chignon from which stray locks were encouraged artfully to escape.

Lady Blaenavon too was dressed with quiet elegance. Slighter and taller than her friend, she too wore her hair tied back, taking a seat beside our hostess and asking quiet questions about the infant.

Their ladylike ways put me in a quandary. At what point — if any — in the evening would it be acceptable to raise the question of the two Sallys? At what point the name of their visitor, Mr Will Snowdon? I fear the anxiety affected my manners: I could hardly hold a coherent conversation.

In the end, as the footman padded around the table, ladling soup, it was Mrs Longstaff who raised the issue of Clavercote. It seemed that we were not expected to

270

talk to our immediate neighbours only. The Longstaffs favoured informal etiquette.

"Only think! The villagers tried to hang poor Dr Campion! And it was only the quick-wittedness of Mrs Hansard's fellow godmother that saved his life." She gave a short and rather lurid account of my near fate.

Lady Blaenavon turned a pair of remarkably fine eyes in my direction — eyes that were somehow familiar? Was she in fact related to Mr Snowdon? "I understood that a Mr Coates was the rector at Clavercote."

"I was there because he had quitted the village," I said cautiously, "and as you may understand, there was work there that only a priest could do."

"Do? What sort of thing do you do? Wouldn't it be better to feed the poor starving bodies than stuff their minds with doctrine telling them that it does them good to suffer?"

Toone nodded enthusiastic agreement.

The comment would have been well beyond the line of pleasing in most gatherings, and it would have fallen to our host or hostess to turn the conversation. As it was, I said as mildly as I could, "Feeding bodies is not incompatible with feeding souls, My Lady. I like to feel that my visits there involved practical as well as spiritual help, largely thanks to my good friend Mrs Trent — the other of Baby Emma's god mamas."

"You can feed the five thousand, can you?"

I intercepted a silent message passing between Lady Blaenavon and Miss Witheridge, who was clearly trying to silence her friend. But I had been to too many insipid gatherings — and had perhaps drunk a little too

271

much wine — to wish the exchange to end with a platitude about doing one's best.

"If I could, do you not think I would? Aye, and ten thousand too. But all I could do was start with one family."

Here Edmund leant across the table to explain about Sarey and her adoptive baby. "Poor Sarey's own babe had died and it was almost certain that Eliza's would too. The poor husband stayed for the burial and then walked away to volunteer and meet his death abroad."

Lady Blaenavon pressed her napkin to her lips. "Dear God, I did not know that the poor woman had died."

"You had made Eliza's acquaintance?"

"Yes." The monosyllable suggested she might be taking her friend's unspoken advice.

I inspected and discarded my more tendentious questions, merely remarking, "To lose your daughter and grandchild in such circumstances . . ." Suddenly a conventional shake of the head was not good enough. "If only they had turned to me! Something could have been done. As it was, I did not even get the chance to bury them. I would have laid them in St Jude's churchyard."

"You conducted Eliza's burial service, I gather?" She cast an agonised glance at her friend, as if she had given something away. And she had. There was something in the turn of the head, the earnestness, that told me I had met Lady Blaenavon before — on the occasion of a bright and willing young man offering to help at Toone's post-mortem examination. Suddenly I felt huge relief that such a person could have had no part in an innocent girl's seduction.

I dared say nothing about her role as Snowdon. First it would draw everyone's attention to her; second, it would reveal to her that I had only just recognised her. But I must and would have a private conversation with her later. Meanwhile, I replied truthfully that I had laid the woman to rest. Then I turned the subject, receiving a swift smile of what looked like gratitude.

Under cover of disconcertingly passionate piano playing from Mrs Longstaff, who had chosen a work by that most emphatic of composers, Herr Beethoven, I managed to murmur to Lady Blaenavon that so long as she wished it, her secret was safe with me.

"A woman — especially if she is a Lady! — is so trammelled and tied by society. To be chaperoned, even at my age — Dr Campion, it is like walking with your legs tied. Consider Mrs Longstaff — a most admirable musician, with three times the talent of her husband — but reduced on most occasions to playing pretty pieces so that others may talk. I suspect that had you not been grateful for the proliferation of notes and chords so that we can converse, you might have considered this sonata less than suitable for a woman."

"You do me wrong. I think it less than suitable for a social gathering, but am hugely impressed by her skill, her musicianship. As I was, My Lady, by your draughtsmanship, not to mention your amazing sangfroid. I believe your skills have helped us to identify the victim and find his killers."

"They have arrested Eliza's husband, no doubt. And who could blame him for taking the law into his own hands? What have I said, Dr Campion? Your face is a study! But I believe we must be silent — this movement is very quiet."

"May I call on you tomorrow?" I mouthed.

She nodded, pressing her finger to her lips.

My route home coincided with the Hansards' for a few hundred yards, as did Lady Blaenavon's and her friend's. We exchanged polite good evenings, and promises to maintain the acquaintance. No mention, however, was made of my call the following morning.

Once we had parted and were well out of earshot, Maria said, "A charming addition to our circle, will they not make?" There was no trace of irony.

"Charming indeed," Edmund agreed. "Tobias, did I notice you in close conversation with Lady Blaenavon — dear me, for all her charm this evening, I cannot think she is better suited to be a woman than a very capable young man."

"Nor I, to be sure. I think we may have passed one test tonight," I said cautiously. "I suspect the ultimate one, however, will be whether she ever lets us see her in her mannish garb."

"And will you flinch, and denounce her from the pulpit?"

Through the dusk, I could see Maria's smile. "Can you imagine Toby denouncing anyone except those who are cruel to others?"

274

The answer, had I had to give it, was that had I not met Her Ladyship, I probably would have done. Thank God it was too dark for them to see my deep blush.

CHAPTER
TWENTY-SIX

"I have devoted a great deal of time and energy trying to run to earth an artistic young man, Lady Blaenavon," I said with a rueful smile, accepting coffee poured with grace by Miss Witheridge. We sat in their morning room, the yellow walls glowing in the sunlight. It was small and not well proportioned but was clearly a room in which to take one's ease: a sketch pad was open on the window sill and an embroidery frame had to be removed from a chair to a side table.

"You might call me Will Snowdon," she corrected me, leaning back and crossing her breeches-clad legs, elegant as any young buck. "And I apologise for not being frank with you."

"I quite understand, and do not need any apology."

"You might. You might need an apology for my way of life. You are a member of the church, after all."

I spread my hands. "As a priest I should be shocked to my core: yours is certainly not orthodox behaviour. As a human being, I am disconcerted — you must have seen that as I walked in to see you dressed thus. But I hope and trust that with honesty and kindness and perhaps forgiveness on both sides — three sides, because clearly we must include Miss Witheridge in this — we will come to deal well as friends."

"You are all kindness, all consideration," Miss Witheridge declared, pressing a handkerchief to her lips.

"If I were, this conversation would not be necessary. I was . . . nonplussed, both yesterday evening and again this morning," I admitted. "But I have already been rebuked by the archdeacon and, more importantly, by my dear mother, for being a prig. Self-righteousness sits like a weight on my shoulders, I fear."

"Just as caution sits on my mother's," said Miss Witheridge. "When we visit Holmleigh Place, we are allocated and keep to separate bedchambers, out of respect for her wishes and to prevent the servants having evidence on which to base their village scandal-mongering. There are no mannish coats and shirts in Lucintha's bags either: she is every inch a demure young lady just waiting for the right man to pluck her off the shelf. As for me, I have a delicate ongoing flirtation with a dear second cousin with no inclination whatever to marry anyone."

I shifted uneasily. "Can you trust your own servants here? Sally, for instance — beg pardon, you have no Sally. Is there a kitchen maid whose behaviour is inconsistent?" I explained.

"You suspect the two girls actually change places? My God!" Lady Blaenavon — Mr Snowdon — paced anxiously about the room. "But why?"

"I have no proof as yet. And it is truly nothing to do with me — but for the fact that you, Lady Blaenavon, arrived at Langley Park offering your services when the ink was scarce dry on the note that I sent Lord Hasbury asking for help. Apparently the note was wrongly read to the servants, and one, known at Orebury House as Sally, slipped out of the servants' hall immediately. She was missing for several minutes — no one is sure how long."

"And our Beth came scampering in, all bright-eyed, with the news that a messenger was going to all the houses in the area requesting assistance. So I became Will Snowdon, and you know the rest."

"I have to ask, dear Lady Blaenavon, why you said nothing at all when we worked together."

"How could I, dressed as I was? You needed me to work without any interruption. One of you might have insisted that I left you immediately, might you not? Dr Campion, tell me on your honour that my relationship with Clara occasions no gossip, no cruel tittle-tattle in the village. You cannot. The change of name and of appearance are a convenient conceit. When Clara and I are alone or when we walk out, I often become Will — for her protection, for my pleasure. Ah, Dr Campion, if you knew what I had to give up when I became a young lady, not a young man! Once I was a capital shot; I could hit a ball better than any boy in the village."

"A dear friend of mine — one I would like to marry — is, I fear, still irked by such restrictions. But I don't think that she would ever wear breeches or pantaloons . . ." My smile was genuine, though my confession about Julia had surprised me.

278

"Would you be shocked if Lucintha appeared in them before this interesting young lady?"

"Alas, Miss Witheridge, my friendship with her will have to progress a great deal further before I can bring her on a visit. By then I trust that we will have no secrets from each other. Are others of our acquaintance aware of your . . . your friendship? I do not want to say or do anything to betray you. The Longstaffs, for instance?"

The women clasped hands and laughed. "Dear me," Miss Witheridge said, "Mrs Longstaff is one of our oldest friends: it was she who found us this delightfully secluded property. And it was she who said that of all the people of her acquaintance, it was you and Dr and Mrs Hansard who could be trusted. Not just to keep our secret, but not to be shocked to the core."

The chiming of a pretty clock reminded me that I had to be elsewhere, and would have to depart more abruptly than was polite. "I am afraid that I have to set out for Warwick gaol in a very few minutes. They have arrested some men for the crime that you saw all too clearly, ma'am." Or should I have addressed her as "sir"? "Before I take my leave, however, may I ask why last night you assumed that the murderer of the man whom you so accurately depicted was Eliza's husband? Why was that?"

She stared as if I was an imbecile. "Good God, with your only daughter ruined, a child not yet fourteen, drowning herself and her innocent babe, what would your reaction be? And your wife of twenty years dying of a broken heart?"

279

"In childbirth, Lucintha," Miss Witheridge corrected her quickly.

She ignored the interruption. "In his place, I am sure I would want my revenge on the vile seducer — or, more accurately, rapist! You say the poor man left the village for good — his conscience probably drove him, like his daughter, to a fast-flowing stream."

"And you are assuming that the man he killed was . . . ?"

She snorted with laughter. "Parson Coates, of course. The only thing that taxes me is how he managed to attach him to the tree. As you must have seen, he was scarce more than skin and bone. He must have had accomplices — but then, the vile creature had cuckolded many men, and then betrayed their daughters, for good measure. Some girls contrived, God forgive them, to take measures to rid themselves of the unwanted babe. You did not know this?"

"I knew about Molly, of course — but how do you come to know this sorry tale?"

"I do not always dress like this, remember. And when a woman finds a girl in tears, she may often engage in a conversation that no man might risk. I became fond of Molly, and despaired when she did not turn to me for help before . . . her end. I was taking food to Eliza when I realised how very ill she was. I wanted to find a midwife to help her, and set off to find one. But I was dressed as a man that morning, and it was clear that if I was observed someone would draw the wrong conclusion."

"Someone did," I admitted.

"By the time I had flung on more appropriate garments and found a midwife, poor Eliza . . . And her baby had been taken in by Sarey, so I left well alone. I planned to do good by stealth, but later found that some good angel was already supporting the Tumps. I am helping another of the evil man's cast-offs, however — I have despatched her to the home of a Quaker friend of mine, who will look after her and her child, and provide work when the mother is able to undertake it."

"May God bless you for your kindness."

She might not have heard my words. "Dr Campion, could you not see the evil in his foul eyes?"

I held up my hands in mock surrender. "Alas, I never met him. Yes, it seems strange, but I have been much occupied with my own parish, and Mr Coates's path and mine simply never crossed. If we were at the same Diocesan functions, then we were never introduced." For the first time I wondered if someone had taken measures to keep us apart. My heart was growing increasingly heavy within me, my suspicions so serious I did not want to articulate them even to myself.

A period of quiet reflection might have helped me regain my equilibrium, but the road was too busy for me to allow Titus to pick his own way. In any case, having once encountered an aspiring highwayman, I was aware I could easily meet a much more efficient one than Dan, for whom I continued to pray.

Why had we so strongly felt that Dan must be removed from the rectory? There was no logical basis, none at least that we discussed. Perhaps my own injuries had prevented any rational discussion, and we had simply followed Maria Hansard's instinct that he was unsafe — a response to her meeting with Archdeacon Cornforth. Perhaps she had articulated her fears to Edmund and Toone, if not to me. But why should Cornforth constitute any danger at all to a sick man? Why should it matter to him that Dan saved me? It wasn't his men who had set on me: the notion of an armed gang of vergers sallying forth to silence me brought a sardonic smile to my face. Perhaps, nonetheless, he feared that Dan would be able to identify someone. In the absence of the assailants I did not even know if they wished to kill me or merely deter me — though the events of my next visit to Clavercote rather suggested the former.

My thoughts had strayed too far for Titus's peace of mind. It was time to take control of him and head with more purpose to the location I dreaded and a task I dreaded even more, keeping my promise to confessed killers that I would forgive them and that their Heavenly Father would receive them as he had received the criminal crucified with Our Lord.

Edmund had already arrived, the gaol gateman informed me, and would be found at a coffee house some two streets away. A coin persuaded him to offer Titus accommodation and refreshment while I sought mine. I saw Hansard before he saw me: he looked old beyond his years, as he stared at his cup.

As he turned and recognised me, his smile was bleak. But he waited till I had sat down and had coffee in front of me before he spoke. "Do you know who confessed to murdering Coates? And who now linger in gaol?"

"Eliza Fowler's husband and his accomplices?" I asked stupidly.

His voice shaking with ill-controlled fury, he counted off the names on his fingers: "Ethan Downs; Luke Stokes; Josiah Stone."

CHAPTER
TWENTY-SEVEN

The three men, two dying, were in the common cell, which stank with a vicious combination of rancid food, filthy bodies, dirty straw and human ordure. I had never come across Josiah Stone before, but it was clear that the old man had no ideas of his own in his head, and very few words with which to express those of others. He had found three pieces of straw roughly the same length and was engaged in trying to plait them between racking bouts of coughing. Dimly remembering his manners, sometimes he would cover his mouth with his hands: they would be speckled with blood, which he wiped on his rough breeches. Ethan and Luke lay side by side near the window, clutching pieces of dry bread but making no effort to eat them.

"They should not be here! None of them!" Hansard hissed in an undervoice. "Whoever got them to confess should be broken on the wheel. And Josiah —" He broke off to speak to the third old man, "Josiah, why are you here?"

"'Cos I was told to look after these poor gaffers, sir. Look, I'm making a little man." He held up the straw.

"Good lad. You can have one of my buttons for a head if you like."

"I got a head, sir." He touched it in proof.

I prayed aloud for all three Clavercote men, and Hansard persuaded Josiah to say "Amen" when it was needful. Prompted by the familiar word, some of the other men gathered round in a loose but attentive semicircle, so I added a few words that I hoped might bring comfort, and asked them all to join with me as I repeated the Lord's Prayer. Some knew the General Confession, others the Creed, and Hansard, borrowing my Bible, read the Beatitudes. That was enough — more than enough for some — so I gave a blessing and, pressing every hand that was thrust at me, left the terrible place.

Hansard demanded to see the chief gaoler, insisting that the old men were moved to warmer accommodation. "Ethan and Luke are dying —"

"Aye, with the Assizes starting next week, I'd say next Thursday at seven in the morning," the gaoler responded, quick as a snake.

"They are very ill, in a great deal of pain."

"I know something that'll put an end to all that," our kind host replied.

"Josiah — he hasn't committed any crime. He's a simpleton. Anyone can see that. How can he be held responsible for murder?"

"That ain't for me to say, masters. That's for the magistrate, who's already said it, or he wouldn't be here, would he? Josiah signed his confession, like the others, he did. All we need now is the judge." He drew a finger across his throat.

In the face of such faultless logic, Hansard changed his approach. "Two of the men need regular draughts of cordial to help prevent their pain becoming intolerable. If the other prisoners knew you were giving them laudanum, there would be a riot — you would be lucky to get out alive."

"That's why I shan't be giving them nothing more than their prison rations."

"Other prisoners get food from outside: I know you allow them to buy in pies and ale."

"So I do."

"Only if they grease your palm first, I suppose," I observed.

"Maybe they do, maybe they don't. But no matter how you were to grease it, I could not give those two laudanum in front of the others. More than my life's worth, as you yourself said, master."

Sighing, I tried a different approach. "When do you move them into the condemned cell? As soon as they're condemned? Why not do it now, my friend, so that you could give them the medicine Dr Hansard prescribes?" I shook my purse temptingly. "Some clean straw? A blanket or two? Some soup and fresh water?"

"That halfwit and all?"

"Unless you want the whole prison infected with consumption I would strongly recommend it," Hansard said. "And take care when he coughs blood."

Hansard was clearly preoccupied on our journey home, so I gave up any attempts at conversation. Much as I would have liked to regale him with my account of my morning, that seemed a lifetime away. Now I felt soiled, inside and out, and could think of nothing more satisfying than tearing off my clothes and plunging under the pump. That, however, would clean only the outside: what would wipe away the darkness that seemed to threaten my very soul?

The question burst from me: "Why have they lied when they are so close to death?"

Edmund reined in his horse. "I have been asking myself the same thing. Were they forced to, or did they offer?"

"Forced by whom?"

"An excellent question, Tobias. And it may be that we never find the whole truth, because if ever a village is good at closing ranks it's Clavercote. We must ask some questions. But not, my friend, while our clothes, our very skin and hair, reek with prison miasma. Maria will already have given instructions to have a week's hot water made ready for us. I dare swear that you would prefer the hair-shirt school of cleanliness, but a soak in lavender-scented water is just what this doctor orders. Our shirts can be boiled, and Marsh will hang our outer garments over a steaming tub. Will such precautions achieve anything? Toone yearns, as you know, to see inside our bodies. I long to look closer at the outside, to see what lies on our skin even when we think we have washed it. If only I had a son to pass my ambitions to . . . But I have Maria, and no man could imagine greater happiness. Not even you, when you win the hand of your inamorata."

We exchanged a smile. Something, however, was making Edmund's horse fidget, and it seemed to be passing its anxiety to Titus. A glance at the horizon was sufficient explanation.

"Will we beat the storm, or will it beat us?" Edmund asked.

"We'll have a better chance if we take to the fields and give the horses their heads," I responded. "And it might make us feel a good deal better."

We arrived back at Langley Park drenched to the skin, something Edmund described, as we stripped off our clothes, as nothing short of the act of a hygienic God. The steaming hip bath waiting in front of a fire in my bedchamber was the act of a well-run household, but I thanked God for it. Will, a change of clothes in his saddlebag, had offered to ride to the rectory to tell them I was safe, an act I attributed less to his conscience for failing to deliver another message than to the fact that Susan had grown a very pretty smile. Young Robert and Mrs Trent herself, of course, would be there "just in case".

By the time I was dressed and had joined my friends for supper — Jem must wisely have decided not to brave the elements — the storm was truly raging. Rain slashed diagonally across the windows, and the wind howled as if we were living in Udolpho, making the candle flames dance and flare even when Burns drew the curtains as he left us to our dessert.

"Your visit to the prison," Toone prompted us. "Clearly something has troubled you."

I let Edmund speak, hardly needing to prompt him. His narrative was received by Maria with gasps of shock. Toone, however, gave his most sardonic smile as, finishing, Edmund downed his brandy as if it were water.

"You fear that these men are being made scapegoats? That they are old and innocent and are being sent simply so that the authorities, having a few to hang, will let the matter drop? Let me offer another theory. That — great heaven, what can be the matter?"

Edmund and I responded as we always did when the bell pealed as if to announce the Last Judgement: we were on our feet, bidding Maria farewell and preparing ourselves for our work. As we stepped into the hallway, we almost collided with Burns.

"The storm, sir — half the houses in Clavercote are blown down, and people have been hurt. Your horses will be ready in a moment — but it's a foul night, sir. We've got lamps ready, and your bag, too, Dr Campion."

Toone, overhearing, joined us. "I'll join you."

"Thank you. Send to Orebury, Burns, and to Lambert Place. Ask for the stewards — they'll be a sight more useful than their masters."

We were greeted by the sight of Lawton and Boddice, struggling alongside the villagers to shift a roof beam, which had trapped a family inside a crumbling cottage.

"Mud walls, you see, Parson, all washing away," Lawton yelled. "We've opened the church for the women and children that we've got out so far. All the men that are able are doing their best to anchor what roofs they can and pull down what they can't." He peered into the swirling darkness. "Is that both doctors? Thank God for that. The church, good sirs, if you please. And Parson — can you lend a hand here? A man your height?"

Should I comfort the dying or try to save lives? For a second I hesitated — then I heard a baby crying within. Thrusting my bag into Toone's hand, I did as I was asked.

I truly had no idea how long I spent with the villagers that night. At first I was indeed most useful with the rescuers; then I was summoned to sit with a dying woman. To my shame I thanked God that it was not Sarey, who, Joseph strapped to her back, was moving amongst the injured offering sips of water. As I watched, Toone summoned her — she was to hold a broken limb as he set it in a rough splint.

Before I could reach the Lady Chapel, a small commotion broke out to greet Mrs Trent, soaked as a drowned rat, who staggered in with two full baskets. The wardens' womenfolk followed.

"They called for you at the rectory first," she called. "We're all of us here, Susan, Robert and young Will. Susan and I have been helping Mrs Lawton make soup. Will and Robert will bring it along shortly." She looked a little guilty. "I came in the gig, Master Toby."

"You did well. Keep our brood safe, I beg you."

We had five bodies by dawn, two old women, one old man and two young men. We had some dozen walking wounded, but not all would survive, Toone said in an undervoice: they were too weak, too malnourished, to deal with the pneumonia and putrid throats he feared would follow their prolonged soaking.

A fierce gale still blew, but the clouds had cleared to the east. The clear skies, the still feeble sun, showed the extent of the devastation. People who had had little enough now had nothing but the clothes on their backs, hardly more than rags in most cases.

Boddice, bleeding from a cut over his eye, joined me by the lychgate. "All these good people thrown on the parish," he said. "And by law some should be sent back to their home parishes. But we can't do that, Parson, can we? Can we? We all strove together; we should stay together."

"Indeed you should. You shall." I would approach every landed gentleman round here and beg, cajole and demand money from them. And I would start with Lord Wychbold, the master of Lambert Place, the man whose failure to provide properly for his tenants had resulted in this carnage.

I encountered him rather sooner than I expected, as I headed with my friends for Langley Park. Toone and Edmund were as ready as I was for another hot tub and a change of clothing — looking at them I suspected that even their expert valets would be unable to rescue their coats and breeches from a whole palette of stains beside the predictable mud and blood. As for me, I clearly must make time to visit a tailor, even one who made me look like a provincial lawyer.

The three of us, riding side by side out of Clavercote, encountered a very natty equipage so badly driven that we had to press our exhausted horses into the bank. It was only as the phaeton passed us that I recognised the driver.

"Hold!" I shouted, bold as any highwayman. "Wychbold, I will speak with you this instant!"

Perhaps his terror was genuine; perhaps he really thought we were footpads. He shouted something at his groom, who remained as impassive as a sphinx.

Hansard was quick to disabuse him, courteously introducing us all. "My Lord, your presence is required in Clavercote. Now."

I moved to his side. With Toone in front, and Hansard bringing up in the rear, Wychbold could scarcely argue. His groom continued silent.

We brought the little cavalcade to a halt beside what had once been the village green. Now it was a sea of mud, with reusable timber stacked to one side, and a great heap of rotten wood and straw on another. A muddy track led to the church.

"What is all this?" Wychbold gasped. "An insurrection? Call the militia!" he squeaked.

"I would if I could," I flared. "I wish I could demand that they arrest you."

Hansard coughed me to silence. Yes, I was making my attack too personal.

"This," Toone said, gesturing expansively, "is what happens when landlords neglect their responsibilities. Half this village has literally been washed away, My Lord, and lives have been lost as a result."

Wychbold paled. "No court of law —"

"Would do anything," Toone obligingly completed his sentence. "No. Because the laws are made by people like you to protect people like you. And just to make sure magistrates and judges are people like you. But these poor people" — he pointed at a group demolishing another hovel — "are not like you. And I am very sure they would like to make your acquaintance."

"Are you threatening me, sir?"

"Not exactly," Toone said reasonably. "I would say that I am blackmailing you. How many guineas are in your purse, My Lord? How much did your horses cost? And the phaeton? I would guess that one-tenth of what you have spent on yourself for today's outing would have saved five lives. So I will relieve you of the contents of your purse to help the parish begin immediate relief. Thank you." He tossed the purse to me. "Now I will accompany you back to your home — Lambert Place, I recall — so that you may make arrangements for a proper restitution. You have a library of national renown, do you not?" It might have been a polite question, but the threat it implied turned Wychbold green.

He began to turn his vehicle. Toone winked at me — this was his opportunity to put into operation some of his revolutionary aspirations. He fell in behind Wychbold. Over his shoulder, Wychbold hissed, "You will pay for this, Campion, you see if you do not."

The groom maintained an admirable composure.

As they bowled away, Hansard said quietly, "The groom's a local lad, I presume. Very well, Wychbold has escaped the lynching Toone would have liked to organise. And Toone will do an excellent job of extorting money from him — far more than you and your fiery temper would achieve. And I, Tobias, not you, will call on Hasbury and your father later in the day. After all, you will be with Boddice and Lawton arranging funerals. Before that we both need rest and sustenance — yes, even we are human."

"So we are. First let me hand this over to Squire Lawton so that he can at least feed and clothe those he worked so hard to save last night. And then — do you think Maria will have saved us some breakfast?"

"I will vouch for it. And for the presence of more hot water in the boiler."

CHAPTER
TWENTY-EIGHT

My first duty, once washed, shaved and breakfasted, was to return to the rectory to thank Mrs Trent and her team and ensure that they too rested. Robert knuckled sleep from his eyes as Titus clattered into the stable, but insisted that he was ready to return the horse to his usual gleaming self. Will would help when he woke up — he jerked a thumb at the next loose box, where the Langley Park lad lay flat on his back, snoring gently. Mrs Trent was not asleep, but stood alone in the kitchen surrounded by towels and bedlinen, checking each item and allocating it to a pile.

I put my hands on one of the stacks. "Have you rested, Mrs Trent? I thought not. And neither have I. So we will agree that that is our first priority. I collect Susan is abed?"

"Has been these last two hours, Master Toby."

"Excellent. Robert will no doubt curl up again with Titus. And as for you and me, whichever wakes first shall knock on the other's door. No buts. The situation in Clavercote is grave indeed, but we will help all the better after an hour's sleep. Dr Hansard's instructions. And neither of us would dare go against them, would we?" I ushered her from the room.

I was awoken by the sound of horses' hooves and the creak of wheels. Maria had arrived, unaccompanied, in her smart gig. In fact, as I saw when I ran downstairs, there was hardly any space for a groom. She and her household might have stayed away from Clavercote last night, but they had not been idle. There were bundles that might have contained linen or clothing, and baskets of bread and vegetables. In fact, she told me with a smile, she had come to reclaim Will, if he was ready to help. A kick from Robert ensured he was. He was to accompany Mrs Trent, having packed my gig with her offerings. A cart, driven by Mr Tufnell with Mr Mead beside him, was weighed down with sacks — gifts, Mr Tufnell announced, from local farmers and their wives. Moreton St Jude's had suffered — I could now see that the rectory roof was missing several slates, but the good husbandry of our local landlords had ensured that the cottages had withstood most of last night's onslaught.

Desperate as I was to help the villagers of Clavercote, I had somehow to keep my promise to support the confessed murderers in their time of need. This was made easier by the arrival of teams of workers from Hasbury and Wychbold's estates: clearly my friends had spoken to good effect. So I begged a loaf and some ale from Mrs Trent's supplies, and set off to Warwick to do my duty.

At least the men had all been removed to the condemned cell. To a man in the best of health, this might not be seen as an improvement, spartan as it undoubtedly was. But at least the cell was quiet, the straw was fresh, and the gaoler had found some blankets. Even the invalids managed a sip of ale and a morsel of bread. Josiah had no problems wolfing down his share and more. None was capable of holding a prolonged conversation, so, reminding them of the power of God's love, I prayed with them and left two to sleep and the third to create yet another straw man.

Before I left, I bespoke accommodation for the days of the trial and executions at the Green Dragon, conveniently close to the courthouse, and ordered food and drink to be sent daily to the three Clavercote men. For a moment I was tempted by the shop window of a tailor — but was truly revolted by such vanity in the face of others' total loss.

The next few days passed in a maelstrom of activity. I found myself feeding children, conducting a deathbed marriage and acting as a joiner's labourer. At some point I fitted in church services both in Moreton St Jude's and in Clavercote, using just the Lady Chapel, since the nave and crossing still functioned as a dormitory. At one point, however, our work was interrupted by the arrival of an absurd phaeton, suited to tooling round London, but hardly appropriate here. Lord Hasbury, perched high above the villagers, dispensed largesse and advice in equal measure. At last he beckoned me over. His groom produced an ignominious parcel, which he handed to me with an illicit wink.

"Seen much of Wychbold?" Hasbury asked, as I clutched the parcel to my chest.

"Not since the day he was . . . waylaid . . . I had not expected to see him so well turned out, Hasbury, nor in charge of such good horseflesh."

He snorted with laughter. "Nor I! After all those years of study you'd think he had completely dried up. And now, all of a sudden, it seems he's in the petticoat line at last — thinks it time to set up his nursery. He's got his eye on an attractive woman, I hear. The *on dit* is that she's a bit of an ape leader. But then, he's long in the tooth himself. Must be fifty if he's a day, and you can't tell me he's worn well."

"Is the lady a bluestocking who would join him in his endless research?"

"Research, you call it! He reads books about nonsense, as far as I can see. He wants to know each religion's view of the devil, he tells me, and not just religions any Christian would approve of. Eastern ones," he said darkly. "Now," he added briskly, "Hartland will be leaving us soon — going back to Derbyshire to finish recruiting his health."

"I would like to pay my respects before he does," I said. But I added a helpless gesture — how could I be spared? "Besides, any of my clothes suitable for visiting a gentleman have been so assailed by the elements, that as you see, I have had to resort to a jerkin and brogues. I could not arrive at your door like this, let alone present myself thus to my father. But please pass on my regards to him, and only spare him any details of my garb if you fear they will cause him an apoplexy."

He did not argue, but I thought I detected a slight cough from his groom.

298

"Will you be attending the trial, Hasbury?"

He shook his head. "Smoky business all round, if you ask me. Reminds me of when I was a lad at Eton. The beak'd tell one of us to own up or we'd all feel his cane. Sometimes we'd put our hands in our pockets and pay one of the fags to confess — he'd probably had nothing to do with whatever he was supposed to have done, not even been there at the time. But for half a sovereign he'd swear on oath that he'd done it. Must have happened in your time there."

"You're right. It did. None of the villagers could afford to pay a bribe — but that doesn't mean you're wrong in principle." I reflected that this was probably the first time I'd ever had a sensible conversation with him.

"Glad to hear it. I'll have a word with that secretary of mine — see if he can have any good ideas. Lord knows, I pay him enough. I'll bid you good day, then, Mr Master Builder." With one beautifully gloved finger, he touched the brim of his hat and bowled off.

Stowing the parcel in my gig, I returned to work. But I was concerned. Any dutiful son would bid his father farewell — even offer to escort him on his journey. Papa would have sufficient postilions to render that unnecessary, but a visit was undoubtedly called for.

At the end of the day, unused to spending my days in such physical toil, I was ready to collapse straight on to my bed when Robert knocked on my chamber door and, with a low bow, handed me Hasbury's parcel, the existence of which I had completely forgotten.

Stripping off the brown paper and string, I found one of the coats I had left behind when I left home, two waistcoats and a pair of breeches. Included were two notes.

The first was from Walker, apologising for taking such a liberty as to send home for more clothes for me, but he believed that if I were to appear in court to give character references for the three accused, I should need to look the part. He himself was more than competent to make a few slight adjustments in the apparel, were it necessary.

The second was from my mother. After two pages of family and estate news, she added,

> Walker tells me that your father has stigmatised your appearance as that of a provincial lawyer. I trust that, subject to a little alteration here and there, these garments will remind him that you are in fact a gentleman.
>
> I do urge you to consider accompanying him when he is well enough to return here or to London.
> Your loving
> Mama

By the time I clawed my way back to wakefulness, there was no sign of my household, just coffee and fresh rolls on the kitchen table.

So there was no one to entrust with my reply to Mama's letter, scribbled and hastily worded as it was. At times like this I could lament, albeit briefly, the convenience of a large household, where one only had to ring a bell for one's every whim to be satisfied. Should I post it myself now or wait till my day's work was done?

On impulse, I sent the letter first.

As a consequence I had time for far less work in Clavercote: sharp showers battered my conscience as much as they lashed the building works. I was in for a wet ride if I were to go to Warwick today. Since I would be going the next day, to take up temporary residence at the Green Dragon, I was terribly tempted not to go. But then conscience, in the form of two village women, reminded me of my duty.

They were so thin, had so few teeth and so little hair I had no idea of their ages: they might have been forty or seventy — I could not tell.

The less bent hailed me. "Sir! Master Parson! Will you be seeing my brother Ethan today?"

"Perhaps not today. But tomorrow or the next." I might have slapped her face. "Why do you ask, ma'am?"

"Because I've made some soup with those vegetables your grand friends sent us. There's a drop left and I thought he and the others might share it. They say they starve them in prison."

I did not want to explain that, thanks to me, their men had good food. "Surely you need every scrap of nourishment yourself."

"Not as much as them, Sir. A little taste of home. Tell them Betty and Martha sent it special and they're to drink up every last drop. And some of last year's elderberry cordial." She produced a bottle sealed with wax.

The other woman held up soup. Despite all the chaos, the poor woman had gone to the trouble of finding a jar, tying a paper lid on with feeble string. I reached for it and for the cordial. "I promise it will get there as soon as I can take it."

CHAPTER
TWENTY-NINE

Toone, catching sight of me preparing to leave, offered to ride with me. We kept up a brisk pace, glad, I think, to escape the apparent chaos that might have made sense to those whose business was rescue and reconstruction. What conversation we had largely concerned Wychbold's change in demeanour, and how it had been brought about. Toone denied responsibility, ascribing it to a sudden realisation that he lacked an heir to carry on his name.

"That does not appear to have bothered him before," I observed, before encouraging Titus to leap a hedge I ought more sensibly to have avoided by using the gate that Toone preferred.

"But perhaps the lady who has caught his eye is one who applauds men who do good works."

"She might want to visit his residence — it scarce merits the term "home" — before she accepts his kind offer. But tell me — when and where did they become acquainted? And do we know the lady's name?"

His response was a gale of laughter. "You are normally the most ascetic of men, Toby, but suddenly you give a glimpse of what you might have been had you stayed in your expected station in life: you would have been just as shameless a gossip as the next man. I don't know the lady in question, or even her name. Come on — I'll race you to that windmill!"

Toone was already fifty yards ahead, and it was time to give Titus his head.

I had forgotten the presence of the soup.

We had regained a suitably sober demeanour when we entered Warwick gaol, and were soon confronted by sounds, smells and sights to wipe any last joie de vivre from our faces. Luke Stokes was on the point of death. The gaoler, angling for largesse, told us he had on his own initiative summoned a nearby apothecary, who was trying to bleed the poor old man. Although at first Mr Keyte was inclined to be belligerent towards us both, not understanding the nature of my own doctorate, he soon realised that there would be no need for him to take the blame if — when! — his patient died.

I said what I hoped would remind Luke of our Saviour's promises, but Toone murmured that he probably heard no more. Nonetheless, I continued to pray aloud until the death rattles ceased and his struggles were over.

We stood in silence as his body was removed from the cell.

"It was too late to offer Luke Holy Communion," I said sadly. "But it would be good to offer it to Ethan and Josiah on the eve of their trial. Would you join me, gentlemen?"

The apothecary agreed with alacrity, though Toone, unsurprisingly, was less enthusiastic. When I offered the wafer and the wine, Ethan Downs was too ill to stand or kneel, but this time at least he did not turn his head from me; and Josiah, though coughing blood and clearly running a high fever, accepted what I offered before returning to his task of making straw men.

I was about to drink the last of the wine when Toone leapt forward, preventing me. Wrenching the chalice from my hand, I believe he was ready to tip the contents on the floor.

"No! The wine has been blessed. It must be finished! I have wiped the chalice with a purificator." I showed him the tiny napkin.

"Nonetheless, give Ethan and Josiah the rest. It is madness," he said, less explosively, "to drink from where the lips of so sick a man have rested, purificator or no. Indulge me, Dr Campion, in this, I beg you."

Between them the two invalids, for it was truly impossible to think of them as vicious murderers, drank the wine.

"That was good, Parson," Josiah said, almost animated. "Fair warmed me through. Ain't got any more have you?"

On his straw, Ethan nodded, holding out a weak hand.

"Alas, no. But I do have some elderberry cordial, sent by your own sister," I said. "A taste of home, she promised."

"My granddaughter, you mean? But she be dead, poor wench. Poor, poor child . . . 'Twas for her I did what we had to do."

"Are you confessing to the murder of which you stand accused? Truly?"

"Did I not put my name to it? Luke too, who bought the nails with the last of his savings? We were sworn, sir, we were sworn. And I am truly sorry for it, and for all the trouble it brought to your door."

Taking his hands, I prayed with him, for him, and for my own ignorance and prejudice. At last he gripped my hands in a feeble farewell, it seemed, and he turned his face from me, and from the world.

The apothecary and Toone had been murmuring quietly in the corner about relieving Ethan's obvious agony, taking no notice of the appalling exchange only feet from them. I could say nothing of it yet, and in fact, now it dawned on me that I was bound by the seal of the confessional, I never could reveal what Ethan had said. To fend off more serious reflections, I produced the bottle of cordial. Mercifully it was still in one piece with the seal intact. They exchanged a glance, the significance of which I did not understand.

"I cannot think of anything more soothing," the apothecary said firmly. "Ah gaoler, might we have a couple of cups?"

First eyeing the bottle, the man scuttled off, speedily returning. He had brought three small tankards. "Can't say I'd mind a drop of that myself," he said. "Carrying the dead is a thirsty business."

I was about to pour a liberal libation when Toone stepped forward. "We will all drink with you shortly, sir, when our business here is done. Allow us a few minutes to complete our examination."

306

Toone opened the bottle, sniffing cautiously. Then he poured a drop on to his finger, tasting it cautiously. The apothecary did the same.

I looked from one to the other. "Gentlemen?"

"We did not want inadvertently to poison them," Toone said. "What you said about a sister alarmed me: I thought I heard say that neither man had any family. I just suspected a . . . benign . . . plot. But I find nothing to alarm me."

Keyte nodded his approval. "Nonetheless, I would advise no more than a few sips after their wine. A drunken scene in the condemned cell would not be appropriate."

"Is it safe?" I insisted. "I pity the men from the bottom of my heart, but I may not pre-empt their trial and punishment, no matter how I might deplore it." I turned my eyes to the two sufferers, dropping my voiced as I asked, "Do you have anything in your pharmacopeia that might ease their suffering?"

"Only laudanum. And we would have to administer a very high dose for it to be efficacious. In a healthy man, it would do no harm; but these are not healthy men."

Somehow I asked, "You mean it might end their sufferings altogether?"

Keyte nodded. "Indeed. There is a hair's breadth between a merciful dose and a lethal one. I am sure that neither Dr Toone nor I would hesitate to administer a draught were either man simply lying in his own bed. But here —" shrugging, he spread his hands expressively. His next words came out with a

307

rush. "In front of witnesses, I dare not, lest I be accused of perverting the course of justice."

"And I dare not, for the sake of Dr Campion's conscience." Toone clapped me on the shoulder in an affectionate gesture.

Shaken from the reverie Ethan's words had induced, I dropped the bottle of cordial.

The gaoler grumbled twice over — at having to clear up the glass and missing his projected treat: he had even brought a tankard to the cell. But Keyte produced a hip flask of good brandy, and poured it all into the tankard. The delicious fumes filled the cell. To my astonishment, the gaoler turned to Toone. "I might spare a drop for they two there?"

It was but a drop in each tankard, but I blessed him for his kindness.

"I will be staying at the Green Dragon for the trial," I said, "so I will see you again. Thank you a hundred times, my man." I dug in my breeches for half a guinea, but found only a whole one. I pressed it nonetheless into his hand — I would not do his job for a thousand times more.

It was too late for Keyte to dine with us when we left our patients, but I invited him to do so when I attended the trial. He undertook to visit the gaol regularly to see how his patients did. I promised to pay his fee.

We parted well pleased with each other. Of Ethan's words I said nothing; surely they had to be regarded as his final confession, and were to be shared with no one. But clearly some sort of justice was being done.

308

Of Betty and Martha there was no sign when I returned the next afternoon to Clavercote to apologise for the loss of the soup. My enquiries elicited a slight hesitation before any of those I questioned responded — usually with a vague gesture that they were somewhere over yonder. I had thought that my efforts on the villagers' behalf had earned me a greater degree of trust, indeed warmth, but today, despite occasional bursts of sun, there was a decided chill in the air. Some of it was attributable to the continued struggle for life of Adam Blacksmith, who had been injured trying to save others during what the villagers all called the Big Storm. Little groups would congregate near the forge, hoping for news. I joined them, even knocking to gain admittance so I could pray with him. Of all those in the village he seemed least keen to be reconciled with me, however; his daughter, a new baby in her arms, hung her head as she begged me to go.

But Lawton and Boddice seemed to make a point of shaking my hand and wishing me good day. By now I was totally confused, and very glad to make my excuses: I had an early evening confirmation class to teach.

Since Mrs Trent was still devoting so much of her time to the villagers of Clavercote, I naturally turned to Langley Park for dinner, to be greeted by three very serious faces.

"And yet I do believe I should quietly rejoice," said Toone, shaking my hand in greeting. "Ethan has died,

309

relatively peacefully, according to Keyte. He fell into a deep slumber soon after we left, the gaoler told him, and never awoke. I am glad he was spared a trial, gladder still that he did not swing."

"I have to ask: does any suspicion attend his death?"

"Lord, no. If there were, Hansard would go on oath that the man was not expected to live so long. As for poor Josiah, it would be a mercy if he had left us in just such an easy way, but it is to be hoped that the judge will allow natural causes to take their course. Damnation, we would not let a dog or a horse suffer thus — why a human being? And do not tell me it is God's Will, Tobias, or I swear I will knock your head off."

Burdened with words uttered under what I believed was the seal of the confessional, I could only speak the simple truth. "I know nothing of God's Will. Does anyone? And I grieve as much as you at the imprisonment of a dying imbecile. There are those who praise those who endure suffering with patience and joy at the prospect of the life hereafter, but Josiah has very little concept of this life, and none, I fear, of the next."

Toone shook my hand. "Forgive me. My tongue ran away with me. Dear God, Edmund, I could use some of your excellent sherry . . ."

CHAPTER
THIRTY

Did the trial judge share the doubts and reservations we friends had expressed? Who knew? But, in the course of the two minutes that Josiah, who had had to be carried into the dock, stood — or rather slumped — before him, he ascertained that he could not understand the charges and therefore could not plead. He recommended his immediate removal to the nearest asylum to live out the rest of his days.

I did not know whether to mourn or rejoice. Neither, I think, did my medical friends, nor Mr Lawton or Mr Boddice.

"I have bespoken a private parlour, gentlemen, at the Green Dragon. I believe we should adjourn there, to hear a few explanations. Squire Lawton, Mr Boddice — you are particularly invited."

The pair eyed each other, like village lads caught scrumping. But since no one else refused my invitation, they could scarcely do so without appearing rude.

Lawton downed his first glass of wine as if he was a harvester slaking his considerable thirst with small beer. I was happy to indulge him, but though I wanted him loquacious I did not want him strident and argumentative.

Boddice was more interested in the nuncheon the landlord had thought to provide.

The rest of us, including Keyte, sipped and ate more circumspectly.

"Squire — Mr Boddice: you have been implicated in this from the start, have you not? You organised the murder of Mr Coates, had him, not inappropriately, hung from a tree in a vile parody of the crucifixion, tried, as I asked questions, to have me killed and then — for what reason I know not — decided to co-operate with me. What say you? The most senior laymen in Clavercote, plotting and taking life! I am ashamed. The archdeacon will know of all this as soon as I have your confessions."

Lawton shook his head, laughing grimly. "It wasn't quite like that, Parson. In fact, though you may not credit it, we saved your life."

"Of course you did," I agreed sarcastically. "It was you who placed Dan where he might save me from a throttling. I'm sure he will be glad to hear it. He is making excellent progress, but not for anything will I divulge where he is staying."

"You were right to fear for his life, Parson," Boddice chipped in. "But not at our hands, I warrant you. That attack had nothing to do with us."

"Nor the lynching? I am to believe it was you who saved me from the mob, not Mrs Trent? I tell you straight, gentlemen, I do not."

"She beat us to it. Believe it or not, 'tis true. We'd not have let you come to any harm, sir."

"Nor did you burgle my home and half those in Moreton St Jude's, I suppose."

Lawton looked outraged. "No. Indeed we did not. And we don't know who was behind it, neither."

"And no one tried to kill my friend's dog as a warning?"

"Kill a dog? What are you talking about? This is the first I've ever heard of it."

"Suppose," I said icily, "you tell me and my colleagues something we can believe. The moon is made of green cheese, perhaps."

Lawton finished his second glass. "Do you have your Bible handy, Parson? Because I will swear on it that what I have to tell you is true, though there are folk who will deny every word of it."

I rang for the waiter. We needed another bottle. No one spoke until Lawton had sipped deeply. Then he continued, "There is a rumour that one of the gentry — a neighbour of yours, Dr Hansard, worships the Devil and such. I know nothing of that, but I do know that there was a far worse man in our village — the Devil himself. Not just any man — a man of God."

"Coates? Good God!" I let my anger spill on to the speaker. "You knew, and did nothing?"

"It wasn't quite like that, Parson," Lawton repeated, with surprising calm and firmness, laying a restraining hand on his fellow warden's arm.

"Exactly how was it, then?" I demanded.

Hansard insisted on accompanying me to the archdeacon's residence, pointing out phlegmatically that there was little point in breaking my neck putting Titus at too high a fence, which my seething anger might well lead me to do. Grudgingly admitting that a witness to my proposed conversation would be useful, I agreed. We set out at a spanking — but not dangerous — pace in Toone's curricle, Toone undertaking to ride Titus decorously back to Langley Park to apprise Maria of the day's events so far.

"What ever happened to vows of poverty?" Edmund murmured as we waited in the gilded library, decked with pictures of Archdeacon Cornforth's smug-looking predecessors. "No, that was for monks, was it not? All the same, what would some of these bloated and arrogant-looking men make of your life, Toby?"

"They would recognise it all too well, I fear." I counted my advantages in life one by one. "I live in a rectory with enough rooms to accommodate as many guests as I would wish. I am blessed with glebe land —"

"Glebe land which profits you nothing, from what I hear."

"There are tithes —"

"Which you refuse to take!" He pointed to another man, whose triple chins overflowed from their clerical bands. "Do you suppose he ever denied himself for Lent?"

"You have to understand, Edmund, that those men probably had to enter the Church — younger sons, with little alternative."

"Younger sons of rich men who brought with them their ambition and sense of entitlement!"

314

"Now you talk like Toone."

"And Archdeacon Cornforth drives an equipage as good as Toone's. What am I to make of it all, Toby? Add Coates into the mix, of course . . ."

At this point, the butler entered and bade us follow him to the blue saloon, where, he told us in sepulchral tones, the Venerable Archdeacon Cornforth would receive us.

The saloon was an even grander room, not least because the curtains and other furnishings had recently been renewed to the standard that my mother would have demanded at home. The result was truly elegant comfort, with good modern landscapes — a Turner here, two Constables there — gracing the walls.

Cornforth was on his feet, holding a piece of paper he set down on a side table. He did not offer us his hand, instead, with a graceful gesture, wafted us to our seats. The butler passed us sherry and biscuits, hovering in the background as if to ensure that any conversation was appropriate to the civilised room.

"The matter I have to broach, Archdeacon," I said, "is of the utmost confidentiality. Indeed, this is not a social call at all, but a matter of serious Church business."

The butler left so quietly he might have evaporated.

I stood to make my accusations.

"Dear Dr Campion," he said, "you tower so dreadfully. Surely we may sit in comfort to discuss what you have to say, like the gentlemen we are?"

"I have to make a serious accusation — so many serious accusations — that I prefer to stand."

"Very well." He sat back, steepling his hands with such an air of patronising tolerance I was glad to have Edmund beside me, his very presence a restraint.

"Firstly, you knew about Coates's appalling activities and did nothing to stop them."

"Oh, Dr Campion, how wrong you are. I did everything in my power to stop them. As soon as I discovered why he had left his previous two cures of souls, for — er — similar reasons; in fact, I spoke to the bishop. He told me that forgiveness was at the heart of Christ's teaching, and that if Coates was penitent and promised to commit no further sin, then we should give him the chance he craved — to serve another parish."

"So Coates had seduced and raped in other villages," Edmund observed.

"In two towns, to be more precise. The bishop hoped that the healing air of the countryside, its calmer way of life, would enable Mr Coates to live a life of quiet reflection."

"Instead it offered him the chance to lead an even more depraved life. As the churchwardens told you."

"As indeed they told me. As indeed I told the bishop. I believe that he himself remonstrated with Mr Coates —"

"Remonstrated!" I repeated.

"Rebuked, if you prefer. And I understand that Mr Coates promised once again to mend his ways."

"But could not keep his word," Edmund concluded. "As a medical man, I have known men who could not stop drinking, though it was killing them, men who could not give up gambling, though it was ruining

316

them. A kind interpretation of Coates's behaviour would be that he was similarly addicted. Cures are possible, sir," he continued, speaking from deep, bitter experience, "but not unless the man avoids the opportunity to indulge his weakness. Surely the Church could have put him in a post where his behaviour could have been closely scrutinised? And repetition prevented? Could you not have demanded that? Failing that, all the information should have been put in the hands of a magistrate! Or did you fear scandal? Or did you suspect that the Church would simply close ranks and deny everything?"

There was no reply.

I continued my narrative: "Coates's conquests — no, Coates's victims! — were dearly loved women, whatever their age or status. And one day their menfolk would tolerate no more. They would have to go to extremes to protect them — am I right, thus far? So they executed a criminal no one else would deal with and then, now fired by vengeance, nailed him to a tree in the vilest parody of the Crucifixion. But you knew about it, did you not, in advance?"

"No. No, of course not. How could I? Heavens, I had a letter in his own hand informing me that he was leaving to take the cure. I thanked God for it, I can tell you!"

I shook my head gently. "I am sure that you received a letter, but it was in the hand of a man who freely admits to being but half educated. You must have seen Coates's handwriting at some time or other. He went to Cambridge, I recall, and that university is not in the habit of accepting men who are barely literate. I don't suppose you kept the letter? Did you pass it on to the bishop? Or send him a copy you wrote yourself? Do you not answer me? Well, I can tell you that one of the wardens in Clavercote was compelled by the conspirators to write it. He freely and penitently admits it, but was sure as he wrote that you would recognise it as a fake and take action. Which you signally failed to do. You still do not wish to speak? Very well, I will make one or two more observations, the first intimately connected with my own safety. You ordered me to lead services in Clavercote: did it not dawn on you that the villagers so loathed members of the clergy that they would prefer to see them dead? Mr Boddice and Squire Lawton did their very best to put me off. But I was persistent, almost with fatal results. On the first occasion, the presence of a vagabond to whom I had done some trifling favour saved my life. You seemed more than interested in this man, whom I housed at the rectory. Did you want Dan removed, murdered even, lest he could identify my assailants?"

At last something I had said struck home. He might control his voice, his hands, even the expression on his face — but he could not stop the ebb and flow of blood to his face. He was ashen-pale. "On no account. Yes, yes — he was a witness to the attack. I thought I would see what a little encouragement — financial encouragement — would do. Because I did know that an attack . . . I confess I asked some men to try to deter you from going back! And look what happened when you persisted," he added, back in the saddle again. "You were nearly lynched! So all I was doing was —"

"Trying to prevent my getting hurt by having me assaulted. I am sure there is logic there I should applaud. But that was not the whole of your involvement, I fancy. One day, before Dan's fortuitous arrival on the scene, you chanced to see, in my study, a half-finished sketch. I will admit my explanation for its presence was not just misleading but also feeble. You were right to be interested in it on those grounds alone. But I suspect that your interest also stemmed from the fact that the sketch was recognisable as Coates, thanks to a very fine artist. And by then you were deeply embroiled in the fiction of your own creation, that he had departed for the Continent — we are at war, sir! So you embarked on a series of break-ins to locate it and destroy it. Oh, you were clever — your henchmen disturbed a lot of other households so that I would not appear to be the only victim. It was highly convenient that Dan could become a scapegoat — though, of course, had a hasty magistrate found him guilty he would in all likelihood have been transported, an experience which would swiftly have proved fatal. You would have sent an entirely innocent man to his death, Archdeacon. I have sent him to a place of safety amongst poor people who value human life." I paused at last for breath. Then I recalled what I had done earlier in the week. "Tell me, was scapegoating three sick old men for the death of Coates your idea?"

"No — but when I heard of it I ... The soup, Campion, and the cordial ... They would have prevented any suffering on their part, had they got as far as sentencing."

Hansard sprang to his feet. "You were prepared to kill them, like dogs?"

Cornforth too rose, walking to the window and pulling back the curtain. "Do you see that fresh-dug mound there? Under the sod lies my faithful dog Horatio. I hope you will forgive the allusion, gentlemen. He was old and weak. He would not have survived without me, and I could not take him to where I am going. So I . . . did what was necessary. And I am about to do something else that is necessary. You see that half-written letter there? I suggest you read it. It is to the bishop."

Hansard was there before me. "You are to quit this post? And join a missionary society in Africa? You know that if a white man can survive there for six months it is a miracle?"

"As the Bard made Edmund say, *Some good I mean to do Despite of mine own nature.* My nature is not naturally bad, gentlemen. Indeed, I have always tried to do good. But events overtook me. I did harm, quite by chance — and became trapped into doing more and more. When I go to Africa I can do good for however many days the Almighty pleases to spare me. That will be my penance. That and the knowledge that I will not have long to wait for a horrible death far from home. I shall miss this house. I already miss Horatio. But not as much as I miss God's love. I must show him how penitent I am, so that on the Day of Judgement my Saviour will intercede for me." He gave me a quizzical, even amused glance. "You are a devout man, Campion — may I ask you to pray for me? And for my work for my new flock in Africa, of course. Thank you. I am sure you will understand if I bid you good day — I have much to finish here before I leave forever tomorrow morning." With some embarrassment he extended his right hand.

I had to shake it, did I not, and forgive him for what he had tried to do to me. "You know it is not in my power to forgive what you did to others. For myself, however, I freely forgive you for the harm you did to me. May God bless you and keep you," I said, my voice gravelly with emotion.

"Thank you. So, gentlemen, farewell!"

It was a very subdued group of friends around the dinner table, free to talk in the absence of any servants. Jem in particular was unhappy. "So no justice is done. Three harmless old men die on behalf of some killers who will never be identified. The churchwardens claim to be good men. The archdeacon, who clearly knew of the dangers Coates brought with him, can skip off to Africa. I do not like any of this, I tell you straight."

Toone nodded. "Some justice has been done, but not all — and none of it in the open. In 1815 we will celebrate the six hundredth anniversary of Magna Carta: have we learnt nothing?"

There was a knock on the door. Burns entered to speak to Edmund, who looked quizzically at me. "There is a man dying in Clavercote. Do we trust the wardens' promise that we are now safe?"

"You will be safer with an escort, if Mrs Hansard will excuse us," Jem said, rising and looking Toone in the eye.

I do not recall anyone speaking as we made our way to the smithy where Adam Blacksmith's daughter admitted us, her face ashen and drenched with tears. Clearly she was no comfort to the grizzling, struggling baby, which Toone removed gently from her arms, taking it out into the evening sunshine.

"No ring, you see, no ring," Adam gasped, pointing a huge accusatory finger. Jem scooped her out his sight, presumably joining Toone.

"She says he promised marriage. Him!"

"Coates?"

Even the steady approach of death did not curb a string of expletives.

At last I asked gently, "Did you help kill him?"

"Not so much kill, as hold him on to that tree while the others nailed him. And I burnt all the clothes he had on. Brave lads that did it: two of them died when that roof fell in, trying to save those inside. One went to be a soldier, they say — he won't have long for this world I dare say, not would he want to, seeing what happened to his wife and daughter. Will that count, do you think, Parson, on the Day of Judgement? Being good to make up for being bad?"

"I hope and pray it will. But now, Adam, it is your own death you must think about, and making your peace with your Maker."

He smiled oddly. "Someone will look after that babe, won't they? Nice little creature, considering its sire. I

322

meant to drown it, like you'd drown an unwanted whelp. But I found I couldn't. I beat my daughter like buggery when I found out. For all that, she's stood by me. Bless her for that. I don't have much to leave, but I want her and the nipper to have it. Can you write that down? It's got to be writ down, to be my Will! Write, write! Then I can sign it and die."

"While Dr Hansard writes, why do you and I not tell God how sorry you are, and how you hope to be forgiven?"

"Your resignations?" I repeated, pushing the two letters from me. I was in the calm of my study but now all around me there was chaos again. "Why, gentlemen?"

Boddice looked at Lawton, then spoke first. "You once said we were the most important laymen in the parish. And it seems to us that knowing what we knew, we ought to have done more. We did what we thought we could, but we should have done more. We should have told Lord Hasbury about the goings on. The bishop himself . . . We should have — we know not what we should have done. So we do not think we are worthy, not anymore. So we want you to look over these here letters to the bishop and tell us if they're all right."

I considered the case. Two ordinary men, thrust willy-nilly into a situation not of their making, driven by their consciences to give up roles they both valued, grovelling to a man so much their social, intellectual and ecclesiastical superior who had helped cause the chaos they had to deal with.

"We should have set an example," Lawton added, "not turned our backs on it all. At least that's what people think. You do yourself, don't you, Parson?"

"I no longer know what to think. I suspect you have less to blame yourselves for than you think. But I applaud you for responding to what your consciences tell you. Tell me," I said, playing for time, "are there any other good and reliable men whom you can recommend to take your places?"

At last Boddice spoke. "Everyone knew something. Every last one of us knew something. But not everything. Not enough to point a finger in accusation. It's on all our consciences, I suppose. But what use is a conscience when your roof is rotting over your head and there's no food to put in your children's bellies? That's what they'd say. It took the Big Storm to make things a bit better, to make people act as neighbours again."

Toone would have nodded sagely, as they supported his angry theory that if you made the world better you would make men better too.

As for me, what did I know? Less than nothing. I could not ask my bishop for help, knowing his part in it all. The archdeacon was heading open-eyed to his penitent death.

"Let us pray together, and see if we can hear an answer," I said at last.

Epilogue

It is the most subdued service I have ever taken, but probably the most important. It is also one the bishop knows nothing of, although the church is full. It certainly has no ecclesiastical precedent that I know of. Together we recite the General Confession. Then, led by their wardens, each man, woman and child rises to confess his or her part in the murder. On our knees we plead for God's forgiveness and each other's. At last, blessed in the knowledge that our saviour died to save us from sin, we rise.

I tell them of the new rector, a kind old man, who will come to work amongst them. They must welcome him, and his wife of thirty years, or they will answer to God — and, more immediately — me.

As I ride away, I have no idea if I have done right. Toone, for one, disagrees, insisting that the bishop should have had to answer to his peers for his wrongdoing. Jem supports this view, but doubts if, being who they are, they would find much fault. Maria and Edmund are more pragmatic, though both continue to hold their breath every time I head for Clavercote without Mrs Trent. If Toone has tried to lure her away from me, I do not know, but she continues loyally with me, occasionally giving me enormous pleasure when she behaves unexpectedly. Robert, despite having a puppy to care for, still prefers the stable as a bedchamber. Susan is wooed by Tufnell's grandson.

Now I have to do something I will permit no one else to do. I must oil my bat for the first match of the cricket season.

Other titles published by Ulverscroft:

SHADOW OF THE PAST

Judith Cutler

Tobias Campion, rector of Moreton St Jude, is delighted to welcome the widowed Lady Chase as his parishioner. Although charming and generous-spirited, she harbours a secret sorrow: her son, Hugo, is missing, presumed dead. Her late husband's nephew, Sir Marcus Bramhall, making a prolonged, unwelcome visit to Moreton Hall, speaks darkly of bringing a court case to declare him the heir. Then Miss Southey, the Bramhall family's ill-treated governess, disappears on the very day that the body of a stranger is found in a local river. When it transpires that the man might have been bringing news of the missing heir, Tobias and his loyal groom, Jem Turbeville, are forced to quit their beloved village to uncover the truth.

STILL WATERS

Judith Cutler

DCS Fran Harman's relationship with Assistant Chief Constable Mark Turner is going well and they are buying a house together. At work, a former protege, Simon Gates, has just become her new boss. But there are complications with both Simon and Mark's daughter. Even the environment is hostile, the water in Fran's village tainted by something in the local reservoir. Some good old-fashioned detective work seems a useful antidote.

Then a dramatic discovery leads to her case becoming a full-blown murder investigation. As the investigation takes its toll on those around her, the waters surrounding both her future in the force and with Mark become increasingly muddy.